DRESS THE NECK BECOMINGLY

DRESS THE NECK BECOMINGLY

SANGUIS ET FAUNA

EMMALINE STRANGE

IRON GALL BOOKS

This book is for anyone who thinks fangs are hot, and/or was a goth in high school.

PROLOGUE

SINCLAIR

I f I squinted just right at the pavement, I could almost still see the bloodstain. Never mind the fact that the night I'd produced the stain and tonight, *this night,* were separated by a dozen decades; never mind the fact that the alley had been repaved with asphalt in place of uneven cobbles.

It didn't matter, because I could never forget that stain —its color, its shape.

How could I ever forget the night I died?

I had followed the history of the building beside the alley since that night, from afar. I watched, and waited, for the property to go up for sale. Fifty years ago, I'd snapped up the deed, but I had never found the courage to return here, to this building, this alley, this city. Until tonight.

Something told me it was time.

It was time to return home, time to learn the truth of how I'd been born into this second life.

If I closed my eyes, I could hear the shouts, feel my ribs

breaking. I could smell the smoke, feel the heat of the fire on my skin as I bled on the stones, listening to my livelihood burn. That entire night rushed through me in an instant where I stood swaying on the sidewalk.

However, I hadn't come all this way to be undone by the sense memory of cruel men long dead, of the slap of fists, by the shuttered windows or the puddles on the street that filled with rain just the same shape as they had a century ago. I was tired, and I missed my home.

I'd been running for over a hundred years.

Living as a shadow left me feeling wrung out and drained. This building had been my home, had been the last place I'd been truly happy. I barely remembered what that felt like, but I thought perhaps it was time to reclaim that feeling.

I'd run from what had happened to me, run from what I'd done. I'd never known the one who made me, and I'd never wanted to know. He hadn't wanted to know me, either. As I lay dying in the alleyway, watching the reflection of flames in the dirty puddles, he'd whispered in my ear, "Do you want to be saved?" I hadn't, but he'd turned me anyway, and left me to transform in the gutter.

I'd fumbled through a hundred years on my own, happy to hide from the memory of the night I'd died. But of late, I'd been struck by some sort of pull, like the opposite of wanderlust. A deep, unshakeable restlessness, a need to fill the empty place inside where most people kept the knowledge of who they were.

I had no reason to believe the one who made me would still be here, in this city that like the rest of the world had changed so much since that night, but it seemed as good a place to start as any.

When I approached the door, I smiled to see it was still

the very same as when I'd left it. The key and its lock were as old as I was, and the satisfying *clunk* of the mechanism sounded like coming home.

I wondered when anyone last set foot in here. The dust settled on everything was thick and soft and pillowy, well acquainted with the creak of the floor, old friends with the spiders in the corners. When I'd purchased the building fifty years ago it had been a dress shop, and ghosts of that life remained in the stacks of faded hat boxes and waifish dress forms, huddled together behind the till counter. I didn't mind them. Ghosts held no malice for me.

I stood in the center of my dusty little kingdom, feeling at peace for the first time in a hundred years.

It was good to be back.

1

PRACTICAL ETIQUETTE FOR SINGLE GENTLEMEN

ROYCE

W hat had I been thinking?

Perched on the stool at the corner of the bar, I took a gulp from my beer. I'd ordered my same old usual. Several, actually. I may as well have been wearing a sandwich board that read, "I don't belong here."

It had taken me six weeks of denial, two weeks of drunken pining, and five days of psyching myself up to get here. I didn't know what miracle I'd hoped to achieve by dragging my ass to a trendy, queer nightclub downtown instead of the pub down the street from my apartment.

No matter where I sat, I was still the same old boring Royce Davis I'd always been.

The same old boring Royce Davis who'd been dumped on his ass nine weeks ago by his boyfriend of three years.

"I need more, Royce."

"More what?" I'd asked, floored, when I'd come home from an eighteen-hour shift to Derek and his suitcase. I'd

just wrapped up an investigation that had left me...
changed. It had shattered the very foundations I'd thought
the world was built on. All I'd wanted was to come home to
my normal apartment, my normal life. Instead, I'd had the
normal fucking rug pulled out from under me.

Derek had shaken his head sadly. *"Just...more."*

Whatever the fuck that meant.

But I guess I knew on some level because here I was
with some bullshit point to prove. I could be spontaneous. I
could be exciting. I could try new things. I could be...*more.* I
would have laughed if it wasn't so damn pathetic.

I'd put on my hippest outfit, such that it was, and
dragged myself out of the house in an Uber. Now I sat here
like a bump on the proverbial log, and all I wanted to do
was go back to my place and crawl into bed. I drained my
beer glass and set it on the bar.

"What are you drinking?"

I looked away from the bar and almost choked on my
tongue. The most beautiful guy on the fucking planet had
approached my lonely seat, any sound of his footsteps
camouflaged by the pounding beat of the club music. He
was short, slim, and pale, dressed all in black and his warm
brown hair swooshed back over the crown of his head. The
apples of his cheeks were round and full, and his entire
heart-shaped face had a generous covering of freckles. I
looked around, trying to find someone else he might be
speaking to because it sure as hell couldn't be me, but there
was no one. Not even the bartender had approached my
little storm cloud in like, half an hour. But this guy was
here, standing far too close, and he was moving in closer.
My knees widened to make room for him like I'd been given
a command. He gave me a soft, shy little smile, one pointy

canine poking out over his plump bottom lip as he fluttered his lashes, eyes fixed on me like I was the most fascinating man in the room.

He was probably drunk.

Or high.

Jesus, he looked young. Way too young for me, and possibly too young to be in this club, which was twenty-one and over. "How old are you?" I blurted.

He laughed, his nose scrunching up, the dusting of freckles on his cheeks drawing my eye as the strobing lights splashed across them. Leaning in, he let his lips brush my ear as he whispered, "Old enough."

When he pulled away, he fixed me with an oddly intense stare. His eyes shone a hypnotizing grey-green out of his smooth, pale face.

"That's not going to cut it for me," I said.

He tilted his head to the side, fiddling with the collar of my shirt, and said, "And why is that?"

"I'm a cop."

Without missing a beat, he let his lips brush my ear again, his breath ghosting over my cheek as he whispered, "In that case, what will it take to convince you to cuff me?"

I huffed out a nervous laugh. "Why don't you show me your ID?" Good *Lord*, what was I thinking? This had to be a new personal low and definitely not a sexy play to run on a prospective hookup. I had truly hit rock bottom: ID'ing some hot twink to figure out how gross it would be if I clumsily flirted with him.

"What shall I call you?" He asked, fishing in the pocket of his sinfully tight jeans. The way he spoke was weird, like he was performing in a play or something.

"Da—Royce," I said. "My name is Royce."

"Royce," he said, like he was tasting it. I found myself instantly warm at the sound of my name in his perfect mouth. "It suits you."

"Thanks," I said, taking a peek at the ID he slipped into my hand. A sensation like vertigo punched through me, and I almost slipped sideways off the stool. He leaned in, steadying me with surprising strength. I caught a whiff of his skin—like fresh mint, woodsmoke, and snow. Confused, I straightened up, and saw him putting his ID back in his pocket, like time had skipped. When had I handed it back to him?

"Now that you have ascertained my age, may I legally buy you a drink?"

I frowned. Maybe I was tipsier than I thought. I opened my mouth, but his intense stare pulled me in, distracting me. "I was about to head home, actually," I found myself saying.

He draped his arms around my neck and brushed his nose against mine. "Even better."

"You're way too young for me," I said feebly, even as desire sputtered to life in my gut. Was I really about to do this?

He batted his thick lashes at me and said, "I don't think I am."

"Is that so?"

He sucked my earlobe into his mouth, then nibbled it before whispering, "I'm an old soul."

I threw way too much cash on the bar, focused more on the smooth pair of lips on my neck, the tongue flicking over my pulse point, and the beautiful body in my arms. We stumbled out the door of the club, and he continued sucking on my neck while I ordered us an Uber.

Buzzed on beer and drunk on my own daring, I slid my

hands down to cup his ass, pulling him closer while we waited for our ride. When I turned to capture his mouth, he placed a finger to my lips. "Not yet," he said.

"Why?"

With an evil grin, he said, "I want all of you, all at once. In private."

Fuck me.

Soon we were in the back of some poor lady's SUV and I could not have been fucked about automobile safety as he climbed up to straddle my lap, grinding against me and teasing my neck with his lips and tongue.

We stumbled through my front door, pawing at each other's clothing, sending fabric flying as we banged into walls and furniture. I was pretty sure I heard a lamp break, but I wouldn't have been able to stop had the apartment been on fire—and when his fleet fingers found their way to the fly of my jeans, I was fucking gone. His kisses were hard, aggressive, lots of teeth and I offered the same, sucking and biting marks into his slender neck.

Tangled up and somewhat naked, we made it to my bedroom, and with a firm hand on my chest he guided me to sit on the edge of the mattress. With practiced grace, he peeled off his skin-tight boxer briefs, kneeling between my thighs to work my feet free of my jeans, which had tangled around my ankles. Lust smoldered in those grey-green eyes, an impish smile lighting his face as he moved to straddle me on the edge of the bed.

"How do you like it?" I asked, leaning in to whisper in his ear the way he'd done to me at the club. I ran my palms down his back, his skin smooth and petal-soft.

His breath caught in his throat as he answered. "Rough."

Music to my fucking ears. I rolled us, twisting to get us

further up the bed with his perfect, lithe body pinned beneath me. I thanked my lucky stars I had some lube, but as I groped in my bedside table, I realized I didn't have a single condom. Derek and I had always used them—but it had been quite a while since we even attempted sex, even before we broke up.

My confidence faltered. Maybe that's what Derek had meant when he said he longed for more. More skill between the sheets, more adventure. More fireworks. He'd never said, but maybe I was an absolute zero in the sack. "Hey." A soft voice brought me back to the present, back to the criminally beautiful, naked guy in my bed *now*. "Are you alright, darling?"

I released an embarrassed laugh around the lump in my throat. *Oh, Christ, Davis. Get more pathetic. Seduce some kid for an anonymous hookup and then sob all over him.* I had no idea why the soft endearment had thrown me so much, but looking into his arresting eyes, I faltered. It was an odd thing for such a young guy to say. Maybe he was, as he said, an old soul. I kissed his nose. "Yeah," I said gruffly, then seized his jaw to deliver a rough, sloppy kiss to his mouth, which he returned eagerly. "I just uh," I stammered. "I don't have any protection."

His gaze burned in the half-light of my bedroom. "If you say you're negative, I trust you. Risk it?"

"Risk it," I confirmed, sounding so unlike myself that I almost stopped. Almost. Thinking about Derek had me reeling, wanting to do something reckless, something stupid, something possibly dangerous. Looking down at the beauty pinned against my pillow, I thought, *what a way to go.*

I raised up on my knees between his splayed thighs,

taking in the tight lines of his body. The adorable freckles on his cheeks spread down over the pale expanse of his chest, and I leaned over to kiss a few of them. He tangled his fingers in my hair, giving the strands a soft tug, like he wanted to remind me he'd asked for a rough fuck, not a tender love-fest.

I growled against his navel, the soft skin of his belly cool and light under my lips. Drawing back, I nudged his hip. "Over," I said, feigning confidence with my gruff tone. He grinned, rolling over onto his hands and knees obediently, and I saw the freckles adorned his perfect ass, too. Hell. I gave one round cheek a gentle swat, and he smiled wickedly over his shoulder before perching with his back arched, his hands on my headboard, knees spread.

I kneaded his sweet, freckled ass with both hands before spreading him wide to get a look at his hole. The puckered skin around his opening was a delicate ballet pink, and I couldn't wait to see what it looked like stretched around my dick. I slicked up my fingers, then gave my cock a few strokes, warming the lube in my hand before massaging his rim with my thumb. I teased until he whined and I pushed my fingers inside, stroking the slick, silky skin of his channel until he begged for more. Pulling my fingers out as slow as I possibly could, I pressed a kiss to his shoulder. "Ready?"

He let out a whispered curse, then softly, "Yes."

I lined up the head of my dick with his sweet little hole and pushed in, slow at first until I was seated inside him and he felt so fucking good, felt like exactly what I needed. I gasped as he squeezed around me, arching his back further. We groaned in unison as we adjusted to each other, and after a few thunderous heartbeats I began to move.

I caressed every inch of his body bent over in front of me, finding the freckles on his shoulders with my lips. As my tongue danced over his flesh, I found a faded scar at the nape of his neck. He shuddered when I kissed it, so I swept his hair aside and lavished attention on the area. Each little shiver had him clench deliciously around my dick.

He'd asked for it rough and I planned to give it to him, but it had been a minute, and I didn't want to humiliate myself by going off too soon, so I started with long, powerful thrusts that had him sighing and moaning on each stroke, pushing his greedy ass back toward me. Soon we fell into a wordless synchronicity, moving together like we'd been making each other come for years.

He didn't have to say out loud that he wanted it harder because I could read the hunger in his body. With my hands on his tiny waist, I drove into him with brutal, blunt thrusts, making sure to angle my dick just right to nail his prostate. I stroked in and out, ramming him harder and faster against the headboard, and if his yelps and moans were anything to go by, he was thrilled to take what I was dishing out. He bucked back against me, surprising strength in his little body like a briefcase bomb, giving as good as he got.

I was close already, but something told me we'd be fucking more than once tonight, so I really let him have it, wrapping a slippery fist around his dick, pumping him till he came into my hand with a pretty moan. With an arm around his torso, I yanked him upright, slamming his back against my chest, gulping for air as he collapsed in my arms. I came hard as I held his body close, filling him with pulse after pulse, groaning with each twitch of my release.

I ran my hands over every inch of his chest, his skin still cool and dry to the touch, while I sweated like a pig. The shame of it curdled the post-nut euphoria and I pulled away, feeling weird and soiled after slobbering and sweating all over the pure-looking angel in my arms. He turned toward me with a small, needy sound as I drew back, his eyes dazed, the very picture of debauched innocence.

"Where are you going?" He fell on his back, stretching.

"Just..." I gestured at my sweaty body and his cum-covered belly. "Going to get something to clean us up."

In a blink, he'd moved to kneel before me, wrapping slim arms around my thick waist to pull me down on top of him, startling me once again with his strength. "I think not," he said, raking his nails across my back.

I shivered. "But..."

"You have a beautiful mouth, Royce," he said, sliding his fingers up into my hair. Pushing gently, he guided my head down his chest. "Why not put it to use?"

Jesus Christ. Okay, so maybe there was a demon hiding behind that angelic smile—perhaps he wasn't the wide-eyed innocent he appeared to be. And to be frank, the idea of getting my mouth on his body had my guilty thoughts melting away like snow in spring. There'd be plenty of time for self-loathing later.

———

SINCLAIR

Leaving my den earlier that evening, I had not the faintest idea what I craved more: a feed or a fuck.

Sometimes, it was difficult to be sure. I'd been back in Douglas Crest for several months now, and while I made every effort to keep to myself, to remain small and invisible, my kind ran in a fairly closed community. I was not the only predator in this city. Never before had I stayed long in a city when I learned I wasn't the only one. This was different. I was finally home, and I had things to learn. When I was first turned, I had no room for curiosity, my mind consumed only with survival, not unraveling the mysteries of the self. Now though...I'd lived long enough to start to wonder.

When I entered the club tonight, I spent some time dancing, twirling, and grinding on the floor to the pounding music with the other writhing, needy bodies, letting the scent of sweat ignite my prey drive until it thrummed below my skin. I searched the sea of revelers with a detached sort of want, still unsure which way my instincts would ultimately lead me.

Laying eyes on the bedraggled, weary-looking man at the end of the bar, I was still unsure, but I knew immediately it was him I wanted. Until I got close enough to smell his blood, I didn't know if I was about to give him the night of his life or put him out of his misery. Judging by the forlorn look upon his sweet, honest face, either would have been alright by him. He was thick and sturdy, with creamy skin that flushed beautifully, and tired hazel eyes. His face was scruffy, his hair thick and brown and curly, and his shoulders slumped. He carried himself like an old man, though he couldn't have been older than forty. The sight of him had me yearning to lift the burdens from his shoulders and smooth the tension from his brow.

Royce, he'd said his name was. A lovely name, truly, a king's name. I hadn't told him my name, yet. But I knew the moment I'd scented his neck that he would learn it soon enough. A hunter's instincts were rarely wrong.

Tonight would not be enough for me to drink my fill of Royce.

After he'd dutifully lapped the seed from my belly, and —to my utter delight—made a meal from the mess he'd made in and around my ass, I was hard again and beyond ready for another romp. Royce took me deep into the silky, wet warmth of his mouth and I was surely a goner. My instincts had steered me well indeed: Royce had a generous and talented mouth and as he swallowed around the head of my cock I released, spilling down his throat as I arched my back off his bed in pure ecstasy.

He sucked my cock until it wilted between his lips before kissing his way back up my chest. God, his lips, his tongue, his entire mouth. Humans usually required something of a refractory period between bouts, and Royce was no different. But he was energetic and amorous, and our bodies came together again and again like they'd been designed expressly for each other's pleasure. After riding his thick cock and then letting him fuck me aggressively into the mattress again, I had made up my mind.

Royce was mine.

It had been simmering in the back of my brain since the club, brewing as he gallantly verified I was old enough to bed, and boiling over now as he bent me in half and fucked me to blissful delirium. After several hours of energetic lovemaking, my darling Royce seemed utterly spent, his human stamina at its end. Or so he thought—he had never spent the night with someone like me before, so naturally, he did not know the heights to which he could be pushed.

I draped over his broad chest, soaking up the warmth of his soft, sturdy body like a snake digesting a meal upon a sunbaked stone. By design, I had lined up our groins so I would know immediately when he was ready again, but his cock-drunk, sleepy face told me he didn't foresee fucking me again tonight.

Pity, because I was surely not done pleasing him yet. I kissed him, softly at first, the corner of his mouth, then nipped his lip until I felt him smile. "I would very much like to make you climax again," I told him.

He slid a warm hand through my hair, stroking my scalp with a tenderness I'd come not to expect from casual lovers. "I don't know if that's possible."

"Afraid of falling in love with me?" I teased, pressing kisses to his chest.

"Afraid my heart will give out," he said with a laugh.

I peeked up at him through my tousled fringe. "Risk it?"

He sighed, closing his eyes, a surrender. I grinned against his clavicle and teased my way down his body, loving the smell of him—he smelled of blood and sweat and life.

I adored sucking cock. There was something about a throbbing erection—it had everything I loved, everything I thrived upon: sex, and blood. Sustenance and pleasure. The urge to feed from Royce was a strong one, but I would not. Not tonight. Not yet.

It took quite a bit of coaxing before he hardened again under my ministrations, allowing me to draw one more orgasm from his wrung body, the taste of his seed exquisite upon my tongue, perhaps even better than his blood would have been.

It had taken quite a while to get him there a fourth time, but of course I did not tire as humans did. I relished in the patience I could take with lovemaking, and clearly Royce appreciated my efforts, seizing my arms and pulling me toward him for grateful kisses and sweet murmurs.

Unfortunately, with night waning, it was time for me to leave.

Royce seemed close to slumber, providing me the perfect opportunity to slip out into the night and return to my den before the rising of the sun. I disentangled from Royce's embrace, loath as I was to do so. He opened one eye. "Hey," he said.

"Go to sleep," I said softly, standing by the edge of the bed. "I should go."

He extricated one hand from the tangled nest of blankets and raised it to brush his callused fingertips over the skin of my ribs, trailing down toward my hip. "Stay."

The intimacy of this gesture had me utterly arrested, and I was powerless to deny his command. I could stay for a little while; there were still several hours before the dawn. When I knelt on the mattress, Royce drew me immediately into his arms, into his warmth, holding me close to his chest so I could feel his heart beating, feel the hollow echo of it in my own, silent chest. I sighed. This was something to which I could easily grow accustomed. I snuggled in, the sound of his pulse, the scent of sex lulling me into a state of purest relaxation.

I could tell by his breathing that Royce was already drifting, but before his heart slowed completely, he pulled me closer. One strong hand cradled the back of my head, the other coming to rest upon my ass, holding me secure like my body was something precious.

It had been quite some time since I had been held like that.

My kind had no cause to slumber, but occasionally our minds would slow, and drift, allowing us to enter a restful state. It only occurred if we were truly at peace, secure and safe. It was a rare thing, so imagine my surprise when I was startled by a fiery stripe of searing pain across my back. I hissed, alert at once with my fangs distending and dripping venom.

Disentangling myself from my sweet, slumbering Royce, I leapt from the mattress. I realized in distress that I'd been so comfortable in his embrace that I'd lost track of time.

It was dawn. The pain lancing across my bare back came from the infernal rays of sunshine slithering through the slats in Royce's sheer window dressing.

If I hoped to make it home to my den without hideous, blistering burns, I would have to transform.

Dammit all to hell. I would have to forgo my attire and effects from the night before, leave it all behind here, which would be very confusing for Royce. There was nothing for it, I supposed. With not even time to leave a note, I called upon the powers of the night and slipped into my bat form, fluttering to the sill. Bats were creatures of the dark, of course, but the sun didn't burn me the way it did when I walked upon two legs. Here, I paused, taking a final look at my new lover sprawled bare on his back, his lovely body rendered boneless and sated by my hand. The thought stirred a possessive flare in my heart as I took in the beautiful array of purple bruises my lips had left like a collar around Royce's neck. I probably shouldn't have marked him so aggressively, but I hadn't been able to help myself. Besides, when he woke, he'd have something to commemorate our first evening together—a calling card, if you will. I'd nipped and sucked my marks on the tender flesh of his throat, down his chest, and a few other places in my passion, leaving little flesh memories of my lips and teeth on his body like a field of violets.

The sight was tempting, to be sure. I longed to crawl

back into bed and wake him with my mouth around his morning hardness, but I had to return to my den lest I be exposed even further to the traitorous rays of the sun. Royce was not ready for the whole truth of me yet, of that I was certain. With one last look at the marvel of his skin against the blankets, so rumpled by our loving, I flew out the window.

2

A MANUAL OF COURTSHIP

ROYCE

"Nuhhh." I flailed with one hand, the other going to wipe the drool off the side of my face. It was early, but a weird hiss and a series of squeaking sounds had jerked me awake. My whole body felt like I'd been hit by a truck. It had been years since I'd had that much sex in a week, let alone one night. Thank God I had the day off to recover. I considered limping out to the kitchen to grab a bag of frozen peas to put on my junk.

I was alone. I shouldn't be surprised that...I frowned. Holy shit. As I sat up in bed, I realized I had no idea what the guy's name was. I covered my face with my hands, wracking my brain—had he not introduced himself? I'd looked at his ID, hadn't I? But I'd been fixated on his birthday—which escaped me, also—and not his name. Jesus.

I got out of bed, sticky with stale sweat and dried cum. A shower would be my first order of business, and then a long morning of coffee and examining my life choices. With the shower steaming away the lingering physical traces of my evening, I allowed myself to remember, hoping to crystalize every moment to recall on lonely nights going forward. That guy had been magnificent.

It was still shocking that of all the people in the club he'd turned those beautiful eyes on me, but I was glad I hadn't looked a gift horse in the mouth. With a soapy palm, I stroked myself casually, rewinding and committing every inch of the mystery man's body to memory. His eyes, his mouth, his skin, the way he'd cried out when I fucked him, the way his freckles made such a nice pattern on the skin of his sweet little ass.

Too bad he'd hightailed it out of here. I should have figured he wouldn't want to stick around—he'd tried leaving somewhere around orgasm number four and I'd begged him to stay. *Pathetic,* I cursed myself. Probably why he left. Maybe if I hadn't been so clingy, he would have given me his number.

Or even his name

After turning off the shower, I toweled myself dry and bent to pull on some clean sweats. I glanced in the full-length mirror behind the bathroom door and almost had a heart attack. I was fucking covered in hickeys and weird little marks, like I'd slept in a bed full of horny spiders. Like I had a hickey necklace, they covered the skin over my collarbones and I found another on my pec, right beside my nipple. There were two on my left hip, and several more on my thighs. Good grief, I even found one on the instep of my right foot. How on earth had that gotten there?

I didn't remember him being that aggressive, and it certainly didn't explain the weird little punctures at the center of each hickey. I dragged my fingers over the bruises, shivering, kind of liking that he'd left his mark behind. I had the sweetest ache in my lower back from pounding him so mercilessly, and I—oh *shit*. Another thing about last night came screaming back to me: we hadn't used protection.

With a mind to schedule an STI panel, I wandered into my living room in hopes of finding my phone with at least a partial charge, and I realized something very, *very* odd.

All of his clothes were still here.

What in the actual fuck? Had he been so full of morning-after regret he had to do the walk of shame totally bare-assed? I dialed my doctor's office, and paced my living room with my phone clenched between my cheek and shoulder as I confirmed every article of clothing he'd worn remained here in my house. Thinking maybe he swiped something clean of mine to wear home—an odd choice, but certainly no odder than strutting down the street naked—I checked my drawers. I didn't have a lot of clothing so inventorying things didn't take very long. Everything seemed accounted for.

"Name and date of birth, please?"

"Oh, *shit*—sorry." I'd forgotten I was on the phone. Once I had my appointment booked, I gathered up the guy's clothes—after checking his pockets, empty—right down to his black Converse, and stuffed them into a bag in my closet. Out of sight, out of mind. Or so I hoped.

Despite the scorching chemistry between me and my mystery lay, it was clear there wasn't going to be a repeat performance. I'd proven I could be adventurous, for all the good it did me. Time to settle down and get back to the real world.

Unfortunately, my real world wasn't any more relaxing.

My commanding officer, Sergeant Stark—or, rather, *Lieutenant* Stark—had just been promoted. He was a hard ass, a stickler, shrewd, ruthless, and unfortunately, I was on the top of his shit list. Or so it seemed to me.

We'd been partnered on a case in the spring, a grizzly serial homicide. The whole thing was insane, and it had proven to me beyond a shadow of a doubt that the city around me harbored an underworld. A paranormal underworld.

After spending months unraveling all the threads of the case, Stark had steamrollered me, chalked the whole thing up to some elaborate hoax. None of the surviving victims had felt comfortable pressing charges, so while the killer had ultimately met his end—it didn't feel like justice.

At first, I'd thought Stark was just stuck in his ways. An old-school cop who didn't want to accept this strange new world we'd stumbled into. I supposed, in a way, I could have lived with that. But the more I thought about it, the more it didn't make sense. He'd been trying to bury the case *way* before we'd found out about the paranormal beings at the center.

Almost like he'd already known.

He'd shown up in Douglas Crest about a year ago, transferring from the much larger police department in Denver, an unusual career move considering it hadn't been a promotion at the time. There was a ton of department gossip about it, and the only thing I could really confirm was that a family death had shaken his mojo, and he'd come here.

I was determined to find out more. The problem, though, with our department finally going digital was that a record remained, an electronic paper trail of sorts, for every file requested, every stone I turned. If I wanted to investigate further, I would have to be careful. I couldn't just put in written requests for every old case file of Stark's before he came to—

"Why are you wearing a scarf?"

My partner, Detective Priya Tanti, wasn't much for small talk, and she caught me off guard as she rolled her chair over toward my desk.

"I wear scarves all the time," I said. There went my hope of it going unnoticed.

"The fuck you do," she said with a laugh, as if I'd come to work with a neon green mohawk out of nowhere. "What, you got a hickey under there you're trying to hide?"

I blanched. "Uh..."

"Oh damn," said Priya. "I was just kidding, but you've been holding out on me!"

"I have not. Can we please just drop it?"

"Yeah, no," she said. "So, who is he? Did Derek come crawling back or are you seeing someone new?"

I huffed, knowing my chances of convincing her to drop this were lower than finding the true identity of the Zodiac Killer. Without meeting her eyes, I said, "Neither."

"Oh?"

"I went to that club, Electric Eel, downtown, and uh."

"Davis!" she smacked my arm. "You got down and dirty with Dr. Strangelove! What's his name?"

I blushed, tugging nervously on my scarf.

Priya let out a low whistle. "Well, well," she said. "Good for you. You needed it."

"What's that supposed to mean?"

"Davis, you've been so pent up I was afraid you'd pop a hernia."

"Ha, ha."

"I'm serious. The pen caps around the office will thank you."

"What do you—"

She nudged my hand up into the space between us, that was indeed holding a pen, with its cap chewed almost to nonexistence.

"Fair point."

"You going to see him again?"

I shrugged. "He took off in the morning before I woke up." I left out the part where he'd neglected to get dressed first.

"But you want to?"

"*Davis!*"

Saved by the bark. I escaped from Priya's probing and hustled to Stark's office. However, I had a sneaking suspicion this would shape up to be an "out of the frying pan into the fire" type situation.

"You wanted to see me, Sir?"

Stark looked up from the paperwork on his desk as if I'd interrupted him and he hadn't summoned me in here. "There's a woman here whose statement I need you to take."

"Oh?"

"Yes. She thinks her son is missing."

"Missing?" I frowned.

"Yes, Detective. Missing."

"Sir, I'm homicide."

Stark fixed me with a ball-shriveling stare so intense I actually winced. "Really? I was under the impression that you were a detective under my command."

"Sir—"

"Perhaps I was mistaken."

"No," I said hastily. "Of course, I'll take her statement."

Before he could give me any other veiled threats, I hauled ass out of his office and into the waiting area. It was uncommon for homicide detectives to work on missing persons cases in our department, especially because so many of them go cold, or, conversely, get taken over by federal investigators. I supposed I should just appreciate getting a new case assigned at all—Stark had been passing me up at any possible opportunity.

The woman in the lounge looked haggard, her eyes sunken, and her skin had the pallor of someone who hadn't slept in a long time. The look of anguish on her face whipped my own gripes from the forefront of my mind. Departmental politics could wait.

"Ma'am," I said, extending my hand. "I'm Detective Davis. My commanding officer says you would like to report someone missing?"

Her hand trembled as it clasped mine. "Detective, thank you for seeing me."

"Why don't you have a seat?" I pulled out a chair. "Can I get you a glass of water or anything?"

"No, no thank you."

We sat in awkward silence for a few loaded moments, but I knew to let it ride. This woman needed to unburden herself.

"My name is Mirabel Taylor," she finally started. "My son, Beckett, is missing."

"Alright," I said. I clicked the top of my pen—see, who needs pen caps anyway?—and flipped open my notebook. "Start from the beginning. When was the last time you saw Beckett?"

"Four weeks ago."

"Four—hold on, and forgive me, why are you just reporting him missing now?"

"He was away at college," she explained. "We spoke on the phone every night until his classes began, and then less often—but then, I stopped hearing from him altogether."

I bit my tongue. Smaller city police departments got dozens of calls like this every fall. Two days from now, chances were, her son would call, apologizing because he got caught up "studying." And by "studying," I of course mean hooking up and partying. And maybe studying.

"I know how this sounds," she said as if she could read my thoughts on my face, and her gaze grew fierce. "But I know my son. Something is wrong. He hasn't even texted me in over a week."

I nodded. "Alright, ma'am. I'm sorry. Please go on—tell me more about your son."

I took down all the details about Beckett Taylor, and told his mother I'd call her when I had a lead. She shook my hand again before she left, and I reviewed my notes, delaying re-entering the bullpen.

Priya was still perched by my desk, waiting for the details of my hookup. When I couldn't stall any longer, I slowly approached my desk.

"What was that about?"

"Just a missing persons case," I said.

"That's weird," said Priya. "When was the last time you worked missing persons?"

It hadn't actually been that long, when I thought about it. While investigating the paranormal homicide this spring, one of my persons of interest in the case had been abducted. But what I said was, "Doesn't matter. I really want to help this woman."

"Aw," said Priya. "You're so sensitive now that you've gotten some."

"Good grief." I tried to convey that I had a lot of important things to do by ostentatiously flipping open my notebook and beginning the process of opening the new case file.

"Anyway, I was thinking," said Priya, clearly not reading the room. "Why don't I swing by later and we can dust your place for fingerprints?"

"Jesus, Priya."

"I'm serious. It'll be a modern-day Cinderella."

"Yeah," I said. "So romantic when I violate his privacy by running his prints! Then I get to see if he's also a violent felon, or just a nudist weirdo."

"Wait. Hold up a minute."

Shit. "Wow, look at the time!" I stood and tried to escape to the breakroom.

"Nudist?" Priya echoed, so loudly a few of the uniformed officers looked around in time to see her chasing me down the hall.

"For the love of *God*," I said. "Be quiet!"

"You better start spilling, Royce." When she used my first name, it was serious business.

I started at the beginning. Priya already knew how I'd been "coping" with my breakup, so thankfully I could skip that part, but she pressed for details about the rest.

"Four times?" she blurted.

I munched on a jelly cruller. "Yeah." I swallowed. "So?"

She held out a fist for me to bump. "Respect."

I couldn't suppress a grin as I bumped her back. I supposed it was fairly impressive, for me at least. "Anyway," I said. "I woke up, and he was gone, poof. But all his clothes were still at my place."

"What the..." she frowned. "Did he get raptured?"

I shrugged. "Your theory's as good as mine."

"Okay, this settles it. I'm coming over tomorrow with a print kit."

"You can't do that."

"Uh, hello? This is practically a missing person case, which is apparently your new forte."

I let my head fall forward onto the table with a thunk.

The next few days were business as usual, which was something of a relief, but I was hitting more than one wall on Beckett Taylor's case. The first few days of a missing persons investigation were critical, and so far I had fuck all. Considering he'd been missing for a few weeks already, things were pretty grim.

I got home, frustrated and exhausted. I grabbed a beer from my fridge, popping the top and taking a long gulp. Priya had made good on her promise to dust my place for prints, and I honestly wasn't sure what I wanted her to find. After our night together, I would have liked to see him again, but the circumstances were weird enough that I kind of hoped her search came up empty. As I sipped my beer, it took a second for me to register a rustling, thumping noise coming from down the hall. *There was someone in my apartment.*

I put down my bottle. Slowly and silently, I drew my sidearm and approached the door to my bedroom. "Police," I said firmly. "Put your hands up, and don't do anything stupid."

No answer from inside, so I cautiously pushed the door, keeping my gun trained into the room. It was empty, except for a small, brownish-red blur zooming spastically around the ceiling, squeaking and flailing.

A bat.

I exhaled, lowering my gun, unsure of what to do. Then, the bat dive-bombed my head. I yelped and hit the deck, definitely more afraid of a possibly rabid bat than I would have been of an intruder. I obviously couldn't shoot it, so I had to stun it somehow and get it the hell out of my house. On my belly on the floor, I spied Derek's old squash racket, lying under the bed.

Wrapping my fingers around the handle, I drew it close to my body and got ready to make my move. When I was pretty sure of the location of the squeaky maniac zipping around above me, I leapt up, planted my feet, and swung the racket. It connected with a soft twang, and the little thing rocketed toward the wall, where it hit, stunned, and fell toward the rug.

I stared, open-mouthed, as the bat fell—almost like slow motion. It stretched and twisted, its fur retreating into its body, its wings lengthening, the wiry membrane between the tiny wing bones pulling back as they became slender, elegant fingers. The bat exploded outward from itself, growing from a tiny creature into an untidy tangle of pale limbs as it—he—hit the carpet with a loud thud.

"*What the fuck?*" I blurted, staring at my very naked hookup from the other night, curled up on my floor, slightly dazed from being struck by the racket.

"Uh," he said, before chewing his bottom lip. Then he sprang to his feet, sprinted past me and dove out my open (fourth-floor) window.

I stood rooted to the spot for several confused seconds before I dashed after him, leaning out the window just in time to see a teensy, erratic speck disappear against the sky.

On jelly legs, I staggered over to my bed and sat down. This wasn't necessarily the weirdest thing I'd ever seen, just the weirdest thing I'd seen in my own bedroom. As I sat, something caught my eye. Someone, and I had a pretty strong suspicion who, had left a note on my pillow.

"*Call me, -S.*" And beside it, a phone number and a little

scribble that looked like...two stick figures fucking? With hearts floating over it?

Jesus. I flopped back onto the mattress, holding my phone to scroll through the contacts list. If this mysterious S was what I thought he was, I was in way over my head. I needed help.

Paranormal help.

———

SINCLAIR

Damn! My head still smarted where Royce struck me with that infernal instrument, but the way he called commandingly into the room when he thought I was an intruder, the flex of his arms as he wound up for the swing—I couldn't help but swell with pride at his tenacity. I was glad to know Royce would not be vulnerable in my absence, but he had spoiled the mystique of my little note.

I had been watching Royce since the evening after our initial coupling, hoping for an opportunity to reconnect. Every new thing I learned about him fascinated me.

He loved jelly doughnuts.

He hunted and apprehended criminals.

He slept on his stomach.

His car was tidy, but his apartment messy.

And, apparently, he played some sort of sport with that wretched stringed club. Each little ordinary piece of his life was something I longed to be a part of.

I felt for him as he struggled to prove the dastardly deeds of the fiends he tracked. The case he worked currently involved a young man who was missing, and

Royce was trying to reunite him with his family, a most noble goal.

I could observe Royce easily after dark, of course, but daylight hours posed a significant logistical problem. Luckily, I did not have to sleep, so I could spend a lot of time at night establishing hidey holes and paths through the city that would allow me to travel from my den to Royce's frequent haunts without risking sunlight exposure. It took me a few days to map my routes, and this would allow me unfettered access to observe Royce, so long as he didn't vary from his routine. I imagined, as a police detective, that he would need to vary his routine quite regularly, but I found he spent quite a deal of time shackled to his desk filling out paperwork. I could tell from where I observed him that he was unhappy. Something was keeping him there, keeping him from being out on the streets, fighting the good fight.

It had been several days since I fed, and the thirst clawed its way up my throat, hunger gnawing at my gut. Loath as I was to abandon my observation of Royce, to maintain focus I would need to feed soon.

When I first began this life, feeding was frightening and violent. The urge was so strong, painful. Agonizing. I'd been alone, bewildered and afraid. It had taken quite some time for me to reach the level of control I now possessed, especially without a sire to aid in my education. I'd learned in my travels that most of my kind were reared by a sire, in a way. Groomed and guided to feed without detection from the human population. Learning on my own had been a difficult slog indeed, but I got there eventually, and now I could feed without creating a big violent scene, as long as I took care to manage my urges.

I climbed the wall outside Royce's bed chamber window, to watch over him as he slept, as I had been doing every night since we parted. As he stripped down for bed, I crouched in the shadows. The night we met, I'd left my marks upon his skin, which I imagined in polite society would convey, "Please do not feed upon this one; they are spoken for!" But the marks faded steadily with each passing day, and as I had learned, the rules of polite society did not always prevail.

I needed Royce to reach out, so he would let me touch his precious skin again, split me open, let me sink my fangs deep into his throat, and perhaps, with his consent, feed on him. Just a hint. I hardened at the thought, the idea of savoring the deepest, most hidden part of Royce during our lovemaking...such things were reserved for only the most intimate of couplings.

It was an exercise in control and devotion, different than feeding off someone you fucked and not really caring how it ended up. Or feeding on prey you had no intention of fucking. That was fairly common. Feeding on one's true lover was a sacred contract. I simmered at the thought of taking that step with Royce, knowing how much pleasure it would bring him, as well.

Pressing a palm to the arousal growing hot and tight between my legs, I continued watching Royce as he sat in bed, blankets around his waist, thumb moving over the screen of his mobile telephone. I could have stared at him all night and never tire, and in fact, I decided to do just that. He had to call me soon. Surely, he must.

Two days later, however, I still waited by the phone. Perhaps I had not done enough to entice this beguiling man. If I was going to win Royce's body and heart, I would have to prove myself a worthy consort.

I would have to formally woo him.

3
ON THE ART OF GIVING PRESENTS

ROYCE

O kay, so. I definitely had a stalker.

It was the third day in a row I'd come into work to find a gift.

The first day, I'd thought there was some kind of mistake because no one had ever sent me flowers before.

But there wasn't any other Royce here, and the bouquet had a card with my name on it. "My darling Royce," it said. With another erotic stick figure drawing.

The flowers weren't like any other bouquet I'd ever seen —they were wild looking, with a lot of green, more greenery than you'd expect in a typical flower arrangement. They weren't wrapped in paper or cellophane but a thin whisp of silk ribbon.

"Woah," said Priya. "Who sent you those?"

"No idea," I lied, with a funny feeling in my stomach. Who else could it be but S?

Priya inhaled through her nose. "What's that smell?"

I held up the bouquet. "Flowers?"

"No shit," she snapped, leaning closer to sniff them. "It smells like that witchy store over on Elm."

I leaned in, too. "Huh."

"Sage," she confirmed, toying with one of the leaves. "That's weird."

"Is it?"

Priya rolled her eyes at me. I liked the sage, though.

Then, the next day, another bouquet came.

Then, another. I was sweating it by then because they got bigger each time. This third one was full of red roses, red tulips, and a bunch of other shit I didn't know the name of. On that day, Priya came over and sat on the edge of my desk. "Okay, so the fingerprint search was a total bust," she said. She leaned over and entered something on my computer.

Priya pulled up an ancient arrest report—so old I was shocked it had even been digitized. I remembered vaguely that the department had interns scanning and saving all the old files from when the Douglas Crest Police Department was founded over a hundred years ago.

"I got a partial," she said with a little scoff, "but obviously this old record is way off—unless you fucked a ghost."

Featured in the top corner of the scanned, hand-written report, was an old photograph.

Of S.

Dated 1857.

"This is from a series of unsolved murders," she said. "Though I really don't know how uncommon that was back then. The suspect was never found again after they brought him in for initial questioning."

"So that's probably not him then!" Priya stared at me because while I'd been aiming for an offhand, sarcastic tone, my voice had come out strangled and brittle. *Did I fuck a ghost?*

"Maybe your mystery lay was a ghost," said Priya, as if reading my thoughts. "Are you sure he wasn't just a steamy wet dream born of a sad, single existence—and a few too many?"

A few months ago, I would have given her theory some serious consideration. Before the flowers. Before the fucking *bat* in my bedroom. And of course, before the case that had proven to me the existence of the paranormal. I chewed my lip, guilt surging through me as I looked at Priya. She was my partner and my best friend, and every conversation we'd had since then felt like a lie. But I didn't want to pull her into all this insanity. And to be honest, I had really hoped to escape the insanity, too.

I had gotten so much pressure from Stark to bury the case. He wanted me to pretend it had never happened, go back to investigating other crimes like everything was totally normal, and God help me, I had been *trying*, but S was making it damn difficult. And now I had no choice but to dive back into that world for advice on my distressing love life.

I had plans after work to meet up with contacts from that case, two young men who I hoped would be able to shed some light on my ghost slash murderer slash bat hookup. Thor Ambrose and Cassian Rhodes went to Fremont University, a nearby college. If anyone could give me advice on S and his penchant for dropping trou and turning into a bat, it was them. Cassian was just an average college kid, but his boyfriend Thor...well. He could transform into a hedgehog at will. And he came from a whole family of people with similar powers.

When I left the precinct, I drove across Douglas Crest to

meet the guys at a little café on Fremont's campus, which made me feel about a thousand years old. Thor and Cas were already seated at a table in the corner sharing a slice of cake and being cute, and making everyone else on the planet feel romantically inadequate. Or maybe that was just me. I cleared my throat. "Hey, guys. Thanks for meeting me."

"Detective Davis," said Cas warmly, standing to pull me into an awkward guy-hug. He'd helped me on the paranormal serial case, and I'd helped prove Cas hadn't abducted and tortured his own boyfriend, so I guess that made us friends. "Have a seat."

Thor was different, small and shy, with glasses and a calculating, guarded look. Prickly as the animal he turned into. He gave me a brief smile before taking Cas's hand where it rested on the table. I had a feeling he wasn't thrilled to relive the events that had brought the three of us into each other's lives, and I couldn't blame him. Luckily, that wasn't why I was here. "I just have a couple questions for you, if you don't mind."

"Is this about a case?"

I cleared my throat again, unable to force the heat from rising to my face. Loosening my tie, I said, "No. It's um, personal."

They exchanged a glance, but waited for me to continue.

"I, uh." Oh, Jesus Christ. I really needed this *not* to come off like I was asking for actual relationship advice. "I met someone." I tried to give them a significant look.

"Oh? That's um, that's great, Detective Davis." Cas shifted uncomfortably.

"Someone," and I added more emphasis on the word, "Someone who I think is like..." I gestured at Thor.

He blinked at me in surprise, sliding his glasses up the bridge of his nose. "A shifter?"

"I believe so."

Thor leaned forward in his seat, looking critical. "Alright, so she's—"

"He."

"He," Thor amended. "He's a shifter. And...what?"

I fidgeted. Was I making a huge social blunder? Was this like, meeting someone from London and assuming they knew every other person who lived in London? I took a different tack. "His behavior was...odd."

"Odd how?"

"We met at a club," I said, my face positively flaming now. *Okay, Davis. Just rip off the Band-Aid.* "And I brought him home with me. The next morning, he left before I woke up."

"Well," said Cas, with the air of one about to drop a truth-bomb as gently as he possibly could.

"I *know*," I said, cutting across him, embarrassed. "That wasn't the weird part." In fact, someone as hot as S skipping out on me after an ill-advised one-night stand was just about the only normal part of this whole thing. "He left all his clothes."

They stared.

"At my place. Then, he came back a few nights later. As—as a bat."

Thor blanched. "A bat? You're certain?"

"Yes."

"What sort of bat?"

"What the—I have no idea? I guess he was kind of, orangey brown?"

Thor looked horrified. "And you're *sure* he was a bat?"

"Yes," I said, glancing between them. Cas looked just as lost as I was. "So...do—do you know him?"

"Emphatically *no,* Detective Davis—"

"You guys can call me Royce."

"Alright, Royce. Well, um." He adjusted his glasses again. "Shifters don't...shifters don't *have* bat *fauna.*"

I knew *fauna* was the term Thor's family and other shifters called their animal halves, but what he was saying didn't compute. "What does that mean?"

"It means your guy is something else."

Cas turned to his partner. "What, are you saying he's like, a Dracula?"

Thor grimaced. "Well, *technically...*"

My heart rate skyrocketed, and suddenly the café seemed very hot. I remembered the arrest report from over a hundred years ago. "Okay, uh. Okay."

"I could be wrong! My research into shifter lore is still in its infancy. There's a lot we don't know." said Thor hastily. He lowered his voice. "Did he bite you at all?"

"What does that prove?" Though I knew perfectly well what that would prove. "You bit Cas!"

Cas blushed and lowered his forehead to the table, and I realized I was being a *bit* loud. I was right, though. I'd learned from Thor that shifters bit their mates—it was a sort of claiming rite. Like a shifter engagement ring.

"Sorry," I said. "But. You know?"

"Let me see," said Thor, "the bite."

The bites on my neck, chest, and...elsewhere had faded, but I had snapped a few pictures the morning after I found them. I opened one of the pics that showcased the bite in an innocent location and slid my phone across the table.

"That's no mating bite." Thor frowned, drawing my phone closer. "But it doesn't look like..."

"Doesn't look like what?"

"It doesn't look like he fed on you."

"Oh, well, gee. That's a fucking relief."

The guys looked startled.

"Shit. Fuck. Sorry." I rubbed my hands over my face. "So, what do I do?

"I don't have a lot of notes on them," said Thor. "But I can check my research. All I know for sure is they're ancient. They're strong. And they're bad news."

Thor's words echoed in my head the entire drive home. They cycled through my brain for the remainder of the evening too, especially when I sprawled in bed, pressing my thumb against one of the hickeys S had left, shivering when I realized how much damage that little love bite could have caused. For good measure Thor's words remained in my head when I plunked down at my desk the following morning. On the plus side, no more flowers.

So why did I feel so disappointed?

———

SINCLAIR

I was at my wit's end with my courtship of Royce. My first offering, a bouquet of fern, sage, and sweet pea was meant to intrigue him. A subtle thank you for our evening together, a hint at my identity, and a nudge toward him using my telephone number. By the time I'd sent along the third bouquet, of the most obvious possible blooms—red roses, for God's sake—I was debasing myself. I may as well have wrapped the flowers around my cock and danced naked in front of him with how forward I was being, but still, he took no notice. I wished to tear my hair out!

My flower shop, Datura, had been several different businesses over the years. When I'd purchased the building from a defunct dress manufacturer, I'd rented it out until I was ready to return home. It had been a flower shop once before, when I first opened it in 1850.

Before I died.

Before I was turned, by parties unknown, and began my second life.

I had always loved flowers, then as now. I didn't often get to see them in the wild because most of them did not bloom at night, so the shop allowed me to capture a sliver of their beauty, and to share it with others. Flowers were truly the language of love, of courtship, of desire. Of passion. But Royce, it seemed, did not speak the same tongue of seduction that I did.

My Royce was playing hard to get.

To be honest, the hunter in me thrilled at the chase, delighted that Royce had decided to put me through my paces to prove my worth. Mere trinkets would not enchant him, no. He required a more personal, intimate courtship token. A gift only *I* could procure, to ensure I was foremost amongst all possible suitors.

Not one to back down from a challenge, I went to the heart of what seemed to be distressing Royce, and fixed it.

Over the course of my long life, I had become quite adept at living unseen. It was a necessity of my kind. We had powers beyond that of our human peers—but there were still ways we were vulnerable. Silver, sunlight, fire, decapitation. There might have been others, but I didn't care to discover them. I had spent my life more hidden than most, and with no sire to guide me, I had to learn most of these things on my own. Rarely did I stay in one place, and I never left myself vulnerable. I quietly haunted the dark places between sleeping and waking, fed no more than I had to, and hid, and hid, and hid.

Royce had me willing to take more risks in a few consecutive nights than I'd taken in my entire second life. I watched his police department building for a few days before I made my move. I learned the comings and the goings of the officers there before returning one night to creep into the basement and raid their dusty old file room.

It would, in theory, have been faster had I simply infiltrated the top floor and utilized Royce's personal computing device to access his files, but in truth, I had never been much good with newfangled tech. Humans were delightfully adaptive, whereas an old cat like me was stuck in his ways. At any rate, the file room, though slower, would serve.

By the time I left, leaving no trace of myself behind, I had a nice list of names tucked into my back pocket.

I had followed Royce through the course of his investigations since we'd entered each other's lives. He was an excellent investigator, to my eye. Always so stern, asking the right questions, catching criminals in their lies, exposing their true selves. Tragically, however, my noble Royce had to navigate the red tape of human justice. Unless he found the perfect evidentiary support, bandied words with defense attorneys, went through the months-long ordeal of a trial, and the scoundrels were correctly convicted, Royce's hands were tied.

Mine, thankfully, were not.

Armed with the chief suspects in four of Royce's open cases, I set out that night to...shall we say, encourage them to do the right thing. The first man, the suspect in a robbery and a killing, was the worst sort of common thug. His name was Blake Roberts, and due to Royce's exquisite note-taking, I found the man without any trouble whatsoever, stumbling out of a local pub sometime after last call.

This would work out splendidly, I decided, since I was absolutely famished. I came upon Roberts, silent as night-fall, stalking his footsteps as he wandered down the street. I waited until he stepped out from below the halo of light cast by the streetlamps above, and pulled him into a dark-ened alley. With my hand at his throat, fingers flexed like bars of iron, I held him up against the bricks. He was taller than I, but my strength allowed me to slide him roughly up the wall until his feet kicked out uselessly into the air between us.

I distended my fangs, hunger burning down my throat, mouth dry, tongue darting out to taste his fear upon the air. "You are Blake Roberts," I said.

His eyes widened and he stammered some nonsense. He struggled, but I planted my feet and held firm. I squeezed my fingers into his neck, and with my full speed and strength, I slammed him to the damp ground at my feet. He let out a squeal of terror, most undignified. Drip-ping venom, I sank my teeth into his throat, and blissfully, I fed.

I fed upon this murderer, ripping my mouth from his flesh just shy of causing permanent damage. It was rough and gluttonous, no finesse. It had been quite some time since I'd fed like that. In this state, he was supremely vulnerable to my powers of suggestion. He would tell the truth. He would be locked away. And Royce would know that I had helped him.

"Did you burgle the man, Joshua Gould, and subse-quently take his life?"

"Yes," Roberts rasped, barely conscious. His hand clasped the wound on his throat, with which I had taken no care to be delicate. It still bled freely between his ugly fingers, and I marshaled my self-control, resisting the desire for further feeding, and told him, "You will walk to the eighth precinct. You will confess your crimes to Detective Royce Davis."

"Alright," he agreed placidly, sitting up. His eyes were far away.

I tied one of my silk floral ribbons around his wrist with a fetching bow for Royce, so he'd know for sure the gift came from me. With Roberts' blood still hot upon my lips, I recalled something from Royce's notes on the case about a missing heirloom. "And," I added, "You will tell me where you secreted the poor man's wedding ring."

ROYCE

If I hadn't taken the confession myself, I would never have believed it. The prime suspect in a months-cold burglary slash homicide case, Blake Roberts, had marched into the precinct with a dazed look on his face, a dirty bandage around his neck, and confessed to everything. He even gave us the name of his fence, another significant collar.

He waved his right to counsel, and blandly explained how he'd carried out the crime. I only wished that he'd confessed where he'd sold the victim's wedding ring, but at this point, the ring was probably long gone. A shame, I'd liked to have returned it to his family. As I finished taking down his confession, something purple on his arm caught my eye.

"What's that?" I asked, pointing at the strip of fabric around his wrist.

"He put it there," said Roberts.

I frowned, pulse quickening. "Who?"

Roberts screwed up his face, like he was struggling to remember. "Didn't say."

Without thinking, I snagged the scrap of what turned out to be ribbon, and the bottom fell out of my stomach. It was a bow, identical to the ones I'd found tied neatly around my bouquets. I recoiled, leaving the interrogation room, and it wasn't until I had collapsed into my desk chair that I'd realized I'd taken the ribbon, and now sat with it clutched in my sweaty fist.

I looked at it for a long time, until Priya came over. "So, that was weird."

"Yeah." I didn't look up.

"What do you have there?"

I shoved my hand into the pocket of my jacket, still squeezing the ribbon. "Nothing."

"Alright." She pulled over her chair and sat down beside me so we could fill out the case paperwork for Roberts.

"Maybe when we bring in the fence, we can get that ring," I said, thinking of the victim's widow.

"Maybe," said Priya. "Long shot, though. Then again, him walking in off the street and confessing was a long shot too, so who knows?"

Feeling out of sorts, I walked home in lieu of taking the bus. By the time I got to my building, I was sweaty and out of breath, and my head was just as muddled as before.

I unlocked my front door, bone tired. It was late, my apartment was dark, and I wasn't even going to turn on the light before stumbling to bed.

"I couldn't wait any longer," came a soft, musical voice from the shadows.

I had my gun out and the light on in the span of one breath, training the barrel on the source of the voice.

My mysterious hookup stood in my living room, grinning sheepishly. At least he looked human this time. At least he was dressed. He raised his hands in surrender.

I didn't lower my sidearm, even as my heart beat faster —not in fear. "S," I said, not a question.

"Did you get my gift?" His eyes shone—innocent, bright, and earnest, like he hadn't sent a half-dead killer to my door.

"Your *gift?*" I echoed, my finger still brushing the trigger.

He showed absolutely no fear of my gun and stepped toward me. "Roberts."

"Yeah, no. I know."

He stuck out his plump lower lip. "You didn't call."

I blinked in surprise. He sounded honestly hurt that I hadn't called him. Under all the coco-nuts nature of this entire situation, I was shocked, on a basic level, that he wanted to continue things between us. "You left," I said, gun lowering a fraction of an inch. "Before I woke up."

Another step closer. *Why wasn't I shooting?* "I had to."

My mouth ran dry. "Why?"

Suddenly, he was right in front of me, and I hadn't seen him take another step. He nudged the arm holding the gun aside. "You know why."

His pupils blew wide as he looked at me, that damned pointed canine sticking out over his lip as he waited for me to speak. Every time he flashed that tooth, I remembered how it felt to have his mouth on my body, and now, I felt a jittery sort of nervousness at the thought of it piercing my skin. My brain sort of melted as I looked down into his eyes. I was close enough to count his lashes. "Uh," I said.

He closed his eyes, inhaling deeply. "You smell intox-icating."

Gross. The word he was looking for was gross. "I'm all sweaty."

Standing on tiptoe, he ran his nose up my neck. I *thought* I was still holding my gun? "Intoxicating," he repeated, and I felt the cool gust of his breath, raising goosebumps.

I shivered.

"I have another gift for you," he whispered in my ear. He drew back, just half a step, and plucked the gun from my limp fingers.

"S," I said because I didn't know what else to call him. I didn't know what else to say.

Something small and heavy and cold landed in my hand. I peered down at it, resting on my upturned palm between our bodies.

It was my burglary victim's wedding ring.

"Sinclair," he said, and it was like a song. "My name is Sinclair."

4
EVERYDAY PROBLEMS IN ETIQUETTE

SINCLAIR

Now that Royce knew my intent, I figured he would be ready for us to take the next step to progress our courtship. However, he still refused to call me. Oh, Royce!

He had me so twisted in knots I didn't know which way was up. I continued to send him flowers from my shop, all while waiting by the phone, watching over him at night, and finding new criminals to deposit on his doorstep.

While this kept me very well fed, the longing for Royce destroyed the savor of each meal.

One morning, after sending two violent ne'er-do-wells along to the eighth precinct—I had been *famished*, and perhaps drinking my romantic woes away—I was startled from my moping by the trill of my mobile telephone.

"Good morning," I said into the receiver.

"Sinclair?"

I released a dreamy sigh. Royce had finally called! "Speaking."

"It's uh." He cleared his throat. "Royce."

How could I have forgotten the sultry, masculine timbre of his voice? "I know."

The line remained silent for some time until Royce said, "I think we should meet."

I couldn't help the little jig I did at the sound of his words, but I had to maintain my composure. "Of course —when?"

"Tonight," he said. "I'll call you."

And he hung up. So brusque! So direct! I could expect nothing else from Royce. He was a man of action, to be sure. But, so was I. That evening, I awaited sunset with even more potent eagerness than usual, dressing in my finest— but still casual—courting attire. I took a taxi to the precinct, knowing Royce would still be working. I wanted him to know that I was no passive partner, so I refused to wait by the telephone any longer, especially given how long it took him to call me the first time.

With the sun barely setting, I had my face cowled by a hood and a pair of sunglasses to protect myself as I ascended the steps. The precinct was dreadfully grimy, and I hated to imagine a vibrant soul such as Royce toiling daily in a cave like this. However, I knew him to be the tough "roll up your sleeves" type of man I had never been able to resist. A man of the people. Of course, he would not consider himself above his peers and—

"Can I help you, kid?"

A beautiful woman with dark hair and sharp, intelligent eyes crossed her arms over her Douglas Crest Police Department windbreaker. I did not know her name, but I knew her to be a close work compatriot of Royce. "Hello," I said sweetly. She didn't seem the type of woman to be easily charmed, but then again, good manners cost nothing. I peeked at her over the top of my aviators. "I'm looking for my boyfriend. He works here."

————

ROYCE

My arrest numbers had been through the roof recently, which would have been cause for celebration, however, the fact that I had criminals confessing left, right, and fucking sideways started to look a bit suspicious. Stark hadn't called me into his office about it yet, but I could feel it was coming. The men were all guilty as sin, I was sure of that, but it was still weird.

I had to convince Sinclair to stop doing whatever it was he was doing. Flirting, maybe. Or at least, that's what I thought *he* thought he was doing. Scowling, I closed out another report—a second drawback. I hated paperwork. I loved being out on the street, chasing down leads and questioning witnesses. I did not love drowning in files.

"Davis," called Priya. "Someone here to see you."

Expecting to see yet another suspect ready to confess his crimes, I looked up to see her crossing the bullpen toward my desk. When my eyes fell on the person next to her, I almost had a heart attack. Sinclair, his face covered in giant aviators and with a hooded sweatshirt pulled up over his head, looked even younger than he had the night we'd met. Ironic, because according to his arrest file he was over a century old. When he saw me looking, he beamed, waving excitedly as Priya escorted him through the maze of desks.

"Royce!" he said, bounding up to me and throwing himself across my lap before I could so much as blink.

"Uh," I said, my face flaming as he kissed my cheek. "Yes. Hi."

Priya was positively giddy as she watched this play out. "Sinclair here was just introducing himself," she said, and it was obvious her composure was hanging by a thread as she barely contained her laughter. I imagined there would be a lecture about midlife crises in my future.

"Oh, good, I'm so glad you two have met," I said through gritted teeth. I turned to Sinclair, who was happily ensconced playing with the collar of my shirt, still sitting in my lap. The officers on duty were either staring openly or trying to conceal their grins—and failing. I'd never had a guy come visit me at work, let alone someone like Sinclair —young, beautiful, and without an ounce of shame about PDA.

Sinclair pulled off his dark glasses and said, "I was so happy to get to know your partner here."

Before I could stop him, he turned to throw Priya a winning smile, giving her a good look at his unobstructed face for the first time. Her smirk fell away so fast it was alarming, and I knew she recognized Sinclair from the picture in that old file. I practically shoved him off my lap, though he landed gracefully on his feet. I grabbed him by the arm and squeezed. "Can you please wait for me in the break room, just over there?"

"But, I—"

I nudged him in the right direction and he took the hint, gliding off through the bullpen toward the door.

Priya stared at me in horror. "Tell me that's not who I think it is."

I was certain I made a guilty face, but I said. "Depends. Who do you think it is?"

"The suspect from a hundred-and-fifty-year-old

unsolved murder," Priya hissed, leaning in close so we wouldn't be overheard. I glanced toward Sinclair, who now scrutinized the donuts in the breakroom.

"How could that be him?" I asked her innocently, kind of surprised at my own daring. But really, there was no way it *could* be him—as far as Priya knew.

She narrowed her eyes at me because of course I had her there. "I don't know, but he's a dead ringer for the picture that matched the prints at your place."

I pretended to consider this. "I guess I could see a resemblance," I said. "Maybe it was his great-great-grand-father or something."

"Come the fuck *on*, Davis. Fingerprints aren't heredi-tary, you absolute walnut."

"I just don't think they look that much alike," I said, and I felt weirdly giddy. This was so obviously a lie, and yet, the truth was clearly impossible—something I could see Priya grappling with as she stared at Sinclair through the windows to the break room.

Priya snorted and seized my computer keyboard, trying to pull up the file. I watched Sinclair, who had picked up a bear claw from the pastry box and sniffed it with distaste. If Thor's theory was correct, I couldn't imagine those were part of his usual diet. *Yeesh.* Heat coiled low in my stomach as I realized that *I* could be part of his usual diet. What would that feel like? Like he could sense my gaze, Sinclair looked up, met my eye from across the station, and grinned.

"What the fuck," Priya cursed softly.

"What?" I turned my attention back to her.

"I can't find the record of that case. I can't even find the record of the fingerprints I scanned in from your apartment to compare." She looked at me suspiciously. "Did you delete the files?"

"How?" And I wasn't lying now. I swung my chair around beside her to examine the screen. "I don't have access to delete case files, Priya."

"But—"

"Come on," I said honestly. "I can barely delete an email."

"Then what happened to your boyfriend's file?"

"He's not my boyfriend," I snapped.

Priya raised her brows with a light scoff. "Have you told him that?" She stalked back toward her own desk. No sooner had her butt hit her chair than a hand landed on my shoulder.

I jumped about a mile and looked up to see Sinclair had returned. "Here," he said. He pulled a small white bag from inside his dark leather jacket. Examining it up close, I saw it had a velvet brocade pattern overlaid on the leather. It looked very expensive. "The pastries in there are a health hazard. And you look pale."

I peered inside the bag, which was stamped with the logo from a fancy boutique bakery across town, and pulled out a doughnut. "I do love jelly," I admitted.

"I know."

I frowned around an enormous mouthful. "How?"

"I have been watching you, Royce Davis."

Flustered, I licked some of the excess powdered sugar from my finger, watching as Sinclair parted his lips, his eyes following the movement of my tongue. "Oh," I said stupidly. Then I frowned again because his words actually caught up with my flirt-dumb brain. "Hold on—you've—you've what?"

"I've been watching you," he repeated softly, "so I could learn what you wanted. What you needed. So I could woo you."

"I'm sorry, *woo* me?" I could practically feel Priya straining her ears from across the room to eavesdrop.

"Did you not enjoy my gifts?" Sinclair looked surprised, and we both knew he didn't mean the flowers.

"Christ," I said. "Keep your voice down."

The look of genuine hurt on his face had me feeling absurdly guilty. He gave me a pout, and I could swear his eyes got bigger, making him look like a sad little anime character.

"You're like a cat dragging in dead birds," I said.

"I'm helping!"

I shot him a hard look. "You can't just bring half-dead criminals here and coerce them into confessing."

"But all of them were guilty. You are an excellent detective, Royce."

"You've followed me on *cases*?"

"Of course," he said, as if this was a normal part of dating protocol. He leaned in conspiratorially. "You look especially arousing when you frown and write things in your little notebook."

"Oh my *God*," I said. "You have to leave."

Sinclair smiled, flashing his pointy canine—on purpose, I was certain. I didn't know how he knew I liked it so much, but he definitely knew. "If you promise to call."

"*Fine*," I said. Priya stared at us over the top of her computer. "I'll call."

He made no move to leave.

I sighed. "I promise."

———

SINCLAIR

I knew I couldn't wait for Royce to call me; I was far, far too excited. The thrill of the chase ignited my prey drive, but what came after the chase—that sent lightning dancing across my skin, filled me with a heat I only felt when I had someone in my sights, and I knew I could move for the— well, the kill literally, or the kill figuratively.

In this case the latter.

I hoped.

There was a risk, of course. I knew my darling Royce— being *such* a clever investigator—had put together most of the pieces of my identity. If I meant to make him truly mine, a deception was hardly sustainable. However, courting a human still required a dance of sorts.

While we had almost reached what I'd consider a romantic accord, I could tell by the way Royce and I had left things that he still did not entirely trust my intentions toward him. To clear my head, I decided to go out for a feed. I'd reached the end of my list of Royce's open cases, so I went to the local park, hiding behind a statue, waiting for the other denizens of the night to emerge. After watching a man for a while, I determined he was there to sell mind-altering substances. I crawled up into the decorative trees and hid until he passed below my perch. When I dropped behind him and punctured his throat, I felt the familiar bliss of feeding. I took a few mouthfuls, just enough to wet my whistle, dosing him with venom to leave him compliant and unlikely to remember my face when the fog cleared.

When finished, I tucked him safely in an alcove beside the fountain where he could recover unmolested. I checked his pockets and found a wad of dollar bills and a few baggies of hallucinogenic mushrooms. No firearms, only a simple butterfly knife, and no more dangerous drugs. I tucked his belongings back on his person and went to cross his arms over his chest beneath his jacket, when I saw something on the interior of his wrist.

A hickey, deep and purple, several days old. Within the circle that was surely a perfect imprint of the mouth that had left it, were several fang punctures. I would know the marks anywhere—in fact, I'd left nearly identical ones on the man's throat.

As I examined the wound, awareness prickled down my spine. I had been so fixated on my courtship of Royce that I'd nearly forgotten something vitally important.

I was not alone in Douglas Crest.

All the more reason for me to establish my bond with Royce as soon as possible, so I could protect him. I hastened back to Royce's abode, climbing up the exterior wall to reach my usual perch outside his window and wait for him to return home. The fire escape outside his bedroom was rickety but plenty strong enough to hold my weight, even in my humanoid form. Crouching on the railing, I peered around the corner of the building into the living room window, far less comfortable than when I watched him sleeping, but I wanted to know the second he got home. Being in such close proximity to him this evening had thrilled me, and I knew it had thrilled Royce too. From where I sat on his lap, I had heard his pulse humming.

The door clicked softly and Royce entered his small den, looking tired. To be sure, he often looked tired. I knew he struggled to sleep well, and watching him toss and turn every night made me think that perhaps he would sleep better with me beside him. I'd have to remedy this as soon as I possibly could. I wondered if perhaps Royce would play hard to get a bit longer, but nigh on immediately upon entering his home, he pulled his mobile telephone from the pocket of his rumpled trench coat.

A high-pitched trill cut the silence. *Damn!* I'd forgotten to put the blasted thing on silent, and Royce looked up immediately, making eye contact with me as I stared through his window. He dropped the phone to the carpet and drew his sidearm, and I'd be lying if I said his quick reflexes did not stir my blood, so to speak. When he realized it was me, he rolled his eyes—presumably at himself for being so prepared with violence! I waved at him enthusiastically through the glass.

With a resigned sigh, he holstered his weapon and approached the window to undo the latch. "Is it true you can't come in unless I invite you?"

"A myth," I said. "Though, of course, I would wait for an invitation before trespassing your threshold."

"You've already broken in," he replied. Then he frowned, remembering. "Twice."

"A special circumstance," I said airily, sliding down from his window sill to stand before him. Now that he'd let me inside, Royce faltered. He appeared uncertain what to do with me, now that he had me.

I licked my lips, standing on tiptoe to press a soft kiss to his slack mouth, merely a greeting, but Royce balked. He seized my shoulders and backed me off half a step. "Hold on," he said.

"Yes?"

"This is—you're—I don't..." he trailed away, scrubbing a hand over his tired face.

"What is it?" I asked him softly. I misliked the crease between his brows.

He shot me a look, like the reason for his chagrin should be obvious to me. As a potential partner, I supposed he had a point—I had to demonstrate my understanding of his innermost workings to prove myself worthy. Despite the way he'd yielded to me so easily on the night we'd met, Royce now seemed determined to make me work for his affections. I expected nothing less.

I clicked my tongue, directing him to sit on the sagging sofa. He rested his head back, staring askance at the ceiling. I knelt beside him on the couch, waiting. When at last he turned to look at me, he jumped, like he hadn't expected to find me so close. "You seem tense," I offered.

Royce snorted and said, "Very."

I swung a leg over his lap, straddling him, interlocking my fingers behind his neck, and lowered my voice to a husky purr. "May I help?"

He was tempted. I could see it in his eyes. I could smell it on him, but before I could taste his lips again, he placed a hand on my chest. It made me shiver. His hand was so strong, so warm and male. I wanted to suck his fingers. I traced one of my own fingertips down the back of his hand.

"Did you kill someone?" he asked me, direct. Blunt.

"Of course," I said without hesitation, knowing that lying to Royce now would assassinate our affair before it had even begun.

To my knowledge, I had only killed a handful of times. It was unnecessary, for the most part, for my kind to kill, and as I aged my self-control only strengthened. The blood-lust was entirely manageable, if one merely had the discipline to keep oneself in check. I was born into this life alone, with nothing for guidance but the names of the men who'd wronged me. The men who'd taken my human life. By the time I'd worked through that list, I'd developed enough control to feed without killing—if I fed often, but fed little from each victim. If I grazed. If I never let myself get too hungry.

Royce closed his eyes and pulled his hand away, and I ached for the loss of his touch. "Tell me."

It was early in our courtship for me to divulge the secrets of my past, and I debated how much to share, now that Royce knew my name.

"In the year 1857, this city was a far less civilized place. No such noble men as you protected the people. I was poor, but happy enough, and I had no family to speak of."

Royce let me continue the tale, and more importantly, he allowed me to take his hand again. I stroked the bones of his thick fingers.

"I had scrimped and saved and pinched my pennies to open a small flower shop," I said. "It was my pride and joy. A beautiful young man used to frequent the shop, and I was utterly smitten. It was...difficult then, for those with romantic proclivities such as ours," and here I sniffed delicately, "to find someone. I became enamored of the young man, who was the son of a city official. He came into my shop so often I thought he returned my affections. I used the flowers to express myself, but I found later he had been courting a young woman and offering my bouquets to her. One night, when I grew bold enough, I made the mistake of speaking the words aloud. He rebuffed me. Quite violently."

I swallowed. It had been nothing but a youthful infatuation, but the memories were still quite painful. Even after all this time. Royce still did not speak, but it seemed to me his eyes had softened.

"He returned to the shop with several comrades, late at night. They stripped me, beat me, tied me to a chair, and set the place aflame."

A small, sympathetic noise escaped from Royce, and I hushed him.

"No matter," I said brusquely. "As they poured oil and lit the match to burn my livelihood to the ground, I pulled free and grabbed a heavy vase from the table. I struck the man with it, in the head. And I ran. His cowardly comrades did not help him, and he was killed in the fire."

I never knew if it was the blow I struck, or the fire, but it was the first life I had taken all the same.

"Self-defense," said Royce quietly. He sounded a bit relieved.

"I suppose," I said, "but there's more to the tale."

"I imagine there would be," he said.

"I collapsed in the alley behind the shop as it burned, bleeding and lying in the muck. In those days we didn't— have the words, but I felt deep inside something had broken. My insides were..." I coughed, because after all these years, I could still feel the phantom of the smoke fill my lungs. "I was dying. I remember lying there, wishing I was brave enough to crawl back inside and burn with my shop."

"But you didn't."

"No," I agreed. "I didn't. I felt a presence in the alley, and I was barely conscious." At the time, I'd thought it was the angel of death come to bring me to the afterlife. "A voice whispered in my ear, 'Do you want to be saved?'"

A shudder rolled through Royce's body.

"I told him no," I said. "I did not want to be saved. He laughed."

I turned my head, tugging on my shirt collar to show Royce the scar on the back of my neck. He brushed his fingertips over the spot that still felt sensitive, even now.

"He saved you anyway."

I grinned crookedly at him. "Did he? I continued to exist, certainly. But it was not what I wanted. He damned me; he did not save me."

When I had awoken, ravenous and thirsting for blood, I resisted as long as I could, fearing I was going mad, fearing I'd been possessed by a demon. My instincts had led me to hunt down the rest of the men from the night of the fire, to feed on them until they were nothing but depleted husks. It was upon my tongue to tell this to Royce, but before I could speak, he cupped my face in his hands, his eyes telling me what I'd shared was enough, for now.

His gaze eventually fell to my mouth, so I allowed the tip of my tongue to dart out, moistening my bottom lip.

Royce groaned softly, and I could not suppress a smile. "Ask me to stay," I said.

"Stay." Royce did not hesitate. With his hands still clasped around my face, he drew me in for a soft, nervous kiss. "But in the morning, don't go."

That whispered plea held me so tight; I could not have refused him anything.

"What is it about you?" Royce mumbled, his hands sliding down to cup my ass.

I shrugged. "Perhaps I have hypnotized you," I teased, before moaning into Royce's sweet mouth when he deepened our kiss.

"You broke into my house," said Royce, as I nipped his square, stubbly jaw. "You stalked me. You killed someone. You—you're not human."

"All of those things are true," I admitted, drawing back. "But do they matter?"

"They should."

"But?"

In answer, Royce fisted his hand in the back of my hair,

pulling me against him for a bruising kiss and I lost myself entirely, biting roughly at his plump lips, tugging back to make him hiss and buck against me from where I had him trapped between my thighs. My fingers flew to the drab button-down shirt he wore, making swift work of it to bare more of Royce's skin. With his shirt unbuttoned, I could see the last, fading remnants of our first night together. My keen eyes could see the ghosts of the marks, but I knew they'd faded too much for human eyes to see. I knew immediately I must rectify that. I locked my lips over one small mark and sucked, flicking my tongue against his heated skin, tasting the salt of his sweat. With my fingers tugging his chest hair, Royce threw back his head and moaned.

Before I could make another move, I found myself sailing through the air as Royce stood, holding tight to my hips to keep me aloft. I locked my ankles around his waist so I would not have to break the seal of my lips on his flesh.

When we reached the bedroom, Royce dropped me unceremoniously on the mattress and shrugged the rest of the way out of his shirt. He pounced on me, pressing his weight on top of my body, pinning me in place, bracketed by his hands and knees. Rolling his spine, he let me get a feel of his rigid cock throbbing behind the zipper of his jeans, like it was fighting to get to me through the rough, thick fabric. With an eager whine, I arched my back to press against him, offering the same tease.

Royce nuzzled against my ear, and then stilled. He placed a small, chaste kiss on my cheek. "We're not having sex tonight."

In a flash, I had swapped our positions, drawing a startled gasp from Royce, to whom I had not yet demonstrated my full strength. "Pardon?"

He recovered quickly from the surprise, looking smug as

he gazed up at me. "You skipped out on me last time," he reminded me. "You know what they say. Fool me once..."

Royce! Of course. *Of course,* I would not get off scot-free after such a sexual snafu. My Royce had far too much self-respect to let some heartless good-time cad wheedle his way into his bed without the offer of everything he truly deserved. Royce cocked an eyebrow, his bravado faltering—just enough for me to see it slip.

"Will you still stay?"

I couldn't resist pressing my hardness against him one more time, thrusting uselessly through my trousers. "Of course, darling."

Royce blushed. He blushed! Oh, heaven above—I would surely perish at this cherubic display from such a burly specimen. He could not know the hold he had over my heart already, could he? I folded my hands on Royce's broad chest to rest my chin upon them.

It was late, and I knew Royce had been out there fighting for the causes of the everyman for the entire day and well into the evening. We undressed for bed, Royce sliding out of his jeans with as much grace as he could muster while still sporting a sizable erection, and into a loose pair of sleeping trousers. "Do you want to borrow some sweats?" He asked me.

If my Royce wanted to tease, then two could certainly play his little game. I slid out of my clothes, leaving on my tight black boxer briefs, knowing they hid everything and concealed nothing. "Thank you, but I should be alright."

Royce grunted, and I knew he was struggling to maintain the iron will with which he had declared we would not be making love tonight. I bent over, arching my back a bit as I turned down one side of his bed, before peeking at him over my shoulder. "Christ," he muttered.

He turned off the light and climbed in beside me, the warmth of his skin flowing over me like the beams of the summer sun used to, before I could no longer withstand their caress. When Royce laid a palm on my bare waist, I hoped he would not burn me just as badly.

5

PREVENTABLE WORRIES

ROYCE

When my alarm went off, I was nervous to open my eyes. I had a suspicion Sinclair had left again. The bed beside me was cool and as I ran my hand over the soft, silky—wait. Sinclair *was* still here. I opened one eye, peering at him, laying on his side like a sleeping angel, eyes closed. Utterly still. My hand, in fact, ran up and down the skin of his side, cool and smooth as fresh linens. With my hand on his ribcage, I should have been able to feel the rise and fall of his breathing, but there was nothing. It was eerie, but in a peaceful way, like the still, glassy tranquility of a lake at sunrise. I slid my palm up to his chest, feeling for the hint of a heartbeat.

Nothing.

"Are you awake?" I whispered, unnerved.

Sinclair's eyes blinked open, immediately alert and focused. "Yes," he said. "I don't sleep."

I startled. "What?"

He shrugged one perfect, freckled shoulder. "I haven't slept since I was turned."

"Your eyes were closed."

"I felt relaxed," he said. "I find peace quite easily with you."

I had no idea what to do with that, but my no-sex gambit suddenly seemed entirely selfish. Did he just...lie there doing nothing? "What did you do all night?"

"Watched you."

Those two words stayed with me all the way to the precinct, and every time they crossed my mind, I shivered. I honestly could not work out if I was horrified or flattered. I thought, perhaps, some combo therein. Sinclair was something else. Something electric, something frightening. He was a dangerous, undead killer, and I knew a longer conversation about what that meant for us was coming like a freight train—but in the meantime, I couldn't help but be intrigued. I hadn't...been intrigued, by something outside of a murder for a long time. Though, being intrigued by Sinclair was perhaps a little too close to that for comfort.

When I arrived, Priya greeted me as always—though her demeanor was a bit cooler than usual. We both knew there was something off about Sinclair, but for most of the population, the word "vampire" wasn't even in the realm of possibilities, so she didn't say anything about him.

"That friend of your missing kid is here," said Priya. "He's waiting in interrogation."

I'd finally gotten a lead on Beckett Taylor's case, though it was a flimsy one. According to his mother, he didn't have many friends, but she'd given me one name: Christopher "Kit" Trent. One look at Trent told me he wasn't the type of friend a mother wanted her son to have. He was hard and mean-looking, and he sported a lot of tattoos—which, on their own meant nothing, but I recognized a few symbols tying him to a local gang, the Ivory Bulls. Trent had the look of someone life hadn't been kind to—but he'd been more than happy to pay the world back in kind.

"I didn't do nothing," he said, as soon as I opened the door to the interrogation room.

I didn't answer right away, but I drew the chair opposite and sat. "You're not under arrest," I explained. *Yet.* "We're just talking."

He narrowed his eyes at me, like he didn't believe me for one second. "Then why am I here?"

"I would like to ask you a few questions about Beckett Taylor."

He stared blankly back at me. "Who?"

I opened my case file and slid a picture across the table toward him.

"Oh, you mean BT? Never knew his last name."

"So, you weren't close," I said.

He shook his head. "What did he do?"

"He's missing." I studied his reaction carefully.

Kit Trent didn't give much away, but based on his body language, he didn't kill or abduct Beckett Taylor—he seemed largely indifferent to his friend's plight. "Bummer."

"Can you tell me the last time you spoke with him?"

"Last month, maybe."

I waited for him to continue, but he didn't seem like the kind to answer an unasked question. Based on the jacket in his file, it was hardly his first rodeo. "Alright, and what did you discuss?"

Trent considered my question. "The thing is, this is just hypo-theoretically speaking," he said, allowing the words to dangle.

I resisted rolling my eyes. "Yes?"

"If BT was involved in something...*something,* my telling you about that would get some other people in trouble, too. Who may also have been involved in the same something."

"People like you?"

He shrugged a shoulder, and I knew that, especially since I wasn't charging him, I wasn't going to get anything if I didn't play ball.

"Well," I said. "Since we're only talking hypothetically—"

"Davis."

It was only through sheer force of will that I didn't jump when the door to the interrogation room banged open. Lieutenant Stark stood scowling on the threshold. "Sir?"

"I need to see you in my office," he said.

"But—"

"Now, Detective." He turned to Trent. "You're free to go."

Kit Trent didn't need to be told twice. With a sarcastic little salute to Lieutenant Stark, he hurried from the room before I could so much as say another word.

Fuming, I got to my feet to follow Stark to his office. Trent had something on Beckett Taylor, I could feel it, and now he had time to revise his story or disappear. "Sir," I started, refusing to take a seat. Stark stood across from me, his desk between us. Stark was a tall, good-looking guy in his early fifties with a scruffy salt-and-pepper beard and hair to match. The crinkles around his eyes, and at the corners of his lips would have been charming on another man, maybe someone who got them from smiling as opposed to constantly scowling. "I was just about to get—"

"Davis," said Stark, cutting across me. "The human trafficking unit of major crimes is taking the Taylor case."

"*What?*"

"The case has been stagnant for some time with no new leads," he said. "And it crosses jurisdictional lines. Messy."

I was mad enough to spit. "You just *gave* me the case."

"Beckett Taylor has been missing for weeks."

"His mother only—"

"Davis, if you don't want to be suspended for insubordination, I suggest you go back to your desk and work on some cases you can actually solve."

The fucking *gall.* The implication that I hadn't found Becket Taylor due to some fault of mine, and not the fact that I'd only been the primary on a weeks-stale case for a few *days,* had me seeing red.

"Dismissed," said Stark, his voice making it clear that my anger had no effect on him.

When I got home that evening, my apartment was empty, but there was another note resting on top of Sinclair's folded clothing from the night before.

"*My darling Royce, this is not the way I want you to get me out of my clothes. Yours, Sinclair.*"

He must have had to leave in his bat form again—perhaps it was the only way he could move around in the daylight. Next time we spoke, I'd need to get a better idea of his Dracula rules of conduct. I wondered why he hadn't just texted me, but if he was as old as his story had suggested, I imagined he was more used to corresponding by letter. I read the note again. Sinclair had beautiful handwriting, almost like calligraphy—though the effect was somewhat spoiled by his inclusion of another pornographic sketch at the bottom of the paper.

I grabbed myself a beer and parked it on the couch, about to settle in for an evening of dumb TV to get my mind off my shitty work day, when my phone rang. I looked down, expecting to see Sinclair's name flashing across the screen, but was surprised to see Priya's picture instead.

"Davis," I answered.

"He's dead."

"What? Who?"

"Kit Trent. The guy you just interrogated."

"*What?*" He'd only been cut loose a few hours ago. How could he be—I clenched my jaw, crushing Sinclair's note in my fist. No. No way. "How?"

"No idea," said Priya. "Uniforms called it in. Seemed like a pop and drop. I have to wait for the initial autopsy to come in."

"Like hell you do," I said, and I hung up. I couldn't wait for an autopsy. I had to know if Sinclair had seen Trent released and been furious about it—furious enough to kill. I had to imagine there was more blood in his past than he'd shared with me last night, but something like this? I'd already told him how I felt about his "gifts", hadn't I? As I grabbed my coat and keys, I tried to recall our conversation. He'd been in my lap—distracting enough, let alone the vulnerability in his eyes as he'd told me about the man he'd loved from way back when. Now that I thought about it, I wasn't certain I'd actually told him off for threatening suspects on my behalf. Some lawman I was.

The night crew at the morgue weren't exactly your top shelf of coroners, but I at least got in to see the body. It was definitely Trent. His face was white as a ghost, even paler than your average corpse. The term "kid" suddenly didn't seem to apply. It looked like he had aged forty years since I'd interviewed him that afternoon, but his clothes and tattoos were a clear match. The coroner had also finger-printed him to confirm identity. I stared at the body, his skin translucent and papery, unlike any body I'd ever seen.

"Initial cause of death is exsanguination," said the coroner, coming in behind me. "Which is the understatement of the year because it seems like he's been totally—"

"—drained," I finished for him.

Shit.

———

SINCLAIR

I now had two sets of clothing at Royce's abode, and no idea when I'd see him next. Of course, part of the thrill of a new romance was the mystery, but I thought possibly it was time for Royce and me to have a more open line of communication, now that our intimacy had progressed to the next level.

I would have waited for Royce to return home from work, but I grew bored. Being trapped inside, dodging beams of searing sunlight that burned through the sheer draperies in his apartment wore on me swiftly. It left me restless, with an unsettled feeling like an itch I couldn't scratch. I puttered about Datura, doing some inventory and preparing a few arrangements for an early pickup in the morning, when my mobile telephone beeped, alerting me to a new text message.

Royce: Come over

Sinclair: So direct.

And then I added a swooning pictograph and an eggplant pictograph. I had recently learned the eggplant was something of a code for an erection.

Royce: I'm not playing. We need to talk.

I frowned down at the device. I could tell by the terse words that this was serious. The swiftest way to Royce's home was as the proverbial crow flew—or the bat, in my case. And considering I had already left some clothing behind at his residence, I figured I could flap my little way right on over.

I landed on the sill of his window, releasing a series of shrill squeaks to get his attention. He rose from the couch and let me in the window, the look on his face so hard and stern I flapped immediately to his bedroom to transform and dress in private. When I returned to the sitting room, Royce waited for me, his face etched with barely controlled anger.

I waited for him to speak, but perhaps the interrogator in him did not want to lose the upper hand. He merely set his jaw, narrowed his eyes, and waited.

His silence was agony, and I had to break it. "Is everything alright, darling?"

"Don't call me that," he snapped, and I flinched. "And no, everything is not alright."

"What's wrong?"

In answer, Royce merely pointed at his kitchen counter, where I spied a cream-colored folder. When I looked inside, I saw a photograph of a dead fellow. Several photographs. A sinking and prevailing sense of dread began in my mouth and slid down my esophagus into my gut. "What is this?" I asked softly.

"Why don't you tell me, Sinclair?"

I turned to Royce. "I didn't do this."

"Bullshit."

"Royce, I swear to you, I did not do this."

"You've attacked my suspects before," said Royce.

"I was trying to—"

"Don't, Sinclair. Just don't." He grabbed my shoulders, giving me a little shake. I could have removed myself from his grasp, of course, but I found myself entirely arrested by his anger, by his commanding, impassioned presence. "Who else could have done this to him?"

It took a moment for this to sink in. "Wait," I said slowly. "Royce, you are aware that I'm not the only one of my kind...right?"

Royce went as white as the poor man in the photograph. He released my arms, his handsome face contorting in confusion, in revulsion. I pulled away, knowing the expression had been caused by me, a grotesque, just as much as my compatriots were. Royce, it seemed, had just allowed himself to remember that fact. My sweet-looking face, and—forgive me—fuckable ass had temporarily distracted him, but no longer.

"I'll go," I said, miserable. "But please, Royce. Be careful." I had no idea who drained the life from Royce's suspect, but the timing of his death was highly suspicious.

"Wait." Royce stared imploringly into my face. "Just— give me a second, here, okay? This is all a *lot*."

"I understand," I said, hesitating. I didn't dare hope he would wish to continue our affair, but at the very least he no longer looked at me like I was a monster.

His eyes begged me. "You are *promising* me that you did not do this?"

"I swear."

"Do you know who this might have been?"

I studied the photograph, wondering. I had seen recent evidence of vampire activity in Douglas Crest, but I had yet to conduct any inquiries. Vampires were definitely not the predominant paranormal parties in this city. For the most part, Douglas Crest was given over to shapeshifters, with whom my kind did not get along—but there was no reason to burden poor Royce with all of this. "I tend to avoid my own kind," I hedged.

Royce cleared his throat, uncomfortable, the blush I'd come to adore rising in his scruffy cheeks. With a smile, a bit like a grimace, Royce said, "I'd ask if you wanted to stay for a beer but..."

I could barely contain myself. "You want me to stay?"

"God help me," said Royce. "I should have my head examined, but yeah. I'd like you to stay."

"Really?"

"On one condition," he said, pointing at me. "Promise me you will not bite any of my perps. Or witnesses."

"What if it's—"

"Even in self-defense."

I pouted. "Fine."

It was not truly a lie. I could leave Royce's investigations well enough alone and never be in danger of starving.

This city was full of bloody men.

6

POLITE ANSWERS TO
IMPERTINENT QUESTIONS

ROYCE

W hen I tried to go to the morgue when the head medical examiner was in, I hit a wall.

"I'm afraid I can only release details to the primary detective on the case," he said. The guy was a stickler for protocols. I had a feeling Stark would assign me as the primary when pigs flew, so needless to say I started my day in a shit mood.

It was clear to me that this murder had something to do with Becket Taylor's disappearance. Glancing toward Stark's office to make sure he wasn't in yet, I pulled up the department directory and called Major Crimes. I got bounced around a few times after asking for the lead investigator on the Beckett Taylor case.

By the time someone from the trafficking task force picked up, I was even more irritated.

"We don't have any files under that name," she said, sounding as annoyed as I felt.

"My CO said you guys requested it. From the eighth precinct."

"I don't know what to tell you," The detective said. "Do you have a case file number?"

"Yeah, hang on—" I put the receiver between my shoulder and my ear and logged into my desktop. After a few clicks, I frowned. "What the..."

The detective on the other end of the line sighed.

"Sorry," I muttered. "There must have been a mistake."

And then she hung up on me. I dug through all my recent files, confirming what I already knew. The information on Beckett Taylor's disappearance was gone. And, if the snippy detective at Major Crimes was to be believed, they didn't have it either. "Impossible," I said to myself.

"What's impossible?" Priya had appeared at my desk.

"Nothing," I snapped.

Priya raised her brows. "Wow," she said. "What's up your butt? Or like, you know, *not*."

"Not today, Priya."

"Alright, Mopey Pants," she said. "Let's go."

"Go where?"

"I have something for you, and you're going to say thank you with coffee and a pastry."

I sighed, knowing I wasn't going to get out of this. Besides, I could always use Priya's advice. When we were a few blocks away from the precinct, I explained to her what happened with Stark supposedly giving my case to Major Crimes and the file disappearing.

"Well," she said thoughtfully, "today's your lucky day. I'm the primary on the Trent murder, and I have a lead on his employer."

"His employer?"

"Yeah," she said. "I figured you might be able to use it to get some info on Taylor."

"I'm not on the case anymore," I reminded her.

She scoffed. "Sure, Davis."

"I'm serious," I said. "Stark threatened to suspend me if I stuck my nose into a case he didn't assign."

"Yes, and you've always been a good little soldier who does exactly what he's told. My mistake. You want the name, or not?"

I took the name to get Priya off my back, but I wasn't entirely sure what to do with it. When had sticking my neck out gotten me anywhere? Stark could make the rest of my career a living hell. Besides, there were a million reasonable explanations for why my file had vanished. Government-funded agencies weren't known for their top-notch inter-office communication, or technology. For all I knew, the file was on its way to Major Crimes and just hadn't gotten reassigned to their server yet. I sighed, vowing to put Beckett Taylor missing person's case from my mind. I wondered if I should tell Priya my suspicions about Stark. She had good instincts, and I trusted her judgment—but at the same time, I didn't want to drag her into this whole mess.

I munched on a jelly doughnut as we walked back to work, and Priya sipped her latte. "This coffee is fabulous," she said. "That place is a little fancy compared to your usual, isn't it?"

I flushed immediately. "Well, you said you wanted a treat." I was learning that I should never consider a career in poker.

"Oh," said Priya, giving me a little eye roll. "Your undead hipster boy-toy likes this place, doesn't he?"

"He's not—Sinclair is—" I stammered. "He's not a *hipster.*"

Priya smirked. "Only you would find 'hipster' the most insulting thing on that list."

I grabbed her arm. "You know what I mean."

"I really don't," she said. "Look, Royce. You're my best friend. I have no idea what's going on with you, and we both know what I'm thinking is technically impossible— but just tell me you're being careful and I'll let you off the hook. For now."

"I'm being careful."

She rolled her eyes again. "Yeah, right."

I left work with an address and a strong desire to change my terrible mood. Sinclair had dropped into my life and home, throwing me off my axis every time he turned up, and to be frank, I wanted the chance to return the favor. Something in my bones told me he'd been telling the truth, and he hadn't killed Trent. I had no idea why I trusted him, and I hadn't ruled out the idea of some kind of vampire hypnosis, but I was, as they say, in it now. Doing a little digging, I'd figured out that Sinclair lived downtown above the very same flower shop he'd once owned. The flower shop was called Datura, had darkened windows and no regular hours, and operated by appointment only.

The small building had a buzzer and an intercom box. I pressed the button, and a familiar voice came through the grainy speaker. "I'm sorry, we are not presently accepting walk-ins."

I grinned like an idiot. "Police," I said, roughing my voice up a bit.

The door flung open within seconds and Sinclair appeared on the stoop. "Royce!" he said, his face alight, his voice breathless.

I had no idea why on *earth* he reacted this way to me,

but to be honest, I dug it. A lot. "Hi," I said, suddenly feeling stupid and tongue-tied.

Sinclair simply stood in the doorway and beamed, like he had never opened his door to something as amazing as me. Poor guy. "How did you find my little shop?"

"You're not the only one who can chase someone down."

He straightened the lapels of my jacket, rising up on his tiptoes and letting his eyes fall closed. "Hmmm," he said. "And what are you going to do, now that you've done so?"

"Can I come in?"

"Of course." And he literally bowed me into the flower shop. I couldn't help being charmed by his mannerisms. Datura was small, tidy, and surprisingly cozy. I wasn't sure what I was expecting, but the space inside was bright and colorful—if a bit dated, with its ostentatious crushed velvet camelback sofa, where I pictured Sinclair playing gracious florist to his clients who had no idea the flamboyant waif designing their bridal bouquets was an immortal killer. He led me over to the sofa, and I collapsed onto it, letting my head fall against the backrest.

"Did you make any progress on your case?" Sinclair asked me.

"Nope," I said.

Sinclair tensed.

"Sorry," I said. "I'm just not used to having someone to vent to about work. My only lead was killed, and then my commanding officer gave the case away."

"He gave the case away? Why?"

I shrugged. Silence fell over the two of us. Sinclair's fingers tangled in my hair, and I let him drag his nails along my scalp because it was like he used his fingertips to pull the tension from the top of my head with every pass.

"Can we go on a date?"

Sinclair startled, and to be honest, so did I. I had not meant to say that, but the words just sort of slipped out. "Pardon?"

"I like you," I blurted. "A lot. I think there's something here, and I'd like to take you out."

Sinclair's smile was so shy and sweet. "I'd like that," he said.

It was late, but I found I really didn't want to leave. The idea of going home alone after a shitty couple of days left me feeling a bit bereft. All I really wanted was to stay here with Sinclair petting my head. Was that too much? Too desperate sounding? I hesitated, but then realized I was being ridiculous. This guy had already broken into my house and calmly confessed to stalking me. I really shouldn't be concerned about coming on too strong. "Would you like to spend the night together?"

"So forward," he said, giving my chest a playful smack.

A feeling like champagne fizzing in my stomach had a stupid smile on my face. I was so fucking gone. I captured his lips in a kiss. "I feel as though we've already skipped a few...early dating steps."

"We have."

I sensed some hesitation in him, which surprised me. Maybe the request was too much. "What is it? Do you not want me to stay?"

"Of course, I do—I just." He chewed his lip. "Perhaps I'd better show you."

Sinclair stood, and I followed him up the narrow staircase, presumably to the door of the apartment he kept above the shop. When we stepped inside, I frowned, puzzled. I spun on my heel, taking in the modest, tidy space. There was something wrong, but I couldn't quite put my finger on it. It seemed like your average studio apartment, except—

"Where the fuck is your toilet?"

Sinclair wrinkled his nose. "I had it removed."

"You had it—what?"

"I don't..." he trailed away, looking embarrassed. He practically whispered the last word. "Void."

I turned this over in my head. "So, you just called the plumber and had them pull out your toilet? Didn't he think you were nuts?"

"Don't be absurd," he snapped. "I did it myself."

I plopped down on his sofa, covering my face with my hands. Just when I thought things had stabilized. "This is insane."

"Yes," Sinclair agreed.

"You...you *feed.* On b-blood." If there was going to be any kind of future for us, I had to cut the coyness and talk frankly about what that would look like.

"Yes."

"But you don't...go to the bathroom?"

"No. Not since I turned."

"So where does all the b-blood go?"

Sinclair blinked at me, cocking his head to the side like he'd honestly never considered it. "I'm sure I haven't the foggiest idea."

"Aren't you curious?"

"At first, perhaps. But some things aren't for us to know."

I stared at him for a long time before the question exploded out of my mouth. "How can you even have sex?"

Sinclair looked flustered and began to pace.

"I'm serious—how can you even..." I lowered my voice

to a whisper, like someone was going to overhear us. "How do you come?"

"I don't like to pull at those threads, Royce." He sniffed delicately.

"You don't wonder?"

He shrugged. "I supposed once I realized I could still climax I figured—take the money and run."

"This is insane," I said again.

"Perhaps," Sinclair said primly. "At any rate, I suggest we stay at yours."

This was *insane*. I'd stopped saying it out loud, but I couldn't stop thinking it. My vampire boyfriend didn't have a toilet. Legitimately every part of that sentence was fucking crazy. I paused. Was Sinclair my boyfriend? I supposed I had just asked him out, somewhat officially, and he had certainly decided some time ago that he had some sort of claim over me. Judging by the bag he carried when he came out of his walk-in closet—again, no toilet, but the man had thirty pairs of shoes—Sinclair had made the executive decision to breeze us right past the casual dating stage of this relationship.

He was quiet in the car, and I felt like I had shoved my foot in my mouth. I hadn't meant to grill him about his bathroom habits, for God's sake, but also, how could I not? I rested a palm on his knee and squeezed tight, hoping he'd understand I wasn't *trying* to be a total jackass. He smiled at me. It was fleeting, and I wondered if I'd screwed this up already. No, he'd still come with me. He'd still packed an overnight bag full of God only knew what.

We were just getting out of the car in front of my building when the phone rang. It was a number I didn't recognize.

"Detective Davis," I said into the receiver.

The person on the end drew a deep, shuddering breath before speaking. "It's Mirabel Taylor," came a thick, shaky voice.

I sighed. "Hi, Mrs. Taylor." Sinclair turned, tilting his head to the side, concern on his face.

"Detective, would you be available to meet with me to discuss my son's case?"

I cursed internally—I should have called, but when major crimes had supposedly taken the case, it would have been standard protocol for them to contact her. "Of course," I said.

"Tonight?"

"Yes," I said again. It was the least I could do. I rattled off the address of an all-night diner where we could meet for coffee. When we hung up, I turned to Sinclair. The look on his face said he'd heard everything.

"Go," he said, cupping my cheek.

"Are you sure?"

"Of course."

I fished out my keys, pulling the spare from my ring to put into Sinclair's palm, and closed my own hand around his. "Go inside and make yourself at home. I'll call."

He gave me a swift kiss on the cheek. "I'll wait."

———

SINCLAIR

I had no intention of waiting.

Of course, I would be at Royce's home when he returned, but with a night to myself, I had no time to waste. It was necessary for me to find out if the other vampires in Douglas Crest were a direct threat to me, or to Royce. I hadn't been lying when I said I told him I didn't know who'd killed his suspect; I had merely left out the part where I intended to find out.

The following evening, I had slipped unseen into the city morgue to examine the corpse myself, to see if the hunter had left any clues behind. What I found flummoxed me. The man had been drained entirely, but he otherwise bore no signs of a vampiric attack. Bruising high up on his thigh indicated the bite point but...there was something odd about the wound site. It didn't look as though it had been made by fangs. I left the morgue with more questions than answers.

Tonight, I returned to the park, searching for the man upon whom I'd recently fed, the man who bore another hunter's bite as well as mine. He was nowhere to be found. I found this more than passing odd. While dealers in illicit substances hardly punched time cards, their haunts were usually fairly regular.

Hidden in a topiary, I observed the other occupants of the park at nighttime. Douglas Crest was hardly a hotbed of the criminal underworld, but it was a city like any other, and the usual fixtures could be found with a little digging, if one merely had the patience. Luckily for me, the park cleaved to the back of a nightclub, and on weekend evenings revelers could be seen cutting through at all hours of the night. From where I hid, I saw a pair of girls stumbling along the path, clutching one another and giggling, clearly fresh off a night of partying. They came to the base of my topiary, one of the girls holding her friend's hair back as she vomited spectacularly against the trunk of a tree. The one still upright made soothing sounds, offering her friend a bottle of water. As she adjusted the collar of the sick girl's jacket, I saw a wound on the interior of her wrist. The wound was quite clearly a fang bite, and said "vampire" much more clearly than the odd wound on the corpse at the morgue.

I waited until she deposited her friend on a nearby bench and moved across the deserted park to refill her water bottle at the fountain. I snatched her before she could make a sound, twisting her arm behind her so I could feed on her exposed upper arm. I punctured her skin with as much care as possible, and when she stopped struggling, I drew back, keeping her held in place against an ivy-covered wall.

"Where did you get the wound on your wrist?" I asked her, keeping an eye trained on the bench, where her friend seemed to have fallen asleep.

"Weird party," she said placidly.

"Where?"

"Loft," she mumbled sleepily. Her blood had flown fast and thin, enough for me to know she was already intoxicated. "Hot dudes. Hot chick. Third Street?"

I nodded. That was a fair amount to go on. I spun her back toward her friend. "You will go, and you will take your friend home." I paused. "You will also never walk home through this park again after dark."

"Okay," she said, stumbling off a step. By the time she returned to her friend, I had taken off around the border of the park, heading for Third Street.

There were a few buildings on Third Street containing lofts, but only one was totally abandoned, with no buildings touching on either side. I figured I'd start there. I melted into the shadows at the base of the building, and immediately got the scent of blood. A lot of blood. Too much blood. That set me on high alert. The evidence of that much prey around a single den implied to me a nest of vampires, not a solitary predator like myself. I knew vampire covens existed, but I had always avoided them. I did much better on my own. In the darkness, I stilled, trying to listen. I heard nothing. The building itself was unremarkable, the kind your eye slid right over as you walked down the street. An excellent location for a nest to hide in plain sight.

I would have loved to discern the number of members this coven boasted, but of course, they most likely were out hunting, just as I was. The building was utterly still, with no evidence of anyone being home.

I searched the base of the building, finding nothing until I went around the back and discovered a bulkhead. When I approached, I thought I heard movement beneath the earth, so I lowered my head to the metal doors to listen. I braced my hand on the handle of the bulkhead to lean down, and immediate, searing pain burrowed deep into the skin of my palm. I leapt back with a hiss of anger and surprise.

Once the pain subsided, I moved closer once again, cautiously examining the metal of the door pulls. The dirty, tarnished handles of the bulkhead door were indeed made of silver. Dirtied up, well-hidden silver, but silver all the same. Upon closer inspection, the hinges of the doors were also made of the same infernal precious metal, and, unless I was much mistaken, silver chains had been welded to the edges of the door, preventing anyone of my kind from working their fingers into the cracks to pry the doors open.

I could still hear feeble movement from behind the doors, but my impetus to investigate had evaporated with the pain in my hands. Whoever these hunters were, they were keeping something in that basement, and the place was rigged to keep vampires out.

Or in.

That thought had me terrified, and I backed away as fast as I could, fleeing the building and retracing my steps to the park. There had been a time when evidence of another vampire in a city would be more than enough for me to pick up and leave, and something that smacked this sinister...well, I would probably have never returned.

Things were different now.

I had come back here intentionally, back home. I didn't want my past to haunt my heels anymore, nor would I be intimidated into fleeing. I did not wish to leave.

And besides, I had Royce.

Royce! As I stalked through the darkened street, the urge to see him grew strong as any hunger I'd ever felt. Before returning to Royce's building, I paid a visit to Datura, settling my nervous thoughts by arranging a bouquet for Royce, hoping to cheer him when he returned home. Royce was so dutiful, always ready to lend his aid. It was one of the many things I'd learned about him that I couldn't help but adore. When I reached Royce's apartment, I waited for him on the sofa as the night wore on, but as the hours ticked by, I imagined my heart hammering in my chest, though of course that was impossible. The feeling of being choked, of being watched, the feeling like I had to crawl out of my skin—I couldn't breathe. Where was Royce? He should have been home by now, surely? I couldn't just sit and wait any longer, knowing there was a dangerous vampire nest in this very city. I had to make certain that Royce was alright. I grabbed my flowers and headed out the door to track him down.

7

GOSSIP ON NAMES

ROYCE

Though I'd been exhausted, the thought of being out and about with Sinclair waiting at home for me had me feeling oddly warm. It was domestic and sweet. I was eager to get back to him, but first I had to get through a really painful conversation with a victim's mother.

Mirabel Taylor already waited in a booth when I arrived, and I gave her a nod of acknowledgment as I made my way through the modest, late-night crowd of diners. "Detective," she said once I'd settled in and ordered a coffee. "Thank you for meeting with me."

"Of course," I said. "I apologize, I should have contacted you sooner."

She sighed, and the poor woman really did look like she had the weight of the world on her shoulders. "You came here to tell me there's nothing you can do for my son."

"Unfortunately," I said, "I was taken off the case. Your son's disappearance was passed on to the Major Crimes

Unit. They have a human trafficking task force but..." I couldn't tell her that my CO had buried her son's case.

"I know how it looks," she said. "No evidence of foul play, a young man off at college, finally free of..." She trailed away.

"Free of what?" I asked, eyes narrow. What hadn't she told me?

Mrs. Taylor shot me a calculating look. "I hadn't told you everything the last time we met," she said. "I was afraid the truth would keep you from taking his disappearance seriously. Apparently, it wouldn't have made a difference."

That stung, because she was right. I hadn't taken the disappearance seriously, and clearly, neither did the department. She'd been let down, and she didn't want to trust me—I'd given her no reason to. But she was a mother. And she had to do something. "I'm sorry, Mrs. Taylor," I said sincerely. "You're absolutely right."

I lowered my gaze to the coffee mug, feeling ashamed of myself, but she reached out and grabbed my hand. "Well," she said grimly. "You can make it up to me by listening now."

"Okay," I said. "Start at the beginning. And this time, tell me everything."

When I left the diner, I was buzzing with adrenaline. With some new details, I thought maybe I could make some headway on what happened to this kid. I had to go to the precinct and check a few things out. It was late, and the lobby was closed, but all the officers had keys to get in and out at all hours of the night. There was also usually a person working dispatch, too. I kind of liked the station at night; it was peaceful. I bypassed my desk and went straight down to the archive room because I didn't want there to be a digital paper trail of my search, considering I was looking into this case off the books.

I pulled the arrest records for Kit Trent and took a few pics with my phone. Beckett's mother had told me a few things that had bearing on the investigation, and a lot of things that really only had bearing on my conscience. Her husband, Beckett's father, died in Iraq when Beckett was a little kid. He'd immediately stepped up as the man of the house, she'd explained, and while he'd done his best at school, he focused more on helping his mother with the bills. Like a lot of young guys in financial trouble, he'd fallen in with the sort of people who promised everything and delivered nothing, but kept everyone in their employ completely beholden to them. I'd met dozens of these guys over the years. According to Mrs. Taylor, her son had worked for one such man, named Vito Garibaldi—and that just so happened to be the very same name Priya had given me, so I figured he would be worth looking into. Digging through the files, I unearthed a few addresses from places he'd been spotted before. He was kind of a catch-all sleazy guy, who'd moved from garden-variety thug to shady middle management. If no one looked too closely, a guy like Garibaldi could *almost* pass for a legitimate businessman. If you squinted, and had a lot of other cases to work. Mrs. Taylor hadn't wanted to believe her son could work for someone like that, but she confirmed Beckett been giving her cash to help make their mortgage. When he'd gotten a scholarship to a school in Denver, his mother swore he cut ties with both Trent and Garibaldi. Maybe Beckett hadn't wanted to risk his education, and Garibaldi hadn't taken kindly to Beckett's retirement from being one of his street-level dealers.

"Detective Davis?"

I just about pissed myself. Lieutenant Stark leaned against the door jamb to the archives room. "Sir?"

"What are you doing down here?"

Shit. "Just double-checking a case file," I said.

"In the middle of the night? What case?"

Despite the fact that Stark had me cornered, I decided to push my luck a little bit. "Well, Sir, I just remembered something important about Beckett Taylor's case—and I wanted to send along a note to Major Crimes, before I forgot."

Stark narrowed his eyes, but didn't say anything.

"Anyway," I said innocently, "My case file was gone. Poof! So, I figured I'd come down here and try to find the hard copy I filed when I first was assigned the case."

"The file vanished?" Stark laid on his show of surprise a little thick, and I could see him fidgeting. If I hadn't already been sure he'd buried the file, I sure as hell knew it now. "That's odd."

"That's what I thought," I agreed. "Anyway, Sir, what are you doing here so late?"

He scowled at me, and up close he kind of looked like crap. Pale, bags under his eyes, even more gaunt than usual. "I don't believe that's any of your business, Davis. Is it?"

"No, Sir."

Stark seemed to struggle with himself for a moment, before saying, "Davis, if you want to get off my shit list, I'd think long and hard about digging into cases you haven't been assigned."

And with that he turned to leave the room. I let a breath hiss out between my teeth, some of the tension leaving my shoulders. The thinly veiled threat rankled, but I found myself full of fresh determination. Obviously, if he was skulking around, trying to figure out what I was doing, I had him on the ropes. He'd also not been as smooth a liar as he hoped to be. After hundreds of interrogations, I knew all the tells. Stark had been lying his *ass* off about my missing file. I tidied up the records room, returning everything to its proper home.

"One more thing," snapped a voice, and I jumped out of my skin for the second time. Stark was back. "Your midlife crisis is here."

My midlife...? Oh shit. I hurried upstairs to find Sinclair standing by my desk, clutching a bouquet of flowers. In my eagerness to get a jump on my new leads, I had completely forgotten he was waiting for me, so now I felt like an asshole. I also didn't love the fact that his pattern of visiting me had caught Stark's notice. "What are you doing here?"

A look of hurt crossed over his face. "I can't visit?"

Well, double shit. "No, sorry. Of course, you can visit. I just wasn't expecting you and I wasn't expecting..." I gestured to the flowers.

"Oh," he said softly. "You don't like them?"

"I love them," I said, before I could think to reign it in. "I just..." I trailed away, uncomfortable. In my experience, gestures like flowers stopped coming once the relationship progressed past the early stages. I hadn't expected Sinclair to keep bringing them now that I'd admitted I was interested in pursuing things between us. "No one has ever bought me flowers like this before. Just because."

Sinclair grinned. "Well, you've never been with someone like me before."

"That is the understatement of the fucking century."

————

SINCLAIR

Now that Royce and I had officially begun courting, I found myself...restless. That was the word I would use—but the feeling was truly difficult to place. The first few times I felt it, I assumed I was hungry. But even after a feed, I still felt it. The ache. The pull. Spending nights in Royce's flat with him was all I wanted, but as a living, breathing man, Royce had to sleep. I lay for hours, curled at his side, listening to his pulse, the beat of his heart. Counting his breaths. Lulled by the strange, erratic gurgle of his intestines—all the music of the human body. We had not made love again yet, and I had a feeling Royce was testing me, my commitment to him, my loyalty. This did not concern me one bit; I was happy and determined to pass any test he wanted to place in my path.

The problem would come in the morning. He would go, out to stalk the streets in search of justice. And I would sit. Or pace. And wait.

The literature never commented on the remarkably dull, banal, day-to-day life of the undead. I had, over the course of my first few days spent at Royce's, mapped the journey of the sun's punishing rays across the apartment. I was certain the plethora of windows in the flat had been a selling point to Royce. To me, they were a veritable obstacle course, a laser grid from a spy film I must take care to avoid. I did not miss the irony of a human searching for a residence that allowed in so much natural light, and then never being home to enjoy it.

I could leave, but either I crept from Royce's bed in the dark, which I'd learned after our first night together was not alright with him, or I flew home in my bat form and left my clothes, mobile telephone, and anything else behind.

Then I'd need to either wait until after dark to return, or return absent clothing *again*. It was, to be frank, a logistical headache. Not insurmountable, I supposed, but it had begun to grate.

Any night spent in my own apartment or prowling the streets was a night spent alone, which seemed equally boring and lonely as a day spent alone.

I was frustrated.

Especially because my noble Royce was moonlighting on this missing persons case. He had his usual work and all of this additional investigative work. It meant he was working later and later in the evening.

Tonight, after I fed, I checked my mobile telephone to find a text message informing me Royce would be working late and wasn't certain when he would be home. I sighed and wondered if this were another test, another hurdle for me to mount to prove my devotion. Stretching my legs, I wandered the streets, and my feet lead me to the city aquarium.

It was a place I loved, but tried not to visit too often because I didn't want them to ascertain my point of entry, as it had taken me quite a while to find it. An old basement room had been converted into a large supply closet, and when it had been converted, the staff had not walled up the small, ground-level window. I was slight enough to shimmy right on through, and I always left a cash donation at the ticket window before I left.

The aquarium was beautiful at night. Peaceful. The tanks were illuminated and the fish and other creatures drifted about lazily. I could watch them for hours, and it was the perfect place to go to quiet my troubled mind. My favorite exhibits were the jellyfish, their luminous, transparent bodies tranquil as they glowed and moved through the tank.

I wasn't sure how long I stood there, but I must have really lost myself because all at once I felt cool breath on my neck and a hand at the small of my back. "Why, hello," said a voice.

Cold all over, I turned toward the voice, but there was no one. I gulped, all the hairs on my body rising to stand on end. A fingertip traced the scar on the nape of my neck, and when I jerked away, I stumbled, straight into someone's chest. I finally got a good look at him as he set me back on my feet. I had lived—and more importantly, survived—long enough to recognize when I was in the presence of another predator.

Something in this man's eyes told me he was a monster in a way I would never be. That he'd always been a monster, and being turned into a creature like me had merely been an opportunity for him to hone his malice. "Good evening," he said, extending his hand. "My name is Clay."

I took his hand, wary. "Good evening."

When I didn't offer my own name, he smiled, and it transformed his face from shrewd and calculating to truly frightening. "I must say," said Clay, reaching forward to straighten the lapels of my jacket. I fought the urge to bat his hands away. "I am impressed you managed to evade my notice for as long as you did."

"Oh?"

"You must be a clever little thing," Clay continued. He stepped away, and he cut quite the striking figure, backlit by the glow of the aquarium tanks. The bluish light transformed from tranquil to eerie when it illuminated Clay, who was tall and thin, his hair slicked back to accentuate the gaunt lines of his cheeks, his pointed nose and chin. The shadows on his smooth, white skin gave his face the appearance of a *Pierrot* mask.

I did my best to remain calm, but it had been years since I'd come face-to-face with another vampire, and longer still since I had felt true, animal fear. Clay stood so still—no attempt to appear more human, no lingering desire to fidget, or instinct to breathe. He didn't even blink. Like he'd forgotten all of what it had meant to be a man. I found his stillness truly captivating.

"At any rate," said Clay. "I don't appreciate anyone skulking around my home."

"Apologies—" I broke off on a gasp, as Clay stood suddenly at my side, his lips nearly touching my ear.

"If I were to find someone placing their sweet little button nose where it didn't belong, I would become very cross indeed."

My teeth clenched and I nodded. "Understood," I whispered.

But he was already gone.

I stood rooted to the spot, staring at the tank without really seeing it. Who was this man? The lingering effects of his visit, the electric, tingling fear, skittered across my skin as I watched the fish. I gripped the railing hard enough for my nails to leave dents in the worn wooden surface—so tense and distracted that shortly thereafter, I received my second shock of the evening.

"Boo."

A full-body shiver of delight rolled through me, a Pavlovian response to the man standing at my back. I turned, and the relief at seeing Royce's face was instant, like sliding into a warm bath.

"How did you find me here?"

Royce grinned. "We got a call from the night janitor

about a small, strange man staring at the jellyfish like he was in some kind of trance. I had a hunch it might be someone I knew."

I was glad that the janitor had left to call the police before Clay had arrived, but my relief soured as quickly as it had come. "Sorry to call you from your work," I said. The words slipped out, more petulant than I'd intended.

Royce touched my cheek. "I know I've been working a lot lately."

With a shrug, I turned back toward the jellies. "It's alright."

"It's not. Listen," said Royce. "For a long time, I had nothing but the job. Then I had Derek—my ex—but I still acted like I had nothing but the job."

I bristled at the thought of my Royce with another man. "Do you miss him?"

"No." He didn't hesitate. "We had other problems. But I don't want to make the same mistakes again, okay?"

"Okay."

"Now, let's go and let Sergei get back to waxing the floors."

I pouted. "I have to stop coming here, don't I?"

"Nah," said Royce. "I think me and Sergei can reach an understanding. Then you don't have to climb in through the window."

When we got back to Royce's, he led me through the front door with a possessive hand on the small of my back. "Can you wait in the bathroom for a sec?" he asked. "I have a surprise for you that I haven't had time to set up yet."

With my curiosity piqued, I allowed him to shoo me into the bathroom. I sat on the tub, and waited. And waited.

And waited.

"Um," called Royce finally, from the bedroom. "When did you sneak all this stuff into my apartment?"

"I didn't sneak anything in."

"My whole top drawer is full of your stuff. Where the hell is all my underwear?"

"Royce," I said loudly. "Can we possibly discuss this once you let me out of your lavatory? I feel ridiculous—"

He opened the door, cracking a grin. "I'm not letting you out of here until you tell me where you hid my underwear."

"I didn't hide it," I said. "I threw out all the pairs that resembled kilts as opposed to plaid boxer shorts. You make a decent living, Royce. Buy yourself some new underwear."

He stepped aside to let me out of the bathroom, and I flounced past him down the hall. "My underwear was fine," he said. "And now I don't have any!"

I smiled at him over my shoulder. "Perhaps you have uncovered my true goal."

When I reached the threshold to Royce's bed chamber, he hovered behind me, and I sensed he was waiting for my reaction to something. I spun on my heel, running my eyes over every inch of the room. I froze when I finally saw something new over his windows. "What are those?"

"Blackout curtains," he said. "I put them up in the living room, too. Sorry it took me so long."

I was touched. Royce had made it so I could move freely about the apartment during the daylight hours. "This is..."

"And check this out," he said eagerly. "You helped yourself to a drawer obviously, but I cleared out this shelf here. I don't know if you like to read or anything, but if you had books you wanted to bring over, or whatever, if you were bored at night when I'm sleeping."

"This is the kindest thing anyone has ever done for me,"

I admitted. I shifted from foot to foot. No one had ever cared for me enough to make room for me in their life. "I don't know what to say."

He shrugged. "You don't have to say anything. I know this relationship is kind of complicated."

I laughed. "That's one way of putting it."

"But, I like you. I want you to know that...you're important to me."

I stood on tiptoe and kissed him, my hands curling in the front of his shirt to keep him close. We didn't break the kiss until Royce needed to come up for air. "Thank you," I whispered.

"Don't thank me yet, there's one more thing I have to show you."

Royce led me by the hand back to his living room, where one wall had been given over to a large corkboard. He had a few file boxes on the coffee table and a haphazard collection of folders. "What's this?"

"Well, some people call it a murder board. It's just a place for us to organize everything we have on this case."

"We?"

Royce nodded. "Beckett Taylor's disappearance is connected to something paranormal. I can feel it."

"What makes you say that?"

"My commanding officer might have something to do with it," he told me. "He buried a big case of mine in the spring that also had to do with the paranormal. And now he's burying this one. My one lead on the case was killed, presumably by a vampire, right after Stark took the case from me and reassigned it. But then he deleted the file and a few others that are related to this whole thing. Including yours."

"Mine?"

"Yeah." Royce flushed. "When we first uh, met, Priya fingerprinted my apartment so we could try to find out who you were. There was an old arrest report on file from..."

"From when I died," I finished. "And Stark deleted it?"

"Yeah," he said. "Burying a current case is bad enough, but why try to hide a century old cold-case unless he knew something about—" he gestured vaguely at me.

"Vampire stuff?"

"Exactly." Silence fell over us as we stared at Royce's empty board. "So, I was kind of hoping you'd help me find this kid, and figure out what the hell Stark has to do with it."

"Of course," I said. Based on what I knew of Royce, his admitting he needed help was a larger, more vulnerable gesture than the rest of the things he'd shown me tonight, combined. With a small smile, I looked at the pile of folders on Royce's table. "Where do we start?"

Royce tacked the first photo to the board, of a hardened-looking man with a tattoo below his left eye. The picture was a mugshot, and he held a sign that said "Garibaldi" across the bottom.

"We start with him."

8

THE ART OF DINING

ROYCE

Sinclair and I had been, to use his word, courting, for a few weeks now. We spent most nights at my place, watching movies, working on our murder board, and not fucking. I was still holding out, for some reason I couldn't quite explain, even to myself. While I slept, Sinclair tailed Garibaldi in hopes that we could catch him doing something shady and use that as leverage to ask him a few questions about Beckett Taylor. He never failed to sneak back into bed before I woke, something that warmed my heart each morning. Sinclair was able to hold so still that when I woke, I sometimes expected an empty bed, only to find him smiling at me from his pillow.

Our one-month anniversary came with some fanfare, including the largest bouquet of flowers I'd ever seen. Priya rolled her eyes when she saw it. She'd been holding her tongue about me and Sinclair, but I knew the more time he spent around the precinct, the more she was building to confront me about him.

But, for once in my life, I was having way, way too much fun to give a shit. I couldn't ever remember a time when I'd been so swept up in a new romance.

Sinclair's over-the-top celebration of our "anniversary" included taking me to a beautiful restaurant on the river. It was called Chez L'Aube and it was the kind of place I never would have spent the cash on myself, but Sinclair was beside himself at the idea of spoiling me. God only knew where he got all his money, but considering he'd been earning it for a hundred years and never had to buy groceries, I didn't question it too much. He'd reserved us a table on a private patio overlooking the water. It was insanely romantic—and, a little weird. Obviously, Sinclair did not eat or drink anything the restaurant could offer. He just sat, watching me hungrily as I worked my way through the five-course tasting menu he'd picked out. With wine pairings, even.

"This is weird," I said, finishing my final bite of an absolutely God-tier tiramisu. "But I love it."

"And I love watching you feed," said Sinclair, and his voice had gone low and husky.

All of a sudden, I was far less concerned about the weirdness of this meal and far more concerned about getting home as quickly as possible.

We hadn't discussed the fact that we hadn't had sex again yet, and we also hadn't discussed when we were planning on it. As I licked the last bit of tiramisu from my dessert fork, I realized we had been locked in a bizarre game of sex chicken. Neither one of us wanted to give.

Tonight, though.

I could tell by the way Sinclair's eyes followed the motion of my tongue that by some unspoken agreement, it was on.

When we got to my building, Sinclair was like a frenzied cat trying to climb me as we stumbled down the hallway toward my door. His lips claimed my neck, my jaw, my ears with little nips and sharp bites that had me wild to get him to bed. Every time we kissed, I felt his fangs brush my skin. Every time we kissed, I longed to feel them deeper. I couldn't explain it, but the danger, the thrill of it ignited something deep in my gut. I had a feeling Sinclair was restraining himself—barely. I wanted to let him know he didn't have to. I wanted to feel him lose control.

For his part, Sinclair finally seemed willing to let me see this side of himself. I had no idea why watching me eat an indulgent meal turned his crank, but I wasn't about to question it.

However.

"I still think you're weird," I said, one arm snaking around his back to hold him close.

"Yes," he groaned, exasperated. "I'm mad as a wax banana. Now, take my pants off."

Laughing, I fumbled between us to pop the button on Sinclair's jeans, a challenge as he wriggled like an eel in my grasp. With one hand shoving the key into the lock and the other working on Sinclair's belt, I finally got the door unlocked and open.

I grabbed his chin, my opposite arm crushing him against me for a hungry kiss. Sinclair allowed me to take what I wanted, moaning eagerly. I slid my hand to brush the teasing swell of his ass before trying to work his jeans down past his thighs.

Then, someone cleared their throat.

I disentangled our lips, twisting around to look toward the source of the sound. "*Derek?*"

He cleared his throat again, cheeks pink. "Uh. Hi."

"What are *you* doing here?" Sinclair asked him, firing up at once. I put a hand on his shoulder to calm him. He snorted angrily, shrugging me off to right his shirt and rebutton his pants.

"We lived together," said Derek, looking Sinclair up and down like he was sizing him up. "I have a key."

"Well," Sinclair said haughtily. "I never needed a key because *mmmph!*"

I clapped a hand over his mouth to stop him before he admitted to breaking and entering. His eyes rounded with reproach over the top of my knuckles, and I said, "Just give us a second, okay?"

Throwing a final glare over his shoulder, Sinclair summoned his dignity and stalked down the hallway. Though I knew from experience he could move with a silent tread, Sinclair stomped the last few steps with gusto and slammed the bedroom door behind him.

"Royce, what the fuck are you doing?"

"I'm sorry, what am *I* doing?"

"Is this some kind of early midlife crisis? Running around, sleeping with Goth Polly Pocket over the—"

"Shh," I said angrily. "He's going to hear you."

"You can't be serious," said Derek. "Come on, Royce. I get it. You're pissed. But we were good together. What we had was real."

I frowned. "Oh, yeah? Real enough for you to kick my ass to the curb, huh?"

Derek took a step toward me. "I know," he said. "I'm sorry. But that was a huge mistake. I know that now—and I think you do too."

"You said you wanted more than I could give you," I said. "You were right. I couldn't give you more because— we weren't right for each other, Derek. Us breaking up wasn't a mistake."

He heaved an aggravated sigh, one I'd heard quite a lot in the months leading up to our split. "Fine," he said. "I get it. You have your pride. If you need to get this fun little rebound out of your system before—"

"Okay, that's enough," I said, raising my voice for the first time. "You can't come into my house and insult my boyfriend to my face."

"Boyfriend? Give me a break, Royce," said Derek. "He looks like a good lay, I'll give you that. But he's too young and way too pretty for you. He's going to lose interest the second something shiny comes along."

"Stop," I said, so angry my hands shook. "Leave your key and get the fuck out."

"Excuse me?"

"I didn't invite you over here," I told him. "And I don't have to fucking listen to this. Get. Out."

Derek huffed. "Fine." He slammed his key down on the table and grabbed his jacket from the peg. "Call me when you get your head out of your ass. Or his."

"Well, that's never going to happen," I snapped.

Derek shot me a weird look.

"Ew, okay. Whatever. You know what I mean. Just go."

As soon as the door shut behind him, I heard a whisper. "Never?"

I turned to find Sinclair wrapped in a robe that fell to his mid-thigh—made entirely of intricate black lace—because *of course* he owned a black lace robe—over his bare skin. I bit my tongue, taking him in from head to toe, but he looked so vulnerable, instead of sexy. Well, okay. Maybe not *instead* of sexy. Because, you know. But he looked small and fragile in that moment.

I cursed under my breath. He'd heard everything Derek

had said, all the insults and everything else. Stupid vampire super hearing. "Listen—"

"It's okay," he said, wrinkling his nose and sliding his toe back and forth across the threadbare hall rug. "If you didn't mean what you said."

Bewildered, I said, "Didn't mean what?"

"That you'd never be done with me," he said, meeting my eyes at last. "It's okay if that was just something—"

I crossed the room in three quick strides and pulled him into my arms. Cradling his face in my hands, I said, "I did mean it."

"Never is a long time," said Sinclair softly.

"Longer for you," I said.

Sinclair rolled his eyes, and I kissed his nose. I had a strong impulse to hide behind the joke, but it felt wrong. My gut told me this thing with Sinclair was something real. Something important. It made no sense; he was dangerous, and frightening, and intense. But he just *fit*. Fit in my life, in my arms, in my bed. My heart. "I'm serious," I said. "I meant it. I'm in this thing, for real."

"That's crazy."

I laughed. "Maybe I'm mad as a wax banana, too."

Before he could reply, I kissed him deeply, trying to put things into the kiss I didn't have the words for yet. Mainly, I wanted to erase the last twenty minutes and get back to what we'd been driving toward when we stumbled through the door.

More than that, though. I wanted Sinclair to know how serious I was about this. About him—us. I wanted him to know beyond a doubt that I accepted him. When at last we'd staggered down the hall and into my bedroom, I broke our kiss.

"Will you..." the request stuck in my throat. I wasn't

even entirely sure how to phrase this. Or why it seemed so important to get it right.

Sinclair cocked his head to the side. "What?"

I didn't think I could say the words out loud, though there was no one but Sinclair to hear them. Making a path of soft kisses up toward his ear, I whispered, "Will you... feed on me?"

The effect on Sinclair was immediate. He turned to stone in my arms for a few heartbeats—mine, of course, not his. Before he drew away, his usually grey-green eyes were all pupil. "You do not know what you're asking."

"I do," I said. "I trust you."

Sinclair trembled against me, vibrating like fine crystal about to shatter when a tuning fork strikes just the right note. "Royce..." he breathed my name, like it was all he needed to fill his lungs.

"Do it," I said, a little breathless myself.

Sinclair still seemed paralyzed by my request, so I kissed him again, sweeping my tongue over the seam of his plump lips before dipping inside to taste. I then kissed his jaw, nipping the sharp corner where it met his neck. As my lips made their way down the column of his lily-white throat, I drew aside the collar of his robe, the black satin hem contrasting beautifully with his pale, freckled shoulder as I bared it. With gentle swipes of my fingertips, I brushed the robe from his shoulders and let it pool on the ground at our feet.

Sinclair naked was fucking art. I said what I said. I'd happily go to a museum if he was the only artifact on display. Hell, I'd buy a season pass and come back every day just to stare at his body. Drawing back to take him in, I said, "So, how does this work?"

His nostrils flared, and he closed his eyes for a moment,

steadying himself. He rolled his shoulders, squaring them, before leveling his gaze at me. There was an odd, hypnotic weight to his voice when he said, "*Sit.*"

I obeyed, unbuttoning my shirt and casting it aside. Sinclair swooped toward the ground, his movements graceful and deliberate, until he knelt between my splayed thighs. He hooked his slim fingers in the waistband of my boxers and tugged them down over my hips. I lifted my ass a bit so he could do away with them. And then, I just had to stare down at him for a moment.

He looked so beautiful on his knees.

"Are you certain?" Sinclair asked, his voice barely above a whisper.

Looking into his blown, hungry eyes, I brushed my knuckles over his cheek and nodded. Sinclair slid his cool palms up my thighs and I shivered, and his eyes never left my face. I cupped his cheek and used the pad of my thumb to push back his upper lip, exposing one of his pointed fangs. I brushed my finger down its length, just a bit longer than the rest of his teeth, really, just enough to give him that strange, unbalanced smile that drove me crazy. The smile that was by turns vulnerable and predatory. He parted his lips, docile, as he allowed me to examine his kind's greatest weapon, blinking at me from his place at my feet. I tested the point of his fang with my thumb, doing my best not to wince at the needle-sharp tip of it pressing into my finger. Sinclair darted his tongue out, hesitant, like he was sneaking a taste of something truly fine, and lapped the pinprick drop of blood welling where I'd pierced my own flesh.

Sinclair trembled, drawing his tongue back between his lips, closing them around my thumb so he could suck. He watched me as he did, and I could sense every particle in him holding on to his self-control. The two halves of him, the hunter and the lover, warred behind his eyes.

Being wanted, equally, by both of those halves, was a heady thing.

"Good boy," I tried, never having been one for such games in bed, but it felt right.

Sinclair liked it too, closing his eyes and preening as he sucked the tiniest savor of blood from the tip of my thumb. I had never felt so powerful as I did with this monster entirely in my thrall, kneeling before me. When I heard the barely-there whine he released as I drew my thumb from between his lips, the little exhale that spoke of his thirst, I almost lost it. I carded my hand through his hair, not missing the way his eyes followed the hand like a cat might follow the flight of a bird before striking it from the sky.

He leaned forward, eyes falling shut again as he trailed kisses up my naked thigh, dragging his tongue and pressing the flat edge of his fangs against my skin. "You taste like heaven," he murmured against my hip, and I thought, even if he snapped and killed me tonight, it would have been worth it just to hear him say those words.

———

SINCLAIR

I had, of course, known the very first night I'd met Royce that I was his. The barely-there taste of his blood on my tongue just now confirmed it. If I had to, I would burn down the world to taste him again. I nuzzled the warm skin of his thigh, the smell of the city clinging to him as always, but beneath that the smell of my Royce, and beneath *that* was the smell of his blood.

I was not certain what Royce expected when he asked me to feed on him, but I didn't think he anticipated this slow exploration. I had to find the right place to bite. Miles and miles of Royce's hot, male flesh exposed, and I could only feed on him for the first time once. The place of the bite held meaning.

I squeezed his waist, thick, and sturdy enough to anchor me before I lost my head entirely, and sucked a little mark above his hip bone, like the ones I'd left during our first night together. Royce huffed, and when I glanced up, I saw him looking down at me fondly, his fingers still slipping through my hair.

Pleasure was a part of feeding, for myself, and my prey. Saliva and venom pooled in my mouth and I let it flow, coating my fangs. The venom allowed us to feed on prey rendered euphoric and docile, but it was like a feedback loop—we felt its effects too, the pleasure reverberating through us could make us vulnerable.

It was alright to be vulnerable now, with Royce. He would take care of me. I could trust him. And he could trust me, too. I would never harm him. I wouldn't even be taking a full meal from his body, more like a sampling, an *Hors D'oeuvres.*

I wrapped my hand around his cock, hoping he wouldn't notice my fingers shaking as I tugged on his length. His eyes became slits in his face, hooded with pleasure, as he let his head drop back. Holding the base of his thick shaft, I wrapped my lips around the head and he gasped; I knew there was a slight fear there, perhaps more than slight, knowing my fangs were so close to his tackle.

The fear was part of feeding, too: the heightened sense of arousal and adrenaline. So, I let him feel my teeth, just the barest whisper, just the smooth flat part of the front of my fang because the predator in me wanted to feel him shudder. He did, but he did not pull away. I rewarded his bravery by swallowing around the head of his cock, taking him as deep as I could, allowing the muscles of my throat to massage his glans. Royce cursed softly, his fingers tugging on my hair, little shocks of pain shooting down my scalp like static. I drew my lips off with a wet plop, kissing the crease where his thigh met his groin, teasing the little valley with my tongue before I reached the jut of his hip. I nipped it, a sharp swift bite. Royce gasped, then released the breath on a shaky moan. The venom worked fast.

"*Oh,*" said Royce, and I glanced up to see his eyes fixated on the spot where I punctured the skin of his hip. The blood welled up and I lapped eagerly at the droplets, the burst of copper on my tongue making my toes curl. That was just a tease, however—a sample for us both as my venom worked through his veins and I sniffed the bouquet of Royce's blood like a fine wine.

Exquisite.

Petting his thighs, I looked up at Royce, asking if he wanted me to continue. He took my chin in his hand and squeezed, staring hungrily down at me. "More," he commanded.

With a little path of kisses, I moved down to the meat of his thigh, the interior of it where the femoral artery pumped life below Royce's skin. I allowed each kiss to show a bit more of my hunger until I had found the spot, like tapping a tree. I latched my lips to the skin of Royce's thigh, sucking a hickey there, bringing all his beautiful blood humming close to the surface, and then I snapped my jaws, piercing his flesh.

His skin burst like a grape.

The salty-sweet copper tang of Royce's blood exploded

in my mouth, gushing down my throat, coating my lips and tongue. With one hand I squeezed his knee, keeping his thigh in place as I hummed around the bite, glutting myself, and the other stroked Royce's cock. Something cold dribbled on my fingers. Glancing up, I watched Royce squeeze some lube onto my hand and his shaft, allowing me to increase the speed and pressure of my strokes, driving him wild as I fed. Keeping my hands so engaged left my own cock aching with want, my hips pumping fruitlessly, stabbing at the air with no relief in sight.

Light-headed, I withdrew my fangs, savoring the last spurt from the bite before soothing it with my tongue. I swallowed a few more drops of blood before filling my mouth with Royce's cock again, the taste of man, of blood and cum, igniting me from scalp to toes making me feral.

Royce yanked on my hair, and I hissed in pain, startled as he pulled me off his cock, and he tugged until I allowed him to tilt my head back. His eyes went dark as he exposed my throat. I parted my lips, gasping, and my hand slid from Royce's knee down his shin so I could take myself in hand —the agony of an aborted feed, the loss of the taste of Royce's cock, it all had me desperate, and I clearly wasn't the only one.

Royce tugged on my hair again. I had no idea what had possessed him, but I wanted more of it. "Up here," he gasped. "I need to be inside you. Now."

Dazed by his command, hypnotized and blood-drunk, I obeyed, moving to straddle Royce on the edge of his bed. He wrapped strong arms around me and pulled me close to plunder my mouth with his tongue, like he wanted a taste of himself before I swallowed the last, lingering traces of his blood. I went to putty in his arms, and he maneuvered me to lay back on the pillows. "You're flushed," he said in awe.

"Your cheeks." He drew his thumb across one. "I've never seen you blush before."

"It's the blood," I rasped. Parting my lips again, I hoped against hope Royce would feed me something—his blood, his cock, his tongue, *anything.*

I simply...needed.

Instead, Royce fed me his fingers. First the thumb I'd pierced before, and I sucked wantonly, as if I could drain Royce's life through the pin point I'd left, nursing the tiniest taste of blood from his fingertip.

Though he had lubricant, right there on the bed beside us, Royce pulled his spit and venom slick fingers from between my lips and shoved two of them deep inside me. I yelped, arching off the mattress at the sudden intrusion, the intensity of the pleasure, as Royce closed his mouth around my cock, hoisting my leg over his shoulder. "*Royce,*" I begged. For what, I wasn't certain.

He released my cock. "Easy, baby," he murmured against the skin below my navel.

I squirmed as Royce's scruff tickled. He loomed over me, fingering me forcefully, but it wasn't enough.

It wasn't enough, and yet when he pulled his fingers back, I mourned their absence. Royce soothed me with a kiss. I bit his lip, perhaps a bit harder than I normally would have, not shy about letting him feel my fangs. Drawing back, Royce grabbed the lube and slicked himself up, groaning as he stroked his own shaft in a way that left me salivating.

"Over," he said.

I obeyed immediately. Surrendering to Royce's commands was intoxicating, just as nourishing as his blood now pumping through me. Linking us together. I arched my back, all but shoving my ass into Royce's face. He slid a palm down my spine, smoothing over one ass cheek, cupping the flesh like he was weighing his options. Then his big hands spread me wide and finally, *finally* he pushed inside. I sighed with relief, relief at being filled at last, but I was far from satisfied. I shoved back against him, fucking myself on his cock as he remained immobile, guiding my hips as I moved. Then, he looped an arm around my chest, pulling me upright and against him, holding me like the first night we'd made love. Only this time, he grabbed a fistful of my hair and held his opposite wrist in front of my face.

"More," he said.

I stopped moving, my body thrumming with thirst and arousal, my already tenuous self-control slipping even further. "Royce," I said. "It's too much—"

"It's not," he said in my ear. "I know you can do it. I trust you. More."

I shook my head, trying to turn away from the enticing web of blue veins in his wrist, the pulse I could hear humming there, just below his skin, like a siren call.

"Do it," he urged. "Feed."

With a soft sob of pleasure, I surrendered, grasping his forearm and pulling it to my lips, licking the tendons, tracing the pattern of his veins with the tip of my tongue before plunging my fangs deep into the papery skin there. Royce groaned again, his forehead coming to rest briefly on my shoulder, his hips stuttering as we adjusted to this new position. I gripped Royce's arm like a vice, and he braced his free hand against the headboard, pulling out and thrusting in hard enough to dislodge my bite and send blood spraying across the pillows. Soon enough I'd latched back onto the wound, suckling from the punctures, my cock aching and throbbing as Royce found his rhythm. It was messy and brutal. He drove into me again and again, and blood dripped from his wrist down onto the sheets and the smell of it made my eyes roll with pleasure.

After a few more blissful, intoxicating pulls, I lapped at the punctures to clean them, hoping I hadn't plunged my fangs too deep. I suckled the blood from Royce's fingers, then laved the wounds till his wrist was clean, the skin around the bite marks raw and pink and wet. Royce dropped his hand down, pinching my nipples as he bit the back of my neck, sucking the skin like he was trying to consume me as well.

I'd become one pure, frayed nerve, and the second Royce's hand wrapped around my cock I shattered, coming with a shrill cry, adding the hot mess of my release to the blood on the pillows.

Royce pulled my hair again, twisting my head so he could kiss my lips, invading my mouth with his tongue, and I felt him quake deep inside me, his cock pulsing as he filled me up. "Greedy little monster," he cooed. "Let me fill you up at both ends."

My head dropped back as I melted, boneless, into his arms. "Yes," I said because that was all I wanted. I mewled as Royce withdrew, pulling me into his lap, stroking my hair. "Yes."

My vision went hazy, and I came back to myself a few moments later to Royce saying, "Jesus, this bed looks like a fucking crime scene."

He was right of course: blood, sweat, and cum had made a truly horrific mess, but it was a horrific mess in which I wanted to live, possibly forever. Our mess.

Royce plied the strands of my hair, featherlight touches on my scalp so different from his rough treatment moments ago, and I could hear his heart rate begin to slow. "That was..."

I cringed, suddenly feeling ashamed. It had gone too far; I had let it go too far. I should never have opened two wounds on Royce. What if I'd lost control? What if—

"...perfect. You are perfect."

Twisting myself, I looked up at him, blinking in confusion. Something peculiar happened in my chest. "Pardon?"

"Perfect," he said again, and his expression was soft. "So good for me, baby."

I smiled against his belly, where I had come to rest my head. We'd somehow ended up curled against the headboard, sitting in a nest of stained, bloodied sheets.

"What?" Royce asked in a dopey, sleepy voice. "I can feel you smiling. You laughing at me?"

"You called me baby," I said. "And...boy."

"So?"

"I'm old enough to be your great-grandfather," I reminded him. "And then some."

Royce chuckled. "Yeah, but 'gramps' isn't exactly a sexy pet name, is it?"

I didn't answer. I merely kissed the soft brown fluff on Royce's stomach, nosing through it to inhale his scent and imprint it on my memory.

Royce did his best to stay awake, but the blood loss coupled with our energetic lovemaking overpowered him. I heard his snores seconds after my assessment of his breathing and heart rate told me he'd fallen asleep. When I was certain he was out, I slid from his arms to stand by the edge of the mattress. Royce had a strong hand in bed, which unlocked a side of myself I hadn't ever explored before, but in reality, I was stronger. I lifted him easily into a bridal carry and walked down the hall, stepping slowly to avoid jostling him, and placed him on the sofa. He wasn't bleeding much, so I turned the heat up on the thermostat and left a glass of juice on the coffee table beside him in case he woke.

I stretched, my bones popping as I shook the afterglow from my limbs, moving with purpose to strip the bed and get the sheets soaking. Now, it must be said, I was something of an expert at laundering blood stains. A cold soak and a good hard scrub with some hydrogen peroxide would do the trick.

Once I had the laundry going, I rummaged in Royce's bathroom cabinets. His first aid accoutrements were woefully inadequate. I searched through the scant supplies for what I needed to patch him up, and made a mental note to purchase some replacement items and give him a more robust home aid selection.

Royce remained dead to the world, draped naked on his back across the sofa, one leg hanging over the edge and the other dangling up over the arm. Carefully, so as not to disturb him, I climbed over his leg to settle between his spread thighs, perched on the cushion. I couldn't help but brush my fingertips over the spot where I'd bitten him, knowing it would scar, knowing he was mine. Still, I had to make sure the wound remained clean and cared for while it healed. I also knew Royce could possibly reopen the wound if he strained his thigh—which I really, really hoped he'd be recovered enough to do soon.

As I dabbed some ointment on the bite, Royce grunted in his sleep, so I took care when applying the gauze and bandages not to jostle him unnecessarily.

When I bandaged his wrist, an entirely different feeling washed through me. The mark was troubling. I had been entirely in control for the first bite, but this second one was impulsive and it could have been dangerous. I'd honed the control over my bloodlust over many decades, and though Royce's was far and away the sweetest blood I'd ever tasted, I couldn't afford to lose that handle on myself.

The way I'd caved so easily to Royce's plea had me feeling soiled and unsure of myself. Vampire venom and feeding sex were intoxicating things, and in truth, I didn't like what this left in my gut. I'd never felt this way after feeding before, and certainly never after fucking—like I'd been flying and then suddenly crashed into a mountainside. How would Royce feel? Would he wake up full of disgust and regret? I bandaged the wound quickly, not savoring it like I did the one on Royce's thigh.

I wanted to hide it.

I wanted to hide from it.

With Royce all bandaged up, and still sleeping, I slid from the sofa to check the laundry and do a few more things to tidy up so Royce wouldn't wake up to see his blood smeared everywhere, reminding him I was a monster. I cringed. He'd called me monster, after. *Greedy little monster.* In the moment, I had loved it, but now...

I felt suddenly like I had to escape my own skin. Like I didn't want to be here when Royce woke. Like I'd ruined everything by being weak and greedy. But I couldn't leave his bed like this. I tore his closet apart, searching for fresh linens. I found them and thanked the stars the blood had not soaked all the way through to the mattress. Had it gotten on the headboard? The wood was dark, but I felt like the smell of Royce's blood was everywhere. He would smell it when he woke, I just knew it. I filled a bucket with scalding water and sought the most abrasive cleaner I could find in Royce's apartment. Armed with a sponge and my bucket I scrubbed the headboard of the bed. No matter how hard I scrubbed, I felt like traces of what I'd done remained. If I could just get it clean—

"Sin?"

I startled, nearly spilling the bucket. Royce stood in the doorway, tousle-haired and sleepy and gloriously naked— though my eyes went first to the bandages on his wrist and upper thigh. Turning away, angry, I dunked my sponge again and returned to scrubbing. "This stain will set," I said. "I just have to clean it up."

Royce approached the side of the bed and reached into the bucket to stop my hands. With a yelp of surprise, he snatched his hand back. "Christ," he said, the sleep totally jolted from his voice. "How hot is that water?"

"Boiling," I said apologetically.

"Sin," he said, and this time I registered his use of the foreshortened version of my name, "Why are you scrubbing my headboard with boiling water at three in the morning?"

A lump formed in my throat. "It's—I—it's dirty."

Royce took my hands, plucked the sponge from my fingers, and moved the bucket to the floor. He brushed his other hand over the spot I'd been scrubbing, and to my horror I realized I had scrubbed the varnish right away, leaving pale scrapes of raw wood. My lip trembled. What on earth was wrong with me?

Royce spun me about so I sat on the edge of the bed, and knelt between my thighs, a mirror opposite of our position from earlier. He braced his palms on my knees and said, "Are you going to tell me what this is about?"

"No," I said, too quickly. "I don't know."

"Okay," said Royce. He kissed my kneecap, and I realized I was still naked, too. I'd been storming around, cleaning the house totally starkers, with a pair of rubber gloves on. Royce must have thought I'd truly gone off my head. He peered up at me, waiting, but all I could think to do was hastily peel off the rubber gloves and toss them into the bucket.

"I'm not certain what came over me," I confessed, feeling jittery and skittish.

Royce nodded, like he was struggling to catch up. "Can you start from the beginning? From, maybe, when I fell asleep?"

"Alright," I said.

Royce heaved himself to his feet and sat beside me.

Crossing my legs daintily at the knee, trying to recapture some semblance of composure. "Well, naturally, I had to get you to the sofa so I could strip the bed."

Royce appeared bemused, like he never would have thought of that.

"And then I had to patch you up," I said, speaking carefully to keep my voice from breaking.

"I appreciate that," said Royce, leaning down to kiss my shoulder. "And the juice. Then what?"

I took Royce's hand, pulling his forearm across my lap, and touched the bandage on his wrist, glaring white and accusatory. "This," I choked out. "I did this."

"Yes," he said, still confused. "I asked you to. Or, well. I told you to..."

I watched him frown down at the bandage, his brows knit together like he was puzzling something out. At once, he seized my hand, bringing my knuckles up to kiss them.

"Have you ever done anything like this before?" he asked me.

"Fed off a lover?"

"No—not that." He dragged his fingertips across my palm, like he was reading my future there. "The um, other parts. The sort of...me telling you what to do. In bed. Parts."

"No," I admitted. "Not in so many words, anyway."

"Me either," said Royce. "It just happened, in the moment. I felt so…"

Disgusted? Horrified? Ashamed? I wanted to cringe from his next words.

"Powerful," he whispered. "Wanted. Needed."

"What?"

"I've never felt that way before. With anyone."

How could my Royce have never felt wanted? I blinked stupidly at him.

"I understand if you didn't like it," he said hurriedly, misinterpreting my silence. "We totally should have discussed it first. I'm sorry I made you—"

"No," I said, pressing a finger to his lips. "I *loved* it."

One corner of his mouth twitched. "Yeah?"

I nodded.

He gave my hand a squeeze. "Then why are you so upset?"

My thoughts were a buzzing, tangled scribble. "I'm not sure."

With one hand smoothing my hair back, Royce tilted my chin up with the other so he could offer my lips a soft kiss. "It's late," he said. "I'm totally spent. I think we need to talk about this more, but I need to crash first. Is that okay?"

I nodded and he kissed me again.

"Uh," said Royce, suddenly bashful. "I know you don't sleep, but…is it okay if I held you for a while?"

His words had my dead heart melting, soothed the frantic thoughts in my head, and I happily surrendered to him tugging me down to curl beside him on the mattress.

———

ROYCE

I woke up with Sinclair in my arms, something I was getting seriously addicted to. I hadn't meant to sleep so late, but having him in my bed improved the quality of my rest by like, a zillion percent. When I opened my eyes, it was to see him peering down into my face, his chin resting on his interlocked fingers.

"Hi," I said, a smile pulling over my lips. It came so easily these days.

"Hi," Sinclair replied.

He seemed to have returned to himself a bit after his strange turn from last night. I still didn't entirely know what to make of what happened, but I was glad he seemed to be in higher spirits. I nudged his cheek with my knuckles. "Sorry if you were bored all night," I said.

He shrugged a shoulder. "I like watching you sleep."

Normally I would have made a joke about how weird he was, but the comment died on my tongue as I remembered how upset he had been. "About last night..."

Sinclair silenced me with a kiss that quickly turned heated. Much to my chagrin, I knew I couldn't let myself be tempted. Not yet anyway. Gently, I pushed him back so I could disengage from his lips and tongue.

"That's not going to work," I chided him.

He made a face. "Fine."

"First of all," I said, adjusting to lean against the headboard, and pulled Sin into my lap. "Are you alright?"

"Yes," he said. "I don't know what happened last night, but it wasn't anything you did."

"Are you sure?"

His hesitation told me everything.

"Come on, Sinclair, what is it?"

He didn't answer straight away, instead contenting himself by playing with my chest hair. Finally, he said, "You can't ask me to do that again."

"Do what?"

"Feed a second time—or just, feed more, in general."

This was about the last thing I expected him to say about last night. "Oh," I said. "Why?"

Sinclair straddled my lap, clasping my face with both hands so we now stared eye to eye. "I could have killed you," he whispered. "When I fed on you the first time, I was in total control of myself. I knew how much to drink, when to stop. I didn't anticipate a second feed and by that point it was...I was too far gone. It was stupid and dangerous."

"Shit," I said. I hadn't realized he'd been so close to losing control—all I could think about was how good it felt, how intense and intimate the connection between us had been. The idea that he'd been so close to the edge had my heart beat faster in my chest. "I'm so sorry, Sin. I didn't know."

He swooped in for a small kiss. "It's okay," he said. "We just should have discussed it first."

"Is that all?"

"Well, that's what started my...."

"Shame spiral?"

Sinclair released a breathy laugh. "Yes, if you want to call it that." His gaze grew serious again, and he said, "I want you to know I enjoyed it, very much. Too much. You simply must promise to *never* push my limits like that again."

"...like that?" I echoed, sliding my hand up the back of his neck to grab a fistful of his hair. "I can push your limits in other ways?"

"I'm going to have to insist that you do," said Sinclair, and he kissed me again, dirtier this time.

I allowed the kiss to continue a bit, rocking against him where he pressed down on my lap. When I paused for breath, I said, "What if we came up with some kind of...safe word?"

He cocked his head to the side. "Safe word?"

"Yeah, like, for both of us. Something we can say during sex and the other one has to immediately pump the brakes, no questions asked."

"I like that," Sinclair said. "So, if you ask me to feed, and I feel like it's gotten past the point of being able to do so safely I just say—"

"Hippopotamus?"

Sinclair cackled. "Hippopotamus?"

"I don't know," I said, face heating. "I think the idea is you have to pick something you wouldn't normally say."

"How about begonia?"

"Begonia?"

"In the language of flowers, it means 'beware.'"

"Begonia. Okay. I like that." I kissed the tip of his nose. "So, uh. How often can we do...what we did last night?"

"Which part?"

"The um. Feeding stuff."

"Not too often," Sinclair said. "It's dangerous. I've never fed off the same person more than once before, so I'm not certain."

"I could look into it," I offered. "Like, people donate blood regularly. That's *kind* of what I'm doing, yeah?"

Sinclair wrinkled his nose and shot me a crooked smile. "I suppose that's one way to look at it."

I reached for my phone and tapped a few words into google. "Hmm," I said. "Consensus seems to be you can safely donate blood six times a year, so like every other month. But that's a pint. Holy shit, did you drink a whole pint?"

"How the hell should I know? I didn't decant it into a measuring glass first."

"Well, alright. Not too often seems to be the word on the street."

"He pursed his lips. "Is that..."

"Is that what?"

"Is that alright? That we can't do what we did last night all that much?"

"Last night was perfect," I admitted. "Possibly the best sex I ever had."

"Me too," Sinclair said, and I was pleased to hear how breathless he sounded.

"But, I think the feeding thing was just one small part of it. At the risk of sounding insanely sappy, I think the fact that it was you and me was the most important factor."

Sinclair blinked at me, mouth open. "Oh," he said softly.

"I liked the...power dynamics we played with, though. Like, a lot." I was determined to have this frank discussion, even if it was so awkward it straight-up killed me. I could feel my face growing hotter by the second. "A lot, a lot."

"Me, as well," said Sin. "I'd be quite keen to revisit that. Often."

"Yeah?"

"Oh, yes," Sinclair said. "Surrendering to you..." he trailed away, bashful. "Felt as natural as breathing."

As natural as breathing, I thought. My heart thudded in my chest. "Okay, so, do you trust me?"

"With my life," he said immediately, and his instant response made my heart swell and my dick hard.

"Okay. Let me do some thinking. And research. For—for next time."

"I can't wait."

9
THE CARE OF THE PERSON

ROYCE

At the precinct the next morning, I finished up some paperwork for a few misdemeanors. It seemed to be the only cases Stark would assign to me these days, like he was determined to keep me off the street and at my desk. But I didn't mind. Misdemeanors had to be cleared, too—and it gave me extra brain power to focus on my off-books case. I had plans to interrogate Beckett Taylor's old boss, Garibaldi, that evening once the sun went down and I could bring my backup. AKA Sin. After a while, my mind drifted back to what we had discussed yesterday in bed. I surreptitiously pulled up an incognito browsing window so I could do some reading up on the kind of kink-lite sexcapades Sinclair and I were hoping to explore.

It was kind of shocking how much was out there—all kinds of terms and gear and even furniture I'd never even heard of. I had a pretty good idea of something I wanted to try the next time I had Sin in bed, but I was also worried about the feelings he'd experienced after our recent encounter. Despite what he said, I had a feeling his shame about overfeeding was a symptom of something larger, not the cause. As I consulted an article that listed some basic roles and terms, I stumbled across something called aftercare.

Aftercare was apparently real important to help mitigate something called "Sub drop," wherein the submissive partner felt an emotional crash after the highs of intense sex. I spent a lot of time reading up on how to care for your partner after kinky shenanigans, and while some of them—like offering snacks or a warm cup of tea—wouldn't apply to Sin, there were a bunch of things I knew he'd like. The idea of pampering him after sex was weirdly intriguing, like I could take him apart and then carefully put him together again. The more I read about it, the more I got excited to have discovered it. Almost more than some of the other stuff.

Almost.

Unfortunately, it also made me realize that I had dropped the ball, big time, the other night. The surge of feelings during any kind of intense scene—the article didn't specifically mention vampirism, go figure—could make a person crash hard, feel depressed and unmoored, and I had to imagine the added connection of Sinclair feeding from me had exacerbated that. Instead of being a responsible Dom—still kind of hard to think of myself like that, but anyway—I'd passed out and left him all alone. Woof. I would one hundred percent be making it up to him next time, especially since I wouldn't be coping with blood loss.

"What the hell is this?"

I jumped, scrambling to cover my screen before Priya could see what I was reading. "What?"

She seized my arm, yanking back my sleeve to reveal the bandage Sinclair had applied to my wrist. "This!"

"I burned myself cooking," I lied.

"Royce, we both know you haven't cooked since 2007," said Priya. She narrowed her eyes at me. "Come on. We're going to lunch. Now."

"But I—"

"*Now*," she hissed, grabbing me by the collar of my jacket. Her eyes slid to my computer screen, which I'd done a terrible job minimizing. "Are you looking at porn?"

"Oh my God," I said, jumping up and slamming the sleep button on my computer monitor. "Let's go. Lunch, right? You pick. My treat."

"But—"

"Let's go." I pushed her toward the door.

Priya was jonesing for sushi, so we grabbed a table at our favorite little spot downtown. "Okay, Davis," she said after we'd ordered. "Spill."

"Spill what?"

"Come on," she said. "We've been partners for years. Don't insult me."

I stared blankly at her, because she was right. She was totally right. Unfortunately, I had *no* idea where to even begin explaining my relationship with Sinclair.

Priya huffed, taking a sip of her green tea. "Okay, fine. How about I start? Stop me when I get something wrong. Your new boyfriend, Sinclair, is not...normal."

Well, I certainly couldn't argue with that. To be honest, part of me was curious about Priya's working theory, if she would even say the word "vampire" out loud, like it was a viable option.

"He's way older than he looks. Like *way* older. Like, inhuman old."

I nodded, inviting her to go on.

Here, she hesitated. "He killed someone," she whispered. "That was his old arrest file, wasn't it?"

"Self-defense," I said automatically, cringing at how feeble the excuse sounded.

"Holy shit," she said. Her eyes fell to the bandage on my wrist and she bristled at once. "Did he do that to you?"

"Yes, but it was consensual. It was like a…"

"Like a what?"

"A sex thing," I said, mortified.

Priya massaged her temple with an aggrieved sigh. "Okay, let's put a pin in that. So, you *did* delete his arrest file? And the results from fingerprinting your place?"

"No, Priya, of course not," I said, a little hurt. "I would never do that."

"Did Sinclair do it himself?"

"Priya," I said, "Sinclair was born in 1837. He calls emojis 'pictographs.' No. I am one hundred percent certain he did not hack the police records database."

"Then who?"

I sighed. Maybe it was time to be honest with Priya about some things she might actually be able to help with. "I don't have proof, but I think it was Stark."

"What? Why?"

"I have no idea," I admitted. "Not really. But I think it has something to do with Beckett Taylor's disappearance."

"This is fucking crazy," said Priya. "I know Stark is kind of a dick, but dirty? Come on."

"He said he was passing my file on Taylor over to Major Crimes. They never got it, and then it was gone from the server."

"But—"

"I don't know, Priya. I have no idea what he's after or

why. But I promise you, neither Sin nor I tampered with the files."

She gave me a hard look. "You're my best friend, and I trust you," she said. "But don't you think it's possible Sinclair is wrapped up in whatever nefarious thing is going on here?"

I shook my head. "No. Never."

"You haven't known him that long—"

"Priya, I'm serious. Back off Sin. He's important to me, and he's not involved with this."

"Wow."

"What?"

She smiled. "It's kind of nice to see you so fired up over someone," she admitted, but then she pointed at me with her chopsticks. "But I still don't trust this guy. Yet."

"Yet?"

"We'll see," she said. And then she stole my tuna roll. "So, what do you think about Stark? Does he have something to do with that big case you worked in the spring? The one with the Ambrose family?"

I startled. "What do you mean?"

"Well," she said carefully. "That case was...not normal, too, yeah? It was big. Then all of a sudden it disappeared and no one was pressing charges...and you walked around with a hair across your ass until...." She frowned. "Until meeting Sinclair, honestly. Huh."

I grinned, and Priya rolled her eyes. "I don't know. I mean, besides the fact that Stark is the one who buried that case, and he is burying this one, I don't think they have much of a connection."

"Except they're both..."

"'Not normal,'" I parroted her choice of words. "Yeah."

Later, I met Sinclair a few blocks from the place we

planned to accost Garibaldi. He had a few known haunts
from where he ran his various shady dealings, one of which
was a dingy office building downtown.

Sinclair insisted on coming with me, "for backup",
which, considering I was working off the books, wasn't the
worst thing. If I ended up having to call for actual backup,
I'd be in deep shit. We posted up at the office building by its
dumpster and waited. I leaned against the wall, and
Sinclair fidgeted, seeming unsure of how to stand. Eventually, he settled on standing beside me with his arms crossed
over his chest in what, I was sure, he thought was an intim-
idating posture.

When our guy finally emerged, I pulled out my badge.
"Douglas Crest PD," I said, and he jumped before turning
around to face us. "Are you Garibaldi?"

"Yeah," he said, shooting us an annoyed look as he
locked the door behind him. "Who wants to know?"

"I'm Detective Davis."

He looked at Sinclair. "Who's the kid?"

"Ignore him," I said, stepping forward, shooting Sinclair
a warning glance. "Can you tell me what kind of business
this is?"

Garibaldi sized us up. "There a specific reason you can't
come through the front door, Detective?"

"What, and let you slip out the back while I bang on the
front?"

"Something like that." He grinned. "So, what is this—
pretty boy is nice cop, and you're the muscle?"

"Trust me," I said. "He's the muscle. But no one has to
be good cop or bad cop. We're just talking."

"Oh, yeah? Well then, I should tell you I got nothing to
say."

"No? You can't even tell me what manner of business

you conduct out of this office?"

"Consulting," he said, too quickly.

Classic catch-all front for something shady. "Consulting for what industry, exactly?"

With narrowed eyes, Garibaldi set his jaw. "Shipping."

"Shipping?"

"And receiving." He turned away from us, shoving his keys into his pocket. "I'm pretty sure you can pull the business license from the permit office."

"Oh, I will."

Grumbling, Garibaldi turned to make his way to the street. I motioned for Sinclair to follow and we casually flanked him as he stepped onto the sidewalk.

"Listen," I said quietly. "I just wanted to ask you a couple questions about Beckett Taylor."

"Who?"

"BT."

Garibaldi snorted. "That fuckin' kid."

"You know him?"

"Let's say I knew him," said Garibaldi.

"Hypothetically?" I said, annoyed.

"Yeah. Let's say if I knew him, and let's say if I pointed him in the direction of a job that could help out him and his mother."

"What job?"

"Doesn't matter," he said. "We're only talking hypothetically, right?"

Through clenched teeth, I said, "Right."

"Anyway, one would have thought that, hypothetically, he'd have some loyalty to someone who helped him."

"Oh?"

"Yeah. Anyway, hypothetically, a kid like that, might get

some ideas about being too good for the people who helped him out."

I threw out my arm, and Garibaldi walked right into it. "Listen," I said, pivoting, putting my hand on his chest to look him in the eyes. "Let's cut the crap. I don't care what business you're involved in. I'm looking for a missing kid. Just give me something, and maybe I don't go pull the business license from the permit office. Maybe I don't look too closely at your books to make sure it all adds up to what you've got on file with the IRS."

Garibaldi seemed to consider this. "Alright," he said. "BT worked for me. Trent vouched for him, and he worked like a dog, never made mistakes, and didn't use, as far as I knew. But then he went off to college. I wanted him to get into moving some of my product on campus. He refused. I asked Trent to lean on him because they were tight. Apparently, BT told him he'd found some other way to make a lot more cheddar. Then Trent talked to you and turned up dead, and a shipment of my product vanished. So now I'm out two street guys and a lot of cash."

I'd have to ask Priya if any "product" was recovered with Trent's body.

"Now if that's all..." Garibaldi turned to go, but almost as an afterthought, he said. "Your name Sinclair?"

We exchanged a look, startled. "Yes," said Sin. "Why?"

Garibaldi shot him a leer. "He said you were pretty."

I waited until Garibaldi was out of earshot before turning to Sinclair. "Who is he talking about?"

Sinclair tugged nervously at the collar of his shirt, looking at Garibaldi's retreating back like he'd seen a ghost. "No one," he squeaked.

I raised my eyebrows.

"Alright, someone," said Sinclair. "I perhaps...may have...ran into another vampire the other night."

"*What?* When?"

"A few nights ago," he admitted. "I'd been trying to see who else might be around. After that body."

"And you didn't tell me?"

"I didn't want to worry you," said Sinclair. "It was my thing. I didn't think he had anything to do with..."

"Well," I said. "Clearly, he does. You've got to tell me everything you know."

———

SINCLAIR

Royce wanted to confer with his partner, Priya, regarding this tangled case and the possibility of Clay's involvement in it. I'd told Royce everything I'd observed about Clay, and vowed to stay away from him in the future. I stopped in at Datura because I had an appointment to meet with a bride-to-be regarding her upcoming nuptial ceremony and its accompanying florals. Because I didn't actually rely upon Datura for income, I could be extremely choosy about my appointments. I had been looking forward to working with this particular young lady and her future spouse.

When I arrived at my shop, I was only about five minutes ahead of our prearranged meeting time, so I bustled in through the front door, heading straight for the cabinet where I kept my appointment ledger. I was in such a hurry, so distracted that I didn't register that something was amiss until I opened the cabinet and a body fell out.

With a soft gasp, I dodged to the side as the body fell to the floor with a surprisingly loud *thud.*

I knelt beside it—her, gingerly rolling the body to get a look at the face.

It was my client.

I placed my fingers to her pulse point where I detected only the faintest hint of life. The hairs on the back of my neck rose seconds before a soft voice said, "I grew bored waiting for you."

I was on my feet, hackles up, in seconds, but the man reclining against my till counter did not flinch. He simply regarded me with mild, almost dispassionate gaze.

"Come now, Sinclair," and the way he said my name had my body prickling with an uncomfortable awareness. Like by saying my name he was looking at me naked. "I simply wanted to speak with you."

"Oh?" I asked, trying to adopt a similar casual demeanor. What could he possibly want with me?

"I thought perhaps you might have wanted to speak with me, as well."

"And why's that?"

Before I could blink, he stood before me chest to chest, towering over me, leaning into my space. "You were sniffing around my nest, were you not? Aren't you...curious?"

My blood turned to ice, and I cleared my throat to cover my fear. I had no idea how he'd found where I lived—unless he already knew, somehow. Perhaps the aquarium wasn't the first place he'd followed me. But no—I was so careful. And I never fed here.

As if reading my mind, he smiled and said, "You are certainly a careful creature," and he stroked one cold finger down my cheek. "But I have been tracking our kind since before you were born, the first time."

It took all my self-control not to flinch away from him.

The familiarity with which he addressed me, with which he moved around *my* home, like he had some sort of right to exist in my world, had me clenching my fists, seething. But something stopped me from flinging myself at him, attempting to tear his flesh to ribbons. He had me pinned, just by the drag of his fingertip on my cheek. His presence was like a magnet, pulling at something deep inside me.

"I merely wanted to invite you to a *soiree* I plan to throw next week."

"Thank you," I said faintly. "I think I'll have to politely decline, though."

"Pity," said Clay. "I find threats quite distasteful, but I suppose they have their place."

"Threats?"

His stare had me rooted to the floorboards, though the animal in me screamed to flee. "You will attend," he said. "Or the next client I visit won't be as lucky as this one."

White hot fury finally galvanized me, and I took a step forward, but Clay only laughed. "I will see you next week, Sinclair." He glanced at the floor, nudging the body with his foot. "You may want to clean this up."

I knelt beside her, feeling again for a pulse, and when I looked up, Clay had vanished. With a curse, I whipped out my mobile telephone. My finger hovered over Royce's name in my list of correspondents, but instead, I dialed emergency services.

"Hello," I said. "I was doing a consultation with a client at my floral shop when she fainted."

The ambulance arrived and I hovered as the EMTs checked her vitals, and by then she was coming around. I could only hope she recovered, and that she didn't recall anything of how she ended up unconscious. When the emergency medics assisted her onto a gurney, I got a glimpse of the nape of her neck where her hair had been swept aside. Just below her hairline was the mark Clay's fangs had left, jagged and raw. It was just like mine.

In sympathy, I reached up and dug my nails into the back of my own neck, knowing her wound would scar. When I was alone again, I sank onto my fainting couch, draping a forearm over my face, trying to gather my thoughts. While phoning an ambulance was definitely the correct response, I remained unsure as to whether or not I should tell Royce of Clay's impromptu visit. I'd sworn to stay away from Clay, but I didn't want to give this man further reason to trespass into my life. It wasn't that I didn't want to tell Royce—it was that putting Royce on Clay's radar turned my stomach. Besides, there was a small, dark part of me that *was* curious about him. I knew Royce would try to convince me not to attend his dinner party, but some instinct told me I simply had to go. I spent the rest of the evening arguing with myself, and in the end, I settled on the justification that Clay's invitation could serve as a fact-finding mission, and I could report to Royce after. There was nothing wrong with that.

Right?

10

IF YOUR CLOTHES TAKE FIRE

ROYCE

What a fucking week.

I spent most of it sweet-talking my way into getting a few other detectives in the precinct to cover my tracks as I started digging into files. I knew Stark was too smart not to have my credentials flagged, but there was no way he had the time to monitor everyone's activity on the precinct servers.

Now that I'd spoken my suspicions aloud, the more I noticed Stark and how off his behavior seemed. One of the perks of a promotion in the department would be that Stark was now in command of his own schedule. Yet I found him working the night shift more often than not, and the days he wasn't, he was already at the office before I arrived—like maybe he'd been there all night. Or at least since the butt-crack of dawn. He looked like hell, and spent most of his time locked up in his office. If I hadn't already been scoping out his habits, I might have just thought he was working a big case. But usually, that would have entailed bringing in at least one other person from the detective squad as backup. Whatever he was working on, he was working it alone.

It was, as the kids said, pretty sus, bro.

I had also started going to the gym.

I know, I know, but enough people had teased me about Sinclair being too young and hot for an out-of-shape square like me that I finally caved. And let me tell you, it sucked. I don't like to paint with too broad a brush, but every person who says they enjoy working out is either a liar or a sociopath.

"Davis, is everything okay?"

I slammed the stop button on the medieval torture device known to some as a "treadmill", and turned to find Priya standing beside me with a towel draped around her shoulders and a huge water bottle in her hand. She looked like she belonged here. I looked like I'd been tricked into being here somehow.

I gulped for air, trying and failing to wipe the sweat from my eyes. "Fine," I gasped. "I'm fine."

Priya chucked me her towel, and I accepted gratefully, dabbing at my face with the terrycloth. "What are you doing down here?"

I knew Priya hit the employee gym just about every day. "I'm always here," I lied.

She laughed. "Uh, okay. Sure," she said. "And I'm sure this sudden health craze has nothing to do with Sinclair and his size zero skinny jeans, huh?"

I scowled at her. "I gotta get back to my workout," I snapped, but the affect was somewhat ruined by the fact that I still couldn't catch my breath, so it came out as a series of gasping, wheezing grunts.

"Okay, man, whatever. Just make sure you eat something with protein."

In the locker room, I checked my phone, and saw a text from Sin, asking if I was working late.

It was a white lie to say yes and that I'd be home shortly, but I still felt guilty. But I wanted to be the kind of guy someone like Sinclair deserved, someone that when people saw me on his arm didn't think "*Him? Really?*"

Meanwhile, I'd been combing my way through a web of red tape that could almost put local government bureaucracy to shame: the ins and outs of higher education. It had taken me forever to get ahold of someone at University of Denver, the college Beckett Taylor had supposedly been attending. I said supposedly because that's the school at which his mother told me he'd matriculated, but getting someone to actually confirm he was a student there had been an absolute nightmare—especially because I didn't have my commanding officer to back me sticking my toe over jurisdictional lines.

When they finally got back to me, they'd confirmed what I already suspected.

Beckett Taylor had never enrolled at University of Denver.

He'd been lying to his mother—presumably, to keep her from worrying. But what it meant was that we'd been looking for signs of him in the wrong place. Chances were, he'd never even left Douglas Crest.

"No," said Mrs. Taylor stubbornly. "My Beckett was a good boy—"

"Mrs. Taylor, I'm not saying he wasn't." I'd broken her the news as gently as possible. In fact, I'd considered not even telling her about his deception, but she might have known something, without realizing she knew it.

"Why would he tell me he'd started college if he hadn't?"

"He...probably just didn't want you to worry," I said, lamely.

She glared at me. "Why do young men always think they know what will make a mother worry?"

"I don't know, Mrs. Taylor," I said. "But I need to know if you can think of *anything*. Anyone Beckett would turn to here, if he got into trouble—any place he'd go to crash since he wasn't staying away at school."

There was nothing, she insisted, and I watched the grief and guilt converge on her face. "I didn't know him at all," she said faintly, and her eyes had gone glassy. "I didn't know my son at all."

And then, I just...let her cry.

When I'd gotten home, Sinclair had perched on the back of the couch like a little gargoyle and petted my hair until I could let go of some of my own guilt. I was running into walls at a million miles an hour—unable to find a door.

Needless to say, by the time the weekend rolled around, I had a lot of pent-up shit that was looking to fight its way out. I needed to forget about the gym, forget about the whole damn precinct, forget about Stark, and spend some time thanking Sinclair for his tireless willingness to help me with the case, and essentially put his entire life on hold to do so. He'd been acting...off for a few days. Even weirder than normal, I should point out. I felt like I owed him something special. Something romantic. Something with...fireworks.

I asked him to meet me at my place at ten, giving me time to get home, shower off the work day and my workout, and prepare for what I had in mind for us. Since this would be our first time consciously dipping our toes into the kink ocean, it's not like I had anything super extreme planned, especially after what happened last time. I didn't want Sinclair to feel anything less than amazing after we finished having sex.

I heard the front door swing open and slow footsteps in the hall; I think Sinclair stepped louder for my benefit. He seemed nervous when he stepped over the threshold into my bedroom, looking around like he expected me to have transformed the entire thing into an elaborate BDSM playroom. Before we explored anything too crazy, I wanted to play out a simple scenario, to remind him that the important part—him and me—was all that really mattered.

"Hi." I sounded breathless. Dammit, I should have practiced my "Dom voice". I wanted to sound confident, sexy, and in charge. But mainly I just sounded nervous.

"Hi," said Sin, smiling. His lip twitched, revealing his little eyetooth, and I had to step forward and kiss it.

"Are you ready?" I asked him.

Sinclair laughed. "Just like that?"

Shit. I hadn't really planned any kind of leadup to our scenario. To be honest, most of my scheming had gone into the actual mechanics of restraining someone with super strength. I'd had to get creative. "Yeah," I said, grabbing Sinclair's chin. I used my thumb to push his lip back again. God help me, I loved his fangs. "Just like that."

Sinclair hitched a little breath, his eyes darting around the room, like the weight of my stare was a lot for him to take. It helped me, stroking my ego a little bit.

Moving my thumb to release his lip, I whispered. "Is this okay?"

Eyes shining, Sinclair nodded eagerly.

"Remember the safe word we picked out?"

"Begonia," he said.

"Good boy," I replied, and Sinclair seemed to melt a bit at that. I took a few steps away from him and said, "Now, strip."

Sinclair hastened to toe off his shoes, the Converse he'd had on the first time we'd met. And then his socks. When he reached the buckle of his belt, I told him to slow down, and I sat on the edge of the bed so I could lean back on my hands and watch. "What about you?" Sinclair asked, shrugging out of his jacket with sensual grace.

I raised my eyebrows. "I'll take off my clothes when I'm good and ready," I said sternly.

He sucked his lower lip into his mouth, his eyes going round as he slowly pulled his t-shirt over his head, revealing his trim torso covered with the freckles I adored.

"Stop," I said when he'd unbuttoned his jeans. I stood, walking around him in a slow circle. Now behind him, I dragged my fingertip across his shoulder blades, stooping to kiss a few of my favorite freckles. I could sense the tension already building in his body, and it made me bold. I continued my slow prowl until I stopped in front of him, raising my hands to explore his chest like I was appraising him. I brushed my thumbs over his nipples until they pebbled beneath my touch. For a dead guy, Sinclair was insanely responsive. When I pinched the rosy peaks, rolling them between my fingertips, he let out a teeny gasp. I stepped away, and he followed, stepping forward to close the gap between us. I laid my palm on his chest and shook my head, retreating to my spot on the edge of the bed. All my self-control went into hiding how much he was already affecting me, but based on the way his eyes darkened, he knew.

I gestured wordlessly for him to continue undressing, and not to be undone in this little game of ours, Sinclair decided to strip out of his pants with his back to me, bending shamelessly at the waist to show off his freckled ass. Part of me wanted to kneel behind him and bury my face between those soft, pale cheeks. I forced myself to be patient. To summon him with a crooked finger to stand between my splayed thighs.

Sinclair grinned like a maniac, clearly loving the attention I lavished on him, and his perfect pink cock was already at full attention. It was the only part of him that flushed without a recent feed. I brushed my fingertips down his shaft just watching it twitch and jump. I closed my eyes and leaned forward, Sinclair immediately tangled his fingers in my hair, thinking I was about to suck him off. Instead, I ran my nose along the vein on the side of his dick, nuzzling into his soft, chestnut pubes before giving his balls a delicate lick. I drew back to look up at him, and based upon the look on his face—the look of a feral predator—the idea I'd had for this scene was just the right one.

With a kiss to his hip bone, I nudged him back and stood.

"Your turn?" he asked hopefully, tugging at the collar of my shirt.

I laughed. "Just lay down, you."

Sinclair hunkered down on the bed, wiggling his hips as he stretched luxuriously, totally at ease with my eyes on him. I thought it was time to change that. I sat on the edge of the bed and reached into my nightstand drawer, removing two pairs of cuffs I'd borrowed from work. Sinclair watched, bemused, and I couldn't lie, the fact that he let his arms go limp and docilely allowed me to cuff his left hand to the bedpost filled my guts with heat. I moved around the bed, repeating with the other hand. As I clicked the cuff into place, I wrapped my fingers around Sinclair's wrist, my thumb brushing along the interior of it, where the skin was extra pale and paper thin. "Is this alright?" I asked him, breaking character for a moment.

Sinclair smirked. "You know I could snap these as easy as breathing, right?"

I released his wrist and stood, walking to the foot of the bed so I could take in the whole picture: him, splayed out, bound and naked, just for me. I started unbuttoning my shirt, taking my time, trying to keep my hands steady. I didn't answer until I'd tossed my shirt over the back of a chair in the corner of my room. "You can," I admitted. "But you won't."

He released a chuckle, letting his eyes sweep over my body in an exaggerated, lingering stare. I had no idea what in the hell he saw when he looked at me, but it was clear he liked it. "I won't?"

I dropped my pants without flourish and crawled naked onto the bed. I wrapped a hand around his cock and gave it a few long, slow pulls. I kissed him, let it get dirty, stroking him until I heard the creak of the handcuff chains straining. Then I drew back. "No," I said cheerfully. "You won't. Because if you do, I'll stop."

Sinclair blinked. "What?"

"If you break those cuffs, tonight's over, and I won't be touching you again for a long—" I dragged my thumb over the head of his cock, then wrapped a fist around it, tugging firmly, "*long,*" I repeated the motion, slower, "long, time."

Sinclair gave a sharp intake of breath as I removed my hand. It was all talk, of course. Empty threats, but we'd sort of entered into this fantasy where it just might be true.

"And," I added. "You know. You'll owe me two pairs of handcuffs."

I watched him struggle with that, the realization

dawning that his strength was suddenly not the advantage in our little game that he'd thought it would be. However, I had to be clear. I leaned over to kiss him softly. "You know that saying the safe word doesn't count, right?" I whispered.

"Huh?"

"Like, if you want to stop. And you say 'begonia' I'm not going to like, punish you or whatever. It doesn't count." My cheeks heated.

"You're nervous," Sinclair said, awe in his voice.

"Of course, I'm nervous," I blurted. "I don't want to fuck this up."

Sinclair's face went soft, warmth in his eyes as he said, "You won't."

"And you know you can say begonia?"

"Yes, Royce."

"So we can keep playing now?"

Sinclair squirmed, shifting his hips up. "*Please.*"

I grinned. "I like when you beg."

I bracketed his thighs with my knees and leaned down so we could kiss some more, sucking hard on his lips, and letting him nip my tongue. I could tell already my little game would pay huge dividends. Sin was huffing and straining, having to concentrate on not snapping the chains that held him. He clenched his fists, the cords of muscle in his thin arms tensing as I moved to kiss his neck. I traced the constellation of freckles on his chest with my tongue until I reached his nipple. I teased it with my tongue, circling it, flicking it, before suckling the tight bud between my lips and testing it with my teeth. Sinclair whined, arching off the bed, like he wanted to pull his arms down, curl in on himself, and the creak of the wooden headboard grew louder as he writhed. Because I didn't actually *want* him to snap and put an end to the scene, I eased off, and he collapsed back onto the mattress, trembling.

His eyes squeezed shut, so I took the chance to shuffle ungracefully to kneel over his chest. There were just so many things I wanted to do to him, but having him trussed up like this, so open, so willing, had me thinking about one specific fantasy in particular. His eyes were still screwed shut, so I gently carded my fingers through his tousled hair until he blinked them open. I wanted him to watch me. With my other hand, I fisted my cock so I could tap the head against Sin's plump lips, and he parted them obediently, eyes round and eager as I fed him inch after inch of my dick. When his nose was buried in my pubes and my balls rested on his chin, I took a second to savor this. While planning this little experience, one thing I'd asked Sinclair was if he actually needed to breathe anymore.

He'd laughed.

He was not laughing now. His lips stretched wide around my shaft as I fucked slowly in and out of his mouth. Every two or three thrusts of my hips I'd pull all the way out, giving him a chance to gather himself, or tell me to stop, or use our safe word, before sliding back into the slick wet heaven between his lips. I could have come down his throat, easily. Not only was the obedient suction of Sinclair's tight mouth perfect, but the knowledge that his deadly, sharp fangs were so close to my dick and he would never dream of snapping them shut was...intoxicating. Sin was a predator, a monster, but he was *my* monster. I wondered if this was how a lion tamer felt, his head between the jaws of a wild animal who could crush his skull.

Fearless. Alive. Powerful.

If I didn't take care, I was going to bust way too soon. I

let my dick pop free of Sinclair's mouth, loving the way he'd drooled eagerly all over it, a string of saliva stretching from the head of my cock to his greedy lips. He chased me with his mouth, like he couldn't get enough of me, part of me wanted to jerk myself hard and come all over his perfect face and then lick him clean, but I had *big* plans, and I wasn't about to let Sin off the hook any time soon.

I rolled off, laying on my side so I could drag my fingertips over his body. Christ, he was beautiful. *Say that,* a voice in my head urged. *Tell him. Make sure he knows.*

"Sin—I," I stammered. "Fuck, you're beautiful."

He'd closed his eyes again, but at my words he opened them, looking shy. He squirmed, like he wanted to hide, but with each light pass of my fingertips on his skin, his cock twitched. I nudged his chin so I could kiss him, shoving my tongue in his mouth before I said something stupid.

I wrapped a loose hand around his cock, a reward, a tease. His hips lifted off the mattress as he fucked desperately into my fist, chasing some kind of relief, but honestly, tormenting him was even more fun than I'd ever dreamed it would be. I stilled my hand, letting him work himself into my fist for a bit before releasing him, moving my palm to rest on his belly. His head dropped back into the pillows again with a groan.

"You alright?" I asked him, unable to keep the smile from my voice.

"Bastard," he muttered, and I could feel the tension in his stomach, could see it in his arms. He had to force his muscles to relax, which used more strength and focus than simply breaking free would have. He wouldn't be able to truly let go.

"We could stop," I said innocently, walking my fingers up his sternum, teasing one of his nipples again. I pinched it, testing a bit more force and Sinclair moaned, confirming what I'd suspected—I could be a bit rougher with him than I would be with someone who was human. I pinched again, holding tight to the little bud before releasing, stroking with a featherlight touch of my fingers. I did it a few more times, maintaining my hold a bit longer, rolling the pebbled skin between my fingers.

"Royce," Sinclair said. "*Please.*"

I stilled my fingers. "Please what?"

"Please, *please*...touch me."

"I am touching you."

Sinclair struggled a bit, releasing a frustrated cry when the creak of wood reached his ears. Tensing, relaxing, tensing again, over and over as he tested the limits of his cuffs, and my headboard. "I can't—"

And I really wanted this to continue, so I maneuvered between his legs, hooking my hands behind his knees to spread his thighs. Sinclair was quite flexible, so I moved my hands to his ankles, spreading him as wide as I could. He turned his face to the pillow with a shy little whimper. "Look at me," I commanded. "I want you to watch what I do to you."

His eyes seemed in danger of popping out of his head like a cartoon's, so I kissed the bone of his ankle and stroked down his calf, kissing my way up his leg before releasing it to rest over my shoulder. His balls were so tight against his body, round and rosy and perfect, so I settled in on my stomach and drew them into my mouth, one at a time, mouthing lazily over his sac, looking up periodically to make sure he was still watching. He was—lips parted, eyes wide and dark, like he couldn't believe what he was looking at. Sinclair's arms may have been bound, but he could still move his lower half a great deal, and my maddening attention had him squirming every which way across the bed. It was hard to tell whether he was trying to escape me or get more of my mouth. I decided for him, pushing his thighs up toward his chest, practically crunching Sinclair's entire body in half so his spine curled off the bed, letting me see his hole. I wasn't one hundred percent certain if one could describe the anus as "cute", but Sinclair's was. A soft, delicate pink pucker that I just had to taste.

I laved the flat of my tongue over his hole, slow, dragging the very tip around the rim before moving up to take his cock in my mouth. I gave the head a hard suck, swirling my tongue around it to taste his precum, then traveled back to his hole once more. I repeated this pattern, stopping occasionally to kiss the side of his shaft, suck his balls, and mix up the rhythm so he didn't know what to expect. Finally, I wrapped my arms around his wiggling body to hold his hips in place and buried my face in his ass. Flexing my tongue, I pushed past the ring of muscle, spearing into Sinclair's core, sucking on his rim as he clenched helplessly around my tongue. His heels dug into my shoulders, hard enough to bruise, but that just spurred me on. Harder. More. Faster.

I didn't know if it was because Sinclair didn't eat, which left his uh, ductwork, naturally clean as a whistle, but I loved the taste of him here, so I swirled my tongue, eating him out with everything I had. I could have eaten him out for hours, but the way the muscles in his legs shook told me he was reaching his limit. I was reaching mine, too. My cock ached, the pressure building rapidly in my groin, a pull. A *need*. Like my hindbrain had taken over and was screaming at me to mount my prey and breed him, to fuck him till he screamed.

I couldn't hold out much longer. But Sinclair didn't

need to know that. I licked a hot stripe from his hole, over his balls, up the underside of his shaft, tasting the shimmering pearl of precum that beaded on his flushed crown. "You better not come before I tell you to," I warned him, which was all big talk. I wasn't even inside him yet and it was taking all my willpower to not nut all over my mattress.

"Then *please*," he whispered, and I saw tears of frustration sparkling at the corners of his eyes. "Please."

"'Please', what, baby?"

I wasn't certain if it were his prim sensibilities that had the words sticking in his maw, but I liked this bashful, needy side of Sinclair. It wasn't a side I got to see too often. He let out a frustrated huff, staring at me and setting his jaw mutinously.

I grinned. "Okay. I'll just have to guess what you want me to do, then."

I got off the bed and wandered slowly to my bureau, trying to walk with purpose and a little dignity—a challenge, given my throbbing erection bouncing ponderously with every step—and selected a bottle of lube, taking my sweet ass time because not touching Sin's body gave me space to ramp myself back down a bit, which I sorely needed. I made a show of dribbling lube onto my fingers, massaging it around. When my digits were good and slick, and I was extra certain Sin was about to snap like a violin string, I traced his rim with my fingertip before applying a bit of pressure. My tongue had paved the way and he accepted my finger beautifully, his tight walls clenching around my finger as I worked him over. Soon I had three fingers in Sinclair's hole, sloppy with lube and my saliva, while tears streamed freely down his freckled cheeks. "Is this what you wanted?" I asked innocently, circling his prostate as I massaged his channel.

"*No,*" he gasped.

"Oh, alright," I said, and I withdrew my hand. "There."

He wailed, like the loss of my fingers was a great tragedy. "Please," he said again.

"Please, what?" I encouraged him. I wrapped my slick fist around my dick, giving it a few strokes to lube myself up, and with my clean hand, I brushed a tear from his face.

"*Just fuck me!*" he burst out angrily. "Stick that dick inside me or I swear to—*ohh.*"

I shoved in to the hilt in one fluid thrust, groin flush against Sinclair's ass, and his words broke off into a moan of sheer relief.

Sinclair was still so tense, his hole so tight around the meat of my cock that I could barely move. It was like a hungry little mouth. Trying to swallow me whole, dick first.

And I still had one surprise for him.

I remained still, letting him adjust, before straightening up. Sinclair was still speared on my cock, still bound, and I knelt between his legs, shimmying my thighs below his ass, so he lay draped across my lap. His cock stood up between us, flushed and angry looking. I gripped his hip so I wouldn't slide out of him, and grabbed a few final things I'd set on my bedside table. Working quickly, I cleaned and sanitized my hands and showed Sin a small, dainty-looking knife I'd bought. His breath hitched, and I laid a finger across his lips.

"Do you trust me?" I asked.

He hesitated for only the briefest of heartbeats before nodding.

"I just want to try something," I said. "I promise, I'll be careful. If you're not comfortable, we can stop. Okay?"

He nodded slowly, his eyes never leaving the knife blade.

I removed my finger from his lips, stroking his hair softly. "What's our safe word?"

"Begonia," he whispered.

"Good boy." I gave a small thrust, rocking in and out, and Sin moaned feebly. "Now, hold still."

Despite my very real nerves, I put on a decent façade of bravado, gripping the knife in my off hand to press the tip of the blade to the pad of my thumb. I'd had it sharpened, so blood welled at the slightest pressure, and I made a tiny, almost painless slice on my fingertip. Once I'd set the knife aside, I showed Sinclair the cut, letting him see how small it was. Just a papercut, really. When I felt him relax a bit, I gripped my thumb with my other hand and squeezed, so a few fat, ruby droplets collected there. I took a moment, watching Sinclair for signs of distress. His pupils blew wide, eclipsing once again the green of his eyes, and I was kind of addicted to that reaction.

Locking eyes with Sin, I brought my thumb to my lips so I could drag my tongue along the cut. Sin's mouth dropped open, and he bared his fangs with a soft hiss like he simply couldn't help it. I darted my eyes to where Sinclair gripped the chains of the handcuffs, the metal straining and groaning as he did. I gave the cut on my thumb a good hard suck, before smearing some of the blood on my lips, and the fact that I had the confidence to even try this spoke to how much Sinclair had changed me already. Holding a mouthful of my own blood, tangy and bitter and just this side of wrong, I leaned down and kissed Sinclair, opening my mouth to feed it to him. He shoved his nimble tongue between my lips, sucking and biting them till they were kiss- bruised and swollen. We passed saliva and blood back and forth until the taste of copper faded entirely, and I started thrusting again, working both of us to a frenzy.

Sinclair, it seemed, was done playing the submissive. Or at least, he certainly thought he was. "Harder," he commanded.

I was happy to comply, slinging my hips, bracing my weight on my forearms. No finesse, no more teasing.

Just fucking.

Sinclair's entire body vibrated in my arms, and his head fell back against the pillow, his eyes squeezed shut. His mouth fell open in a silent plea as I railed him. I wanted him to lose it, I really did, so I shifted my weight and scooped his legs over my shoulders once more, pressing his knees to his chest so I could fucking let him have it.

When I sunk back in, the new angle allowing me to go deep, Sinclair found his voice, a wordless cry bursting from his lips as I pounded him into the mattress. The creak of the bedposts, the steady thump of the headboard hitting the wall, Sinclair's helpless begging, it all added up to a soundtrack that was hot as hell. Sinclair was fucking flying, I could see the ecstasy etched in every line of his face, and I knew he was seconds from detonating. Sweat beaded on my forehead and rolled down my back, and I didn't know how much longer I could hold out, but I wanted—*needed* to make sure he got there first.

"Let go, baby," I urged.

"I—I can't," Sinclair said, anguish making his voice pitch high and breathy. "I can't."

This, this was exactly what I had planned: his body was so tense, every muscle pulled tight like a coiled spring of pleasure, every particle and fiber of his focus in use to keep him from snapping the cuff chains. He was way too tense, too in his head, to get there on his own. He needed help letting go. He needed *me*. "You can," I grunted in his ear, releasing his shaking legs, allowing them to slide down and catch on my hips. Doing my best to maintain the grueling pace I'd set, I kissed him, hard, demanding, until I had to pull away to gasp for breath. I bit his bottom lip. "You can. Come for me."

"I—I..." he turned his head to the side, muffling a sob in his own shoulder.

I curled my spine, changing the angle of my thrusts and burying my face into the side of his neck, scraping my teeth along the rigid tendons of his neck.

"Let go," I said, wrapping my hand around his cock, stroking him rough and dirty. "Let go for me."

And with a yelp from him and one final deep thrust from me, I held him against me and unloaded, my cock pulsing and his ass clenching down so tight my vision whited out. Sinclair erupted, his flushed cock firing spurt after spurt of cum all over my chest as my hips moved against his ass, stuttering half-thrusts as I fucked him through our shared release. I heard the shriek of splintering wood and his arms came around my back, his trembling hands clawing my shoulder blades as his body bowed beneath me, arching off the bed like he would have ended up on the ceiling if I wasn't there holding him down.

I wanted to keep grinding against his ass, the feeling of my cum painting his hole and gushing out around the base of my dick felt way too damn good, the pleasure-pain of my raw nerves at once way too much and not enough. Sinclair clung to me, his ankles locked around my waist, like if he let go, he'd completely shatter. I'd kept him in a state of hyper-arousal since I'd instructed him not to break the cuffs, and it seemed like his body wasn't ready to disengage from that yet. As good as it felt to stay inside, I pulled out with a wince and slowly disentangled Sinclair's limbs from my torso. His chest heaved, his lashes fluttered, and he might not need sleep but I could tell he was about to crash hard, and I was determined not to fuck up like I had last time. I worked swiftly to undo the cuffs from Sinclair's wrists. To his credit, Sin hadn't actually broken the cuffs; the strain and abuse had instead shattered both my bedposts, leaving two jagged, splintered spikes on the corners of the head-board. I massaged his wrists and fingers, rubbing his palms with my thumbs before bringing his hands to my lips, so I could kiss his fingertips, his knuckles, the delicate little bones of his wrists.

"You did so good," I told him. "So, so good."

Sinclair wasn't ready to speak yet, his body still wracked with spasms from what I could only hope was the most explosive orgasm of his long life. He whined as I moved from the bed, reaching blindly for me. I brushed the tear tracks from his cheeks with my thumb, leaving a tiny smear of my blood across his freckles. Why was that so fucking hot? "I'll be right back, sweetheart," I soothed. "Don't move."

In the bathroom, I turned on the tub, adjusting the knob to get a pleasant, balmy temperature. I knew Sin didn't like the water too hot. I added a fizzy bath bomb and some scented oils to the water, and while the tub filled, I cleaned myself up. With a fresh cloth, I returned to the bedroom, where Sinclair indeed seemed unable to move, and cleaned his chest and belly, his ass, and the remaining tears on his cheeks. Not in that order. I scooped him into my arms and brought him into the bathroom. He'd closed his eyes, so when I lowered him into the tub he yelped and hung onto my neck like a cat threatened with the same.

When he realized it was just the bath, he relaxed, shuddering as he entered the soothing water. I turned off the tap and knelt beside the bath.

He reclined against the back of the tub, turning his head toward me, blinking lazily. I brushed the hair from his eyes. "You know," I said mildly, "it's really not fair that after sex like that you don't sweat at *all*."

Sinclair grinned, tilting his chin to nuzzle my palm. "I like when you're sweaty," he said, his voice rough and gravelly. "You smell so good."

"Gross," I said. I leaned into the tub and kissed his forehead. "Just relax in here for a bit, okay?"

He lifted his hand up and let it fall, splashing back down into the water at his side. "Alright."

"I won't be long," I promised.

Back in the bedroom, I threw on a pair of loose pajamas and changed the sheets. I gathered up the two lethal-looking spikes Sin had snapped off my bed posts, but this left me unsure of what to do with the remaining parts. I finally figured out a temporary solution, and I was putting the finishing touches on it when a soft voice asked, "Are those oven mitts?"

"You're supposed to be in the bath!" I said. And yes, they were, duct-taped to the top of my bedposts, looking like bizarre mitten-shaped finials with a bacon and egg print. "And, you know, wooden stakes and vampire boyfriend didn't seem like the safest mix."

Sin smiled. He'd pulled on his lace robe and clutched it tight around himself. "That's a myth."

"Oh. Well, still." I set the duct tape on the bureau, where I'd also laid out some massage oils. "Do you want to get back in the tub?"

He shook his head and crossed the room in slow,

graceful steps, almost like he could glide. "I want to be with you."

I pulled him into a hug. "How do you feel?" I asked the top of his head.

"*Mmm,* like all my bones fell out."

"In...a good way?"

He nodded against my chest before pressing a kiss there.

"Come on, then," I said. "Lay down on the bed."

Even though our game was over, his obedience was just as intoxicating as it had been before. Sinclair shucked out of his robe and lay down on his belly, pulling one of the pillows close to squash against his face and chest. I'd never really given anyone a massage before, but in this case, I kind of felt like it was more the intention behind the act that mattered. I rubbed him down, working the oil into his skin until he was plied supple and shining, and I pressed kisses to his shoulders, down his spine, his thighs. Sinclair made soft little mews of appreciation, occasionally peeking back over his shoulder to watch me work.

I'd always been a bit tongue-tied in the romance department; I babbled like an idiot when it wasn't needed and clammed up when it was. Sinclair, though. He made me bold. I was never going to be any kind of smooth talker, but I knew he needed to hear the words, no matter how awkward, just as much as I needed to say them.

"This was everything," I said softly. It was a bit easier when his face was buried in the pillow and he couldn't watch me stammer and blush. I kneaded the spotted flesh of his butt.

"Yes," Sinclair replied simply, releasing a soft sigh, arching his back a bit to push his cheeks against my palms.

Leaning down to plant a kiss on his tailbone, I lingered

there, letting my lips travel lazily up the dip of his lower back. There wasn't any sense of urgency, just a slow press of palms, a gentle exploration of flesh, soft kisses, the drag of fingertips. I accompanied the movements of my hands with soft words of praise. Sin rolled and arched, moving his body so I didn't miss an inch of it, like he wanted my fingers to map the terrain of his skin.

All at once, Sinclair rolled onto his back wrapping my wrists in his small, powerful fingers. He yanked, pulling himself up so he sat cross-legged, cradling my hand in his lap. "You didn't have to do this," he said quietly, his finger whispering over the cut on my thumb. It was little more than a papercut, but he lifted it to his lips, pressing a chaste kiss to the wound.

"I know," I said. With my free hand, I grabbed the back of Sin's neck, tugging him close so our foreheads pressed together. "I did it because I thought it would be hot."

A fang poked out. "It was."

"I know." I kissed him. "I won't spring something like that on you again. I just kind of thought after last time you'd be too in your head to try something we might both really enjoy."

"My Royce," he said, his voice a purr. "So wise."

When I coaxed Sin into laying back against the pillows, I recalled how I'd thought he looked like an angel when I'd first brought him home with me. My throat grew tight, looking at him now. No one had ever made me feel like Sinclair did. *Needed.* Like I was something worthy, like I was something special. I hoped I made him feel that way, too.

11

ANIMAL JEALOUSIES

SINCLAIR

When Royce text messaged me that he would be working late, for once I was relieved.

I had received my formal invitation to attend the "soiree" hosted by Clay. It was wretched of me to keep this from him, but I held out hope that Clay merely wanted to count coup, as it were. If I attended his brouhaha, and agreed he was the scariest vampire in town, perhaps he would leave me alone. I got the impression that he wasn't the kind to set up a permanent residence. Most of my kind didn't—especially those who killed when they fed.

He would grow bored of Douglas Crest eventually and move along.

Or so I hoped.

In the meantime, I could assess the level of danger his coven posed to me—and Royce, by extension—by attending whatever little gathering he had planned. Clay was certainly one for posturing; he sent a town car to collect me in front of Datura. Of course, I was no stranger to these sorts of games and accepted graciously. The driver was human, and I idly wondered what they'd been told about their employer.

When we arrived, Clay waited in the flesh to escort me inside. He was dressed immaculately in a three-piece suit in a stunning shade of crimson, his hair slicked back and tucked behind his ears.

He offered his arm, which I reluctantly took, and allowed him to escort me inside. My skin crawled when he rested his opposite palm on top of mine, but I did not flinch or draw away. "Clay," I said.

"Sinclair," he said warmly as if we were old friends. "I am delighted you could make it."

I put on my most gracious smile, like the invitation hadn't been a threat. "Of course," I said. "I wouldn't have missed it."

Clay escorted me around the back of the dingy building as if he were walking me down the red carpet at a film premier, and I resisted rolling my eyes with immense difficulty. When we arrived at the bulkhead doors that had been reinforced with silver, I couldn't help but tense up. Clay gave my hand a squeeze, and his presumptuousness took my breath away—what made him feel as though he had any sort of claim, any sort of right to touch me? "It's alright," he said, and thankfully removed his hand from mine in order to snap his fingers imperiously.

A man stepped from the shadows and I startled. He was undoubtedly human, and dressed as a valet. "Sir," he said, making a small bow. He leaned forward and unlocked the bulkhead, pulling the doors open and bowing Clay and me through.

"My familiar," said Clay under his breath. "John."

"Familiar?"

"Yes," he said. "He's a human that longs to be one of us. In exchange for loyal service, I will turn him."

"Really?"

Clay laughed, high and cold—a madman's laugh that set my teeth chattering. "No, of course not. But he doesn't know that. You simply must get yourself one. They are easy to kill and easy to replace if they outlive their usefulness. I always keep several on retainer."

I clenched my jaw, forcing myself not to react to the blasé way Clay regarded human life, and said nothing. We descended the steps and the smell of blood intensified, as did my trepidation. Part of me wondered if this was some sort of test he had in mind for me—could I control myself around blood? Was I civilized? The twisted part of me that I did my best to hide pricked up its ears. Not only was the scent of blood like being summoned to a feast, I was curious, *so* curious, about Clay. He prowled Douglas Crest like it was his home—not merely a place he'd stopped to hole up. Had he been here before, and if so—when? Watching Clay, I wondered when he'd been turned. He carried himself with poise, with the grace that only came with age. The intimate way he spoke to me, it was more than ego.

It was familiarity.

My breath caught, a vestigial reflex from my human need for oxygen. Could Clay be the one for whom I'd been searching? The one who'd turned me so long ago? The rasp of the voice in my ear as I lay dying—it was a voice I thought I'd never forget, but memory was cruel and fickle. I couldn't be certain.

I set my jaw and tried to marshal my focus. This was a fact-finding mission, not a trip down memory lane. My personal quest could be shelved in favor of the more pressing matters at hand. What, in the now, did Clay want with me?

I tried to brace myself for what sort of gathering this would be. A dinner party of sorts? An orgy? I hoped Clay did not expect me to participate in an affair like *that*. My desire to ingratiate myself went only so far.

When we reached the earthen floor, I was actually somewhat disappointed. The room appeared to be simply a rather dreary, average-looking basement. After the pomp and flourish of Clay's reception, I had expected something lavish. The only things in the basement not covered in a layer of dust were five ornate antique chairs set in a row to one side, and two were occupied at present. The room was large, but had a low ceiling, and smelled of sweat, blood, and silver.

"Come, Sinclair, I'll introduce you." He led me over to the occupied seats. "This is Louise," he said, indicating a black woman with a shaved head, "And Randall."

Randall, who was pale, portly, and handsome, stood and bowed, gesturing for us to sit. "Pleasure to make your acquaintance, Sinclair," he said, clasping my hand. Louise inclined her head politely, then turned bored eyes to the center of the room where I noticed a thick wooden post affixed with iron rings, lit sinisterly with a single spotlight.

The unsettled feeling in my stomach intensified as I took my seat beside Clay.

The man called Randall leaned over to engage Clay in conversation. "I believe we have finally secured a contender to best your champion," he said.

Clay scoffed. "I doubt it, but I certainly hope so. I begin to tire of watching him win time and time again."

Had I still possessed a pulse, it would have quickened. What was I about to witness? Clay's "familiar," John, approached us from where he had stood by the stairs, and stooped to whisper something in his ear. Clay nodded, flicking his wrist, dismissing the man to parts of the basement I could not see. "Forgive the décor," said Clay, and it seemed he couldn't address me without an accompanying touch—my shoulder, this time. "By its nature, this sort of venue is transient."

I nodded, as an actual answer did not seem required.

Clay hummed, and his icy fingertips traveled from my shoulder to my hairline. "You should wear something here," he whispered, scraping his nail over the scar on the back of my neck. "An affect to hide this rather unsightly scar."

I pursed my lips, wanting to elbow him in the face, but for some reason, I remained like a statue as Clay tugged my collar up a bit higher. I said nothing, but I was certain he could feel me trembling.

"It's a pity it's no longer *a la mode* for men to dress the neck becomingly," he said, cupping his palm around the column of my throat. "A high cravat, or a collar perhaps..."

"I don't mind the freedom," I said, finding my voice at last.

Clay withdrew his hand with a wicked smile, flashing his teeth—much bigger, and far more obvious than mine. Then he leaned in to whisper in my ear, so quietly I had to feel the words instead of hearing them. "Whoever put that there should have considered it more carefully, no?"

When John returned, he dragged an enormous bundle of muslin behind him until he reached the center of the room. When he untied the bundle and revealed its contents, I bit the inside of my cheek hard enough to taste my own blood: a woman, groggy with drugs, bound hand and foot.

I opened my mouth, but Clay patted my arm condescendingly and shushed me. John looped thick rope through the bonds on the woman's hands and used it to hoist her limp form against the post in the center of the room. Before I could so much as blink, he drew a cruel blade and slashed her forearms, wrist to elbow. The knife must have been sharp; the flesh parted like crepe and the blood sprayed grotesquely, and John worked quickly to gather a few ounces into each glass on a tray of crystal flutes.

He came over, poised and prim as any fine dining sever —though his vest was spattered with red—and bowed low, offering us the tray. The others took theirs without so much as blinking, and Clay's cruel stare told me I would be expected to share their toast. There was one remaining glass upon the tray after we had each selected one.

"*Salud*," said Clay sardonically.

We drank, though the blood tasted of ash in my throat.

John bustled away with our tray as the woman bled quietly under the spotlight. The position of her arms slowed the arterial spray, so she didn't die as quickly as I would have expected.

"Would you care to release your combatant?" Clay asked Randall, and the man nodded eagerly.

"I'll take your familiar, if she wins."

"Done," said Clay, before turning to look at something behind where we all sat. "Ah, Mr. Stark! Glad you could join us."

I jerked my head in time to see Royce's scowling commanding officer cross the basement with long, purposeful strides. "Apologies," he said brusquely. His eyes swept over me, and while I was certain my mouth dropped open in surprise, Stark did not give any indication he recognized me.

"Not at all," said Clay, playing the benevolent host. He summoned John and his tray once more, and he offered Stark the remaining crimson flute. "Just in time for the toast."

"Excellent," said Stark, regarding the woman bleeding out in the center of the room with cold detachment. He took his glass, and his seat. Without moving his eyes from the dying woman, Stark downed his glass of blood in one.

My mind whirred, furiously churning over this new piece of information. Lieutenant Stark was a vampire. Well, thank goodness I had accepted Clay's invitation—this fact-finding mission had already yielded large, if distressing, results.

"If you will all excuse me, I must see to my own contestant."

The arrival of Royce's boss had distracted me, but Clay's words brought me back to the present with a jolt of fear. I now had a strong inkling where this night was headed, but I hoped to be proven wrong.

The sound of feral hissing filled the room, growls and screeches that were like nothing human. Two doors opposite one another flung wide, and from one emerged a rail-thin young girl with mad eyes. She parted her lips, tasting the air like a serpent, and I could see her fangs glinting in the half-light. When her eyes fell upon the poor woman in the center of the room, she flung herself forward with a shriek to feed. Before I could blink, she was on the floor—another vampire had emerged from the adjacent chamber. He was massive, with the same unhinged look about him that the girl had. I flinched as he howled and tore a chunk of flesh from her arm with his teeth before turning and plunging his fangs into the open wound on the bound woman.

"Newborns," Clay explained.

I no longer tried to hide my look of revulsion. "What did you *do* to them?" Turning back to the carnage, I saw the two grappling furiously. Each time one of them circled closer to the prey—or bait, rather—the other would pounce. The fight was brutal, the screams jolting through me like white-hot knives. The poor woman on the post was being torn apart as they fought over her bleeding corpse like rabid dogs.

"We turn them, and keep them locked up for days. Fledglings always have the most vicious bloodlust."

I watched in horror as the two fought, clawing, biting, and beating each other as they both sought to claim the prize in the center of the arena. Clay watched the proceedings with distasteful elation. Louise examined her fingernails, and Stark stared at me instead of the fight. He still had not let on to Clay that he and I had met. Turning away from his gaze, I forced myself to watch the barbaric tableau playing out before me, and received another gut punch.

The young male fledgling turned his face toward our spectator seats for the first time, and as he met my eye, I recognized him from the photograph on Royce's murder board.

It was Beckett Taylor.

With a soft gasp, I watched Beckett dig his fingers into the side of the female fledgling's neck, like he was hooking them under her jaw, and with a savage jerk of his massive arms, he ripped her head clean off.

Before her body had even hit the floor, he was back at the post, feeding greedily like a hyena on a carcass, glutting himself on his hard-won prize.

I truly thought I was about to vomit for the first time in over a century. I couldn't, of course, and as such, my guts clenched impotently, twisting like they just wanted to expel *something*.

While he was distracted, Clay gestured to Stark, who donned thick leather gloves, like those a falconer might wear, and picked up a chain from the corner of the room.

"I told you," said Clay. "No one can best my champion."

Randall only laughed, like he'd lost a hand of cards— not two lives.

My eyes were on Stark as he advanced on Beckett, approaching cautiously with the chain. When he swung it up and over Beckett, wrapping it around his torso, Beckett screamed in agony, and the sizzling burn of his flesh told me the chain was silver—perhaps it was the only way for them to restrain the newborns.

"What do you think?"

I jumped. My attention had been on Stark, now locking Beckett Taylor behind the door from which he'd emerged. I could hear the young man howling and throwing himself against the door. "Pardon?"

"It is a spectacle, is it not?"

"Indeed," I admitted. He had me there.

Clay dragged a fingertip over my cheek and I shied away. "A clever little thing like you should be able to see that I have very little to fear."

I gulped, and said nothing.

"So," he whispered in my ear, "you best stay out of my way."

His plan revealed—intimidate me into compliance with his activities, or at the very least into taciturn sufferance of them. To be frank, I wanted nothing more than to stay out of his way. I wanted to turn tail and run, and never be cursed by the memory of what I had seen. But I could not. I forced a small smile, paid Clay some over-adulating lip service, and extricated myself.

I *was* a clever little thing, thank you very much, and I couldn't allow myself to leave this vile locale without something of worth. I perched myself on a nearby scaffold and waited. Soon enough, the bulkhead doors threw wide, and the rear end of John, Clay's familiar, emerged. The man had bundled the human victim once again in muslin, and shortly after he cleared the steps, Stark followed, carrying a similar bundle—the deceased female newborn.

They loaded their cargo into a vehicle parked behind the building, and I heard them discussing the railyard on the edge of the city. When they drove off, I weighed my options. Given city traffic at this time of night, I could get to the railyard almost as fast as a car if I cut through the alleys and ran the entire time. However, if I were mistaken about the destination, I'd lose them and miss them disposing of the bodies and any other intel. On the other hand, if I didn't take that direct route, I'd miss the intel anyway.

Obviously, if I flew, I would have beaten them by a significant margin, but then I'd be left observing criminal activity with my bollocks in the breeze, an idea I did not relish. I would just about make it on foot if I established a swift hunter's gait, but only if I didn't dither any longer.

As I'd planned, I arrived at the railyard, just in time to hear the heavy footfalls and breathing of John, who now dragged one parcel, and then the other. Stark surveyed this, issued some terse instruction, transformed into a bat, and flew off. John picked up Stark's clothing and added it to his bundles.

Another man approached, and I immediately recognized the dealer Royce and I had interrogated, Garibaldi. With feigned nonchalance, the familiar dropped a backpack he'd been wearing to the ground and leaned against one of the shipping containers. "Were you followed?" Garibaldi asked him.

"No," said the familiar. He unzipped his backpack to show Garibaldi its contents.

I smirked to myself. Fool.

"Douglas Crest PD, freeze!"

Oh, hell. I recognized that voice: Royce's partner, Detective Priya Tanti. This night was shaping up to be a right kerfuffle. She must have been tailing Garibaldi in connection with her homicide case. John dropped his backpack and raised his hands.

"You don't want to do this honey," said Garibaldi, raising his hands with a cocky smile. He kicked the backpack with his foot, tipping it over. Rolls of cash spilled out onto the ground. "Why don't you grab that bag and be on your way? We'll call it a finder's fee, and we can all pretend this never happened."

Priya had her weapon and a flashlight trained on the men, and a radio strapped to her vest. It crackled to life suddenly, and ice flowed through my veins as I heard the garbled approximation of Stark's voice come through the speaker. Did he know she was here, on a scene he helped create? Was he distracting her on purpose?

The call from her superior officer split Priya's focus just long enough for John to dive at her, bowling her over. My tongue caught in my throat, and I moved into a crouch. A scuffle broke out, and I hesitated, unsure of what to do.

John wrestled Priya's gun away from her, and after a brutal two-on-one, Garibaldi twisted her arm behind her and shoved her up against the side of the shipping container.

"Now what?" he panted.

John leveled the gun at Priya's temple. "Now we clean up this mess."

"You guys really don't want to do this," said Priya, maintaining what I thought to be a laudable level of composure, considering the fact that she had a cut on her forehead, a split lip, and her face was squashed up against the side of the shipping container. "Drug possession is a hell of a lot less jail time than assaulting a police officer. Especially if you talk."

Apparently Priya had yet to see the two corpses, discarded in the shadows.

"She's right," Garibaldi put in. "I didn't sign up to kill cops."

John cocked his gun. Whatever promises Clay had made him had his loyalties ironclad. "Either we kill her, or he kills us."

In that instant, I knew these two men had nothing to lose, and while Royce had informed me never to interfere with his criminal suspects, I had a feeling he'd appreciate the extenuating circumstance here. I dropped to the ground beside John, silent as snowfall, and had my fangs in his throat before he could blink. It took less than a heartbeat for me to force his arm upward, so when he squeezed the trigger of Priya's sidearm, it fired uselessly into the sky. The sound split the night, causing both Priya and Garibaldi to dive instinctively for the ground. My own ears rang and I hissed, releasing John to crumple to the gravel, clutching his throat. Whirling toward the distorted, faint sounds of Priya fighting off Garibaldi, I focused on them just in time for him to pull his own gun and fire a round into Priya's shoulder as they struggled. She fell, and he stood over her, cocking the gun once more.

Before he could fire again, I lunged for him, crushing

him against me so I could sink my teeth into the side of his neck. I drained pull after pull until he went limp in my arms, his blood flowing down my throat, filling me with power and rage. Before I could dislodge my bite and go again for John, who was still alive and crawling away, Priya scrambled back, reclaimed her sidearm, and trained it on...me.

"*Freeze,*" she shouted, but her face was a mask of pain. I dropped the body. "You have—Sinclair?"

"Uh." I lifted my hands skyward in surrender.

Priya grunted, her eyes sliding in and out of focus. She kept her gun pointed vaguely toward me, but her hand shook so badly I knew she wouldn't be able to hit the broad side of a barn if she fired it. Finally, she dropped it, cursing, and slapped her hand against the radio on her good shoulder. "Dispatch," she said, leaving a smear of blood on the button. "Emergency and all available units to McGinty Railyard, southside. Two suspects wounded and..." she grunted. "Officer down."

She released the radio, collapsing back against the shipping container. "Get your ass over here," she barked, and it took a second for me to realize she was talking to me.

I scurried over.

"Put some fucking pressure on this."

I whipped off my tee and balled it up against the wound on her shoulder. Holding my breath, I focused on not allowing the smell of her blood to addle my brain. I didn't need to breathe, but my lungs still worked. I focused on stilling them, on not drawing in the particles of blood floating in the air around us. Thankfully I'd fed a *lot* during the skirmish.

"Thanks." Priya groped for her gun once more, pointing it behind me this time, but her brows knit together in confusion. "Sinclair," she said, voice faint. "Where'd they..."

I twisted around, frowning. Both men had vanished. That was *not* a good sign. "Don't worry about that now," I murmured. I cocked my head, listening. "Help's almost here."

"How can you—" she broke off as the sound of sirens grew close enough for human ears to hear. "What the fuck are you, dude?"

Luckily for me, she didn't seem to need an answer.

Luckily for her, emergency services arrived seconds later, and I heard a shout from my favorite voice in the world.

"*Priya!*" Royce had arrived on the scene, body armor vest on, sidearm out, springing into action. He skidded to a stop in front of us, sending gravel flying as he crouched beside his partner. "Sin? What are you doing here?"

"Saving my ass," said Priya, but her voice was far weaker than I would have liked it. "He took out two perps like it was nothing."

I expected to be bathed in praise for my heroics, but Royce had nothing for me but a scowl. The emergency medics raced over to get Priya onto a stretcher, and Royce grabbed me by the meat of my arm and hauled me to my feet. "You're coming with me," he snapped.

I followed him warily, pulling my stained shirt back on. "Royce?"

"Save it," he said. We arrived at his car, the siren on top still flashing, though without sound. "In."

"But—"

"In!" he barked again.

I truly could not fathom what had Royce so upset, so I didn't budge. "Talk to me," I said.

"Your face is fucking covered," said Royce, his voice shaking. "Your hands are covered. You...you fed from someone."

Bewildered, I said, "Royce, I had to! They were about to—"

"Turn around," said Royce. "Sinclair, you're under arrest."

"*What?*" Paralyzed with sheer confusion, I allowed Royce to cuff my hands behind my back and guide me into his vehicle.

We didn't speak for the entire car ride, and by the time we arrived at the precinct, I had transitioned from bewildered to furious. Royce escorted me inside, past a dozen officers sitting in the bullpen into an interrogation room. It was humiliating. Everyone in the office knew I was Royce's boyfriend. Now I was a suspect. Royce attached the restraints to a metal bar bolted to the center of the table and then left the room without even glancing my way.

When he came back, I sat and watched him pace. The more silence stretched between us, the more betrayed I felt. I could easily break out of these cuffs, like I could have the other night. And Royce knew that. But, like that night, he knew I wouldn't.

When Royce didn't speak, I finally asked. "What are the charges?"

"You killed someone."

The way Royce spoke told me there were no actual charges laid against me. I shrugged a shoulder. If he was going to do it like this, I wasn't about to make it easy on him. "I don't believe a body was recovered at the scene."

Royce cut me a look. "Sin," he said, "What the hell did you do?"

"You seem to already have some ideas of your own, Royce."

He glowered at me, a stare I was certain melted many a criminal's resolve, but it would not melt mine.

"I was in the railyard," I said carefully, "And I stumbled across Detective Tanti attempting to apprehend two suspects. She was flanked and overpowered, and I stepped in to help."

Royce narrowed his eyes, like he knew there was plenty I wasn't saying. "Then what?"

I gave Royce a quick rundown of the fight. He didn't make a move to write down anything; he simply continued to pace. So I said, "Would you like to tell me what this is really about?"

He stopped in his tracks, turning to me, eyes cold. "Have you looked in the mirror?" He sneered, and it felt like a slap. I didn't know my Royce's face could look so cruel. "*Can* you even?"

His question told me that we were alone in the room. Normally, I was certain he would be recording an interview with a suspect. I could, in fact, see my own reflection, but Royce's flippant question made me defensive. I glanced over his shoulder, staring at myself in the mirrored glass. My face and hands were covered in blood, and I couldn't even lift my hand to wipe it away if I wanted to allow Royce his illusion of dominance. A cruel joke.

"Why were you at the railyard?" asked Royce.

His question caught me off guard. Now was not the ideal time to explain about Clay, about Stark, and explain that I had, in fact, located Royce's missing man, but unfortunately, I had no choice.

I sighed heavily. "Royce," I said. "I found Beckett Taylor."

"You—hold on, what?" Royce gaped. "That's not who..."

"No, of course not," I said. "Clay has him. Clay, the one who is, like me."

"As in—"

"Yes."

"Fuck." Royce collapsed into the chair opposite me. "Is Taylor...?"

"He has been turned."

"Jesus Christ," said Royce. He was silent for some time, and while some of the fight seemed to have gone out of him, he made no move to uncuff me.

"Royce..."

"You fed from someone," said Royce again.

I blinked, confused. "Why does that make you so angry?"

"Because..." said Royce, frustrated. He scrubbed a hand over his face.

I set my jaw and met his eye. Let him look. Let him see me. *Monster.* This was who I was, and there was no way to change that. "Because what?"

"What we did," Royce said. "You fed from me while we were...I thought..."

So this had very little to do with the investigation, and a lot more to do with being unfaithful. "Royce," I said softly. "I have to eat."

"And you lied to me. You told me you'd stay away from Clay."

I chewed my tongue because in this instance, I had no defense. I had lied by way of omission. But at the same time, I would never betray Royce's trust the way he was implying. He should know that. "I had to," I said. "Don't you even care what I found—"

"So, you just feed with anyone, from anyone," said Royce, firing up again. "Did you fuck him too?"

The question, after everything I'd been through tonight, was like a knife thrust to my heart. I went cold all over. Sliding my fingers under the manacle on my opposite wrist, I snapped the metal and let it fall to the table with a clatter, and stood. "You go to hell, Royce Davis."

———

ROYCE

Standing in the interrogation room, watching the door swing shut behind Sinclair, I felt like the world's biggest piece of shit.

"Huh," I said to myself. "Maybe we really are all bastards."

My body hummed with adrenaline; my heart pounded in my ears. Tonight had gone from bad to worse. It started with a mountain of useless busywork and ended with me arresting Sinclair when we both knew it was total bullshit. Oh, and in between, my partner had been shot.

I hadn't technically dismissed Sinclair, but I hadn't technically arrested him either—not really. And I could hardly blame him for walking out. I wouldn't blame him if he never spoke to me again. In fact, I could hardly believe the words had come out of my mouth, and if I had one wish right now it would be to recall them. Seeing the blood on Sinclair's lips, someone else's blood, had been like a sucker punch. Seeing Priya, hurt, and knowing I wasn't there to back her up was worse. Hearing from Sinclair that he'd been keeping stuff from me had been the cherry on top.

And that's before we even *got* to the fact that I was too late to save Beckett Taylor.

Someone else's blood.

Someone else's blood.

I felt humiliated and dirty just thinking about it. Sinclair's mouth on another man's neck, his fangs—the fangs I was so crazy about—piercing someone else's skin, the taste of *someone else* on his tongue...I knew it wasn't fair, rationally. I knew it.

But it still felt like he cheated.

Was it really a betrayal? I tried to reason with myself, but images of his lips exploring the skin of another man invaded my brain, made me feel sick.

He was right, though. He needed to eat. Somehow, I'd forgotten that. More like, I'd let myself forget.

So, what now?

I went to visit Priya at the hospital because the thought of going home and seeing Sin's things, with no Sinclair in the apartment, was way more than I could deal with right now. I flashed my badge so the nurse would let me in even though visiting hours were over. It was the middle of the night and Priya was zonked out in her hospital bed. She seemed okay. The floor nurse told me she'd needed an emergency blood transfusion and surgery to remove the bullet and repair the damage to her shoulder. She would need physical therapy, but otherwise would make a full recovery.

I hunkered down in the visitor's chair, putting my feet up on the windowsill to watch her sleep. Partly because I hadn't been there to back her up when she needed me, and I wanted to make sure she knew I was here for her now if she woke up. The other part of me, the guilty, cowardly part, was hiding out here instead of facing my lonely bed.

What if Sin had gotten his things and vanished by the time I got home? That was the kind of soul-crushing revelation that could wait. It was future Royce's problem.

I must have drifted off because I woke up to a plastic fork hitting me in the face.

"Finally," said Priya. "I finished my breakfast an hour ago."

"Huh?"

"You snore." She gestured toward my lap, where a few other pieces of cutlery had landed.

I gathered them and set them on her tray. "How are you feeling?"

"Like I got fucking shot," she said, but there wasn't any real heat behind it. She shifted, grunting in pain as her shoulder jostled against the bed.

"Want me to call a nurse?" I sprang to my feet.

"No, Christ. I don't need anyone hovering. Did they say when I could get out?"

"It was the middle of the night when I got here," I said. "They didn't want to tell me much since I'm not family."

Priya clucked, adjusting the blanket with her good hand. "May as well be."

"Yeah, but they don't have a spot for 'bestie' on the HIPAA form." We sat in silence for a bit, until I finally said, "Priya, I'm so sorry."

"Why are you sorry?"

"I should have been there to back you up."

"It's okay. Apparently, you sent along the big guns. I was covered." She squinted at me suspiciously. "Where is Sinclair, anyway?"

I averted my eyes, mumbling.

"What was that?"

"I kind of, uh, arrested him?"

"Okay, now I know they must have given me the good shit because you did *not* just say you arrested the guy who saved my life."

"Maybe a little."

"Jesus, Royce. Why?"

"He killed someone," I said. And why did that sound like such a feeble excuse? It should have been an ironclad excuse, but it wasn't, somehow.

Priya screwed up her face, remembering. "I think both of the guys took off," she said. "Did uniforms bring them in? Or a body? Any bodies?"

I sighed. "No."

"Then you don't *know* he killed someone."

"Priya, we're police," I said. "I can't be with someone who 'might' have committed manslaughter."

"Come on, you know it's not that black and white. Besides, it was a clear-cut case of self-defense. Or, me defense. She defense. Friend defense? I don't know. I'm on drugs."

"It's complicated," I said. "He's..."

"I know." She frowned at me. "What else did you do?"

"I accused him of cheating."

"*What?*"

"Priya, I don't know. It's not like there's a *Loveline* series for 'My boyfriend's a blood-sucking demon of the night.' It *felt* like cheating."

"What did?"

My face heated.

"Oh my *God,*" she said. "You let him...?"

"Maybe?"

"Damn. That's—that's—"

"Horrifying? Masochistic? Against the laws of nature?"

"Kinda hot."

"*Stop.*" I picked up the plastic fork and threw it back at her.

"Okay," she said. "Fine. So, then what did you do? Have you apologized?"

"No, I came right here to see you!"

"Royce, I love you, but please. Get the fuck out. Go apologize to Sinclair."

"But—"

"I'm fine, and we can talk about the case later."

"But—"

"*Go!*"

I went. The fact remained, however, that I had no idea how to make things up to Sin. Or where he was. Or how to reconcile that the only way he could eat was to assault someone. Or what to tell Beckett Taylor's mother. Or what to do about this other vampire named Clay. Yikes. Standing on the sidewalk in front of the hospital, I sighed. One thing at a time.

Sinclair had mentioned before a knowledge of floriography, the language of flowers. I'd never really heard of it, but it seemed like a good place to start. I weighed the possible angst it would cause him if I patronized a flower shop besides Datura, versus the angst of not making an apology.

And not just any apology. The *right* apology.

With a little research, I had the perfect bouquet picked out to symbolize remorse, and how much I valued Sin, and how much I did actually trust him. The more I thought about it, the worse I felt. While it was absolutely my fault for being a jealous asshole, I still wasn't remotely sure how we could move forward. It really wasn't okay for me to condone Sinclair's particular diet.

Was it?

Before I even started figuring that out, I had to get him

to talk to me again. I hadn't realized how much I'd come to accept and expect Sinclair's presence in my periphery. He really did follow me around as much as possible, and some instinct within me recognized the lack of his hovering. I missed it.

A lot.

Armed with my flowers, I buzzed the door at Datura.

The speaker crackled, but no one spoke. I sighed, and pressed the button again.

"We're closed," came Sinclair's voice, before the speaker cut out.

I buzzed again.

"You can find our telephone number on the website," he said snappishly through the intercom. "Please call to make an appointment."

I pressed the speaker button on my end. "Sin," I wheedled. "Come on. Please let me in?"

"Go away, Royce."

"Please?" I said. "I know I fucked up. Just let me in and we can talk about it."

"I'm busy."

"With what?" I was starting to feel like even more of an idiot, standing out here on the stoop, having this conversation through a door.

"Who's to say," he said, voice dripping with sarcasm. "I could be entertaining a dozen lovers in here."

I groaned. He was not going to let me off the hook. "Sinclair," I said. "*Please.*"

I waited for a while in silence, and just when I was about to go home and try again tomorrow, the door buzzed open. *Thank God.* I hadn't realized I'd been holding my breath. I walked through the darkened, cramped hallway and entered the receiving area of the flower shop. Sinclair greeted me with a hard look, lips pursed, arms crossed over his chest. Somewhere deep inside me, my suppressed fight or flight response reminded me that entering the lair of an angry predator was beyond stupid, but I'd long since put my trust in Sinclair not to kill me.

I held the flowers, which he eyed with distaste. "I brought you these."

Sinclair cut me a withering look, before gesturing at his work table. He then stomped over to one of his fancy couches and sat down. Nervous, I approached his workstation. It was meticulously organized. I knew fuck all about flower arranging, but something told me asking for his help or advice was not an option. I found a pair of scissors, and selected a vase from below the counter. With my focus on the flowers in front of me, I didn't hear Sinclair get up and cross the room.

"White orchids," he said softly. "Hyacinth, lily of the valley..." he reached across the counter to finger the blooms.

"Sin, I'm so sorry," I said. "Please. I didn't mean what I said."

He looked up and met my eye, and I could see how much hurt I'd caused. "I would never be unfaithful to you, Royce. Ever."

"I know," I said. "I was an idiot." I bit my tongue, hard. It was a knee-jerk reaction to get defensive, to offer reasons and excuses, but something told me Sin didn't want any of that.

He considered my amateur arrangement, tugging a few leaves, before he seized the scissors from me. Snipping the stems with a practiced, methodical hand, he said once more, "I have to eat."

"I know," I said again. My guts twisted.

"You might be sorry about what you said the other day, but..."

"...but it doesn't really change anything, does it?"

"No," he said. "No, it doesn't."

I found myself trying desperately to swallow around the lump in my throat. *Were we breaking up?*

Sinclair met my eyes again, looking miserable. "I'm not really certain how to move forward."

No way. I refused to give up on us. There had to be some alternative. There had to be.

12

ANECDOTES OF UNSELFISH ANIMALS

ROYCE

Two nights later, Sinclair and I stood hand in hand on the sidewalk in front of a cozy-looking old house that had been converted into apartments. I'd visited the building a few times before, but never with as much personal skin in the game. Once we'd calmed down (and made up), Sinclair had explained in far greater detail everything he'd witnessed the night he'd saved Priya's life, including the fact that my commanding officer was a fucking vampire.

I must have been getting better at compartmentalizing because I hadn't had a mental breakdown about that. It was coming, sure, but it hadn't hit yet. For now, I was desperate to save my relationship with Sinclair. We could figure out the rest, together.

With a squeeze of Sinclair's fingers, I lead him up the front steps to ring the bell for number three, beside which a small name plate read "T. Ambrose & C. Rhodes."

"Are you certain about this?" Sinclair looked doubtful.

"If anyone can help figure out any alternative...dietary choices for you, it's Thor Ambrose."

Sin pulled a face.

"What?"'

"My kind and his..." Sinclair trailed away. "Don't mix well."

"His...kind?"

"Shifters."

"You *know?*" I'd been kind of hoping to blow his mind a bit with that reveal.

His nostrils flared. "Of course, I know. This building smells like a barn."

"Do *not* say that to him when we go in." When we reached the top of the staircase, I knocked on the door to number three. "Thor? Cas? It's me—us."

The door swung open, and Cas stood beside it wearing a strained smile. "Hey, guys. Come on in."

"Cas, this is Sinclair. Sinclair, Cas." They shook hands. I gestured to where Thor stood in the living room—arms crossed, eyes narrowed, hackles raised. "That's Thor."

"Pleasure," said Sinclair drily, staring down his nose at Thor.

Thor said nothing.

Cas scratched his head and gestured toward the kitchen. "Can I get you guys anything?"

Sinclair rolled his eyes.

"Right," said Cas hastily, his voice rising half an octave. "Can I get *you* something, Detective Da—Royce?"

"Coffee," I said, hoping to cut the awkwardness. "Coffee would be good."

I followed Cas into the little kitchen as he bustled around fixing coffee. He had also laid out a cheese plate because he had absolutely no chill whatsoever. I nibbled a cracker, and Cas stood nervously at my elbow. Thor and Sinclair stood in the living room, glaring at each other like they were preparing for a duel.

"It's like the clash of the twink titans," Cas muttered, setting a coffee mug on the counter in front of me.

I made the mistake of snorting. Sin and Thor both snapped their gazes to me, and if looks could kill...

Thor cleared his throat, sliding his glasses up his nose. "So, let me make sure I understand," he said, addressing me. "You want him to go off his diet of human blood?"

"Excuse me," snapped Sinclair. "*Him* is right here, and can speak for *him*self."

"Alright," said Thor. "*You* want to go off your diet of human blood."

Sinclair looked at me, steeling himself. "Yes."

"Is it even possible?" I asked.

"I've done a lot of reading," said Thor, moving around Sinclair to the stack of books on the coffee table. "It's wildly inconclusive, but I have some theories."

We waited for him to go on, and he selected a particular book from the pile and brought it to the kitchen.

"I did find some fascinating histories that suggest—"

"—maybe we could cut to the chase?" Sin examined his fingernails, like he had better things to do.

Thor glared, but otherwise, let the comment pass unremarked. "Some histories that suggest our peoples' respective origins date back to the story of Romulus and Remus."

"The founders of Rome?"

"The very same," said Thor. "I've found several accounts of the story that one brother was a vampire, and the other a shifter."

"And?"

"*And,*" said Thor, "that implies that you and I share common ancestors—perhaps even physiological traits. At any rate, I think there is something we could try as an alternative to blood." Thor flipped to a page in the old book, which depicted a rather grisly drawing of a wolf devouring a sheep, opposite a man devouring a sheep. "With shifters," he said, "we can eat things in our *fauna* form that we can't eat in our human form. My cousin Ragnar, for example, regularly consumes raw mollusks and sea worms while wearing his animal skin."

"And what is his *fauna*?" I asked, curious.

"A walrus."

I snickered, and Thor glared at me again. "In my *fauna*, I eat all kinds of things I wouldn't eat as a man."

"So?"

"So…it follows from this that…"

We all stared blankly at Thor.

He sighed in exasperation at us. "If shifters and vampires share some genetic commonalities, there's a chance your bat form can consume things your humanoid form cannot."

"That's insane," I said.

"All of this is insane," Cas reminded me. "Your boyfriend is a hundred years old and he turns into a bat."

"He has a point," I allowed.

"Have you ever tried it?" Thor asked.

"No," said Sin. "Why would I?"

"No reason I can fathom," said Thor, rolling his eyes.

"Okay—enough." They all turned to me. "So, what does this mean? How do we test this theory?"

Thor eyed Sinclair critically. "That depends. What kind of bat are you?"

"I beg your pardon?"

"There are approximately..." Thor pulled out his phone. "...fourteen hundred bat species worldwide."

"And?"

"*And,*" said Thor. "They don't all eat the same thing, do they?"

"No?" I asked.

"Correct." He turned back to Sin, gesturing at his body. "So, what kind of bat are you?"

Sin crossed his arms. "I don't know."

"You don't?"

"It never came up."

"Alright," said Cas. "Let's see, then! I bet we can figure it out."

Sinclair looked disgruntled. "It's not a party trick."

"Sin, *please,*" I said. "We've got to try."

"We don't even know if this theory will work."

Suddenly, I remembered something. "You can't go outside in the sun, correct?"

"Not without enduring unspeakable agony and eventual death, no."

"But you flew out of my house as a bat," I said excitedly. "And you weren't burned."

"So?"

"*So,*" I said, "to Thor's point, there are differences between your bat form and your human form."

We all stared expectantly at Sinclair.

Sin smiled, showing his fangs in a mischievous sort of leer. He pointed at Thor. "I'll show you mine if you show me yours."

"Oh, for heaven's sake," said Thor under his breath. "I'm trying to help you, you know."

"Come on," Sin urged. "Tit for tat."

Thor sighed and removed his glasses. He handed them

to Cas and in the span of a breath, he'd vanished, like he'd been raptured. The pile of clothes on the floor twitched, and a tiny hedgehog emerged from one of Thor's sleeves. I hadn't actually ever seen him transform before, so I couldn't help flinching in surprise. Cas stooped immediately and picked up his boyfriend, setting him on the counter beside the pile of books. He was cute. I knew better than to say so, however. With a resigned sort of expression, Sinclair disappeared too, his clothes falling in an untidy heap beside Thor's. With a few squeaks, the small tan bat I recognized from my bedroom wriggled out of the neck of Sinclair's shirt. I picked him up and set him beside Thor on the counter.

"Okay," said Cas, vibrating with barely suppressed glee. "I could just take a picture and I'm sure me and Thor could ID the bat species."

I grinned. "You better send me the pic."

"Okay, scoot them next to each other," said Cas, pulling out his phone. At a glare from hedgehog-Thor, he added. "For size comparison!"

"Of course," I said, nodding seriously. "Very important."

———

SINCLAIR

After debasing myself for the mischievous delight of Royce —whom I still wasn't certain I'd fully forgiven—and his charming young friend Cassian, we retired to Royce's apartment. The silence was fraught and thick. Neither of us said aloud what it would mean if this little experiment failed.

But I wanted so desperately to keep Royce that I was willing to try anything.

In the meantime, he needed me to give him the details of what I'd found out at Clay's horrifying little party. He took the news about his boss in stride, but the realization that he was too late to save Beckett Taylor weighed heavily on Royce, I could tell. I tried not to take it personally, the sad, defeated way he reacted to the young man's fate. He was like me, now, something that was like a blow to Royce. He didn't say it in so many words, but I could read it on his face when we discussed the investigation. He hadn't wanted that for Beckett—hadn't wanted anyone to end up like me.

However, it did seem to fill both Royce and myself with a fresh focus: we had to rescue Beckett Taylor, expose Stark, and put a stop to Clay and his cohort. Listed that way, it seemed quite daunting. We added what new details we had to Royce's murder board, after which, I felt drained. Despite the fact that, physically at least, I did not tire as I did when I'd been human, I felt exhausted. Royce suggested putting on a film, and we changed into our respective loungewear —silk and lace robe for me, flannel sleeping trousers for Royce—and settled into the saggy sofa in his living room. Neither of us made a move to switch on the television set; we simply sat side by side and stared at our reflections in the silvery grey surface of its screen.

I could not think of one single thing to say to break the silence. Luckily, I was saved from needing to do so by Royce's mobile telephone, which chirped on the coffee table. He scrambled for it and showed me the screen when he saw it was a message from Cassian and his...rodent.

Thor Ambrose: Obviously I'm not a bat expert, but comparing the photos to some stuff online, I think Sinclair transforms into a Little Golden-Mantled Flying Fox.

"*Little,*" I scoffed.

Royce shot me a lopsided grin, before tapping out a reply to Thor.

An ellipsis appeared, followed by another message.

Thor Ambrose: Cas insisted I send you this, too.

And then, a photograph came through of myself and Thor the rodent sitting on the counter beside a coffee mug. The spines on top of Thor's head stood erect, giving him the appearance of a rather spectacular set of irate eyebrows, and I thought I could see something of the human man in the hedgehog's expression.

Royce shifted, brushing his thumbs over the screen of his phone. "Looks like the little golden-mantled flying fox is a fruit bat," he said.

"Bully for me," I grumbled.

Royce stood and walked to his kitchen. He opened his refrigerator and stared inside for several silent moments. "I don't have any fruit in the house," he said.

"That's a crying shame."

He shut the refrigerator with a snap. "Sin?"

"Yes?"

"Are you sure this is…something you want?"

"I want you," I said simply. "Relationships are about compromise, are they not?"

"That's the rumor," said Royce. "I just feel like you're acting a bit…reluctant."

I considered my next words very carefully. "What happens if this little theory of Thor's doesn't pan out?"

Royce sighed. "I don't know."

"That's why I'm reluctant," I said. "Trying this…if it fails, it proves that our lives are incompatible. That we're incompatible."

"Not necessarily," Royce hedged. He sat down beside me once more and grabbed both of my hands in his. "Can we maybe just try this first? Before we worry about what happens if it doesn't work?"

"For you, anything."

Which was how I found myself the following morning, standing naked in Royce's kitchen with a veritable smorgasbord of fruit spread out before me. "Go ahead," Royce urged.

Reluctantly, I summoned the powers of darkness and transformed, flapping about Royce's head a few times before landing on his countertop.

I nosed over a few of the offerings before selecting a cube of melon. It smelled sweet and fresh, but my stomach was a mass of nerves. What if my constitution rejected the fruit straight away? I hadn't even *tried* to consume anything in my bat form before. I hadn't eaten anything but blood in over a century, so this simple act carried a lot of weight that I couldn't quite explain, even to myself. I darted my tongue out, giving a tiny lick to the side of the melon.

Sweet juice exploded on my tastebuds, assaulting me with something besides the copper tang of blood, something I'd forgotten. All at once, I was a man again, crumpled on the floor, retching, my throat tightening, tears pricking the corners of my eyes. Royce was there, crouched beside me, wrapping me in his arms. "Are you alright?"

I spat on the floor. "Yes," I rasped, struggling to get a grip on myself. "It simply—it caught me off guard."

The look on Royce's face told me I was not sufficiently disguising the raw emotion in my voice. "We can stop," he soothed, brushing the hair from my eyes with his warm fingers.

I caught his palm and pressed a kiss to it. "No," I said. "Let me try again."

I transformed once more, and allowed Royce to lift me

onto the counter this time, and set me beside the cube of melon. Sidling up to it, as if it were about to become a predator and devour me whole if I approached it wrong, I gave the melon another small lick. The flavor was just as staggering, but I'd braced myself this time, and managed to swallow a small mouthful of cool, sweet juice. I realized in that moment I was ravenous. Throwing caution to the wind, I took as big a bite as my small mouth could manage, chewing thoroughly, turning the pulpy mass over and over in my mouth. All sorts of things came back to me as I pulverized the fruit. Candy, wine. Chicken with crisped skin. Roast potatoes. Crusty bread still hot from the oven. Most of those things would remain lost to me, but the sense memories that came with each of them came crashing into me like a tidal wave, punching the breath from my lungs.

I'd thought memories of my human life had lost their power to stop me in my tracks, but apparently not. I gorged myself on cubes of melon while Royce watched until my tiny stomach felt full to bursting. I squeaked repeatedly at Royce, forgetting he couldn't understand me, but it seemed like the point got across. I waited until all the taste of fruit had dissipated from my tongue before attempting another transformation.

Human again, I stood and staggered sideways, dizzy. Transforming so many times in rapid succession took a toll on the body, and I felt a hollow, weak sort of ache in my stomach. Hunger. Thirst. I turned to Royce helplessly. "I'm still hungry," I said.

"Why didn't you try eating more before shifting back?"

"I couldn't. I was full..." frowning, I reached for the melon and gave it a hesitant sniff. The smell remained as enticing as it had to my wee bat nose, but my stomach lurched and roiled when I brought the flesh to my lips. It was like my esophagus closed, my tongue rebelled, and my mouth simply would not allow the fruit to trespass within. I put it down on the counter.

I turned to Royce, and he took a startled step back. "Woah," he said.

"What?"

"Your eyes—they...they've gone dark."

"Dark?"

"Like when you're about to feed," he said.

I could hardly deny it; my throat burned with thirst. "I do not care for this."

"Should we forget it? Maybe there's something else we could try."

I shook my head. "No. But perhaps you could tell your rodent what the results of this first test were."

"I don't actually think hedgehogs are rodents," said Royce.

I glared at him.

The next two weeks were pure misery. I could only get fruit down in my bat form, and the stomach capacity of a little golden-mantled flying fox was far too small to sustain a man. I lost weight. I weakened. I actually slept, which was disorienting. It scared the daylights out of poor Royce, who thought he'd killed me. I woke with a foul taste in my mouth, groggy and disoriented. I'd bitten my lips, chewed my fingers in my sleep, trying to drink from myself as this body slowly starved.

"There's a thought," said Royce. He bandaged my fingers, a worried look on his face.

"What?"

"Can you live off vampire blood?"

"No," I said.

"Are you sure?"

"Yes. We can drink from our own kind, but not enough to sustain. Living off our blood would be like you trying to live on champagne and candy."

"I think maybe it's time to give this up," said Royce.

I shook my head stubbornly. "It's working," I said.

"It clearly isn't," said Royce. "You're killing yourself."

"If that were true, I'd be dead already."

"You look dead," said Royce bluntly. "I can't watch this anymore."

"What choice do we have?"

Royce chewed his bottom lip, and my stomach swooped. I wanted to bite that lip. I *needed* to bite that lip. I lunged across the space between us, kissing him hungrily, dragging my fangs along the plump flesh of his lip, feeling drunk. He pushed gently on my shoulders. "Easy," he said softly. "Give me a reason why I shouldn't let you feed from me right now," said Royce. He reached into a drawer and pulled a knife from within. He held it to his palm. "Or I'll do it, I swear."

The thought of getting a taste of Royce's blood had my cock hard in seconds, and I went weak-kneed and dizzy. "Put that down," I said, wrapping my fingers around his wrist. I was so hungry—if I fed on Royce, I didn't have faith I'd be able to stop.

I had tried something just that morning while Royce was at work, and it proved that our experiment was working, albeit slowly. "I won't be able to show you until tomorrow," I said. "But you have to trust me."

"Sin..." Royce pleaded, tightening his grip on the knife.

I held up my hands, trying to placate him. "If I were truly starving, I would have fed."

"What?"

"I would not have been able to stop myself," I insisted.

"Instinct would have taken over, and I would have bitten you. Or someone else."

Royce lowered the knife, but his expression was still suspicious. "Are you for real?"

"*Yes,*" I said. "Just wait until tomorrow."

He cupped my cheek and pulled me in for another kiss. "Alright," he said. "Tomorrow. And if you don't have something to prove this is changing a damn thing—besides giving me grey hairs—you're going to feed, for real. Promise me."

"I promise," I said solemnly.

I spent the remaining hours of the evening as a bat. Over the past few days, I realized I was more comfortable in my bat form. A few hours before dawn, however, I transformed and lifted the blackout curtains by Royce's bed. I stood at the foot of the bed, in shadow, watching the glow of the rising sun spread slowly across Royce as he slept, curled up like a sweet manly cherub. Another side effect of this new diet was that I had been able to summon zero energy for lovemaking. That alone would have cracked my resolve if it were not for what I was about to show Royce.

When the sun crept across his sleeping face, he blinked awake. "Hey," he said, and I loved his sleepy, raspy voice. He squinted at the window. "What did you do to the curtains?"

Instead of answering, I braced myself for the pain and stuck my arm directly into the beam of sunlight streaming through the window.

"*Baby!*" Royce scrambled out of his blankets, at once alert. He grabbed my arm, trying to shield my skin, but... "Wait," he said.

We both watched my forearm turn pink, then red, over several long, silent minutes. This much direct sun exposure would have caused instantaneous, hideous blistering before I'd begun this little dietary experiment. It was still painful, and I winced, gritting my teeth as I tested the limits of my tolerance. I glanced at my mobile telephone, upon which I had activated the stopwatch feature. At five minutes, a soft hiss and slight blistering appeared on the skin of my arm. I yanked my hand from Royce's grasp, back into the shadows. He stood on the mattress to pull the shade down once more, before plopping down beside me, cradling my sunburned arm in his hands. "What does this mean?"

Looking down at the angry, but intact, skin on my arm, I grinned. "It means I'm changing," I said. "It means it's working."

13

TABLE SERVICE ETIQUETTE

ROYCE

I swear, Sinclair's transition to a fruitarian diet was taking *years* off my life. He only spent a few hours a day out of his bat form, and I was nervous this transition was doing irreparable damage to his body. The fact that he could withstand the sunlight had seemed a positive sign, but he was still weak, feverish, and occasionally delirious.

His lips were swollen with self-inflicted bites, and I'd taken to making him sleep in mittens if he was in his human form because he kept chewing his fingers. After not sleeping at all for a hundred years, Sinclair's circadian rhythm was not what one would call normal. He'd fall asleep in the most random locations and positions, and after only an hour or two, he'd wake up like he was coming out of a decades-long coma.

It had been two weeks of him trying to live off whatever fruit he could eat in his bat form, and the hunger and thirst were taking their toll on him, big time. And me, to be frank.

Meanwhile, I was trying to tail Stark and prove his involvement in all the shit that had been going on, without letting him know I knew his secret. I thought back over everything I could remember about Stark since he came to our precinct. When he first got here, I was pretty sure he moved around in the daylight, so maybe he'd been turned recently?

Perhaps Clay had turned him to have a plant in the police department. Given the man's level of organization, it didn't seem outside the realm of possibility. I reflected that I'd never noticed his teeth, or fangs rather, the way I noticed Sinclair's—but Stark never smiled. Ever. I couldn't spend my shifts at work staring at his mouth, either.

The two men Sinclair had fought off at the railyard had turned up dead. They hadn't been drained, but clearly this Clay had humans working for him too, including his now-deceased "familiar". A bag of cash and a case full of ketamine had been recovered at the scene, apparently Garibaldi had been more involved than he'd let on. There was a piece to this mess that I was missing—something that would make all of this make sense, and it was driving me insane that I couldn't put my finger on it.

Priya had still not been back on active duty since being shot. She badgered me day and night about getting back into the field, and complained constantly about her physical therapist who kept saying "one more week" to signing off on her recovery.

Finally, she was cleared to return to work, and I took her out to celebrate. Sin was resting at my place, and had been in quite a foul mood, encouraging me most vociferously, to give him some space. After a few rounds, Priya and I were more than a little tipsy, and since we were close to my place, she asked if she could crash on my couch.

Normally, I wouldn't have thought twice about it, but I hesitated. My rum-and-Coke addled brain wasn't quick enough to come up with a decent excuse.

"Come *onnn*," she said, linking our arms together as we staggered down the sidewalk.

"Sin's kind of staying with me," I said. "He's...sick."

"He's home sick and you're out partying?" She poked me in the chest. "Ruh-roh."

"No ruh-roh," I said. "Just...it's a delicate situation."

"I promise," said Priya, dragging a finger across her heart. "I'll be good. And if I'm hungover tomorrow, Sinclair and I can be miserable on your couch together."

"Okay," I said. Priya already mostly knew everything about Sin. How bad could it be?

Very bad, as it turned out.

I heard a ruckus on the other side of my door, and when I pushed it open, my apartment looked like it had been fucking ransacked. Sin was bouncing off the walls, literally, chaotically shifting back and forth from man to bat, squeaking and throwing himself around the kitchen, knocking doors off the cabinets and pictures off the walls as he careened around the place. I slammed the door shut and planted myself between Priya and the threshold. She stood on the welcome mat, confused. "What the hell is going on in there?"

"Nothing," I said loudly, trying and failing to cover up the distinctive sound of a lamp breaking.

"Nothing, my ass," said Priya. "Why won't you let me in?"

"Sinclair is..." I cast around for an excuse. "On drugs."

Priya stared at me. "Drugs."

"Yes."

"Royce," she said. "You're a cop."

"Yes."

"I'm a cop."

"Also yes."

"So, you're saying we should remain on this side of the door," she said. "And your reason for that is there's illegal drug activity going on in there?"

"Um. Yes?"

She sighed, pushing me aside to open the door. "I am way too drunk for this shit."

I followed her into the apartment, and Sinclair seemed to have stopped shifting, but he now crouched naked on top of my refrigerator, gnawing on a can of something, snarling like a wild animal.

"Sin?" I said gently, approaching the fridge.

He growled at me, then bared his fangs. Then he went back to biting savagely at the can, chewing it viciously until he managed to puncture the side of it like he was about to shotgun a beer. Something sticky oozed out, and I got a glimpse of the torn label between his fingers. It was some kind of nasty fruit cocktail in syrup—which possibly had been in the cabinet when I moved in because I sure as hell didn't remember buying it.

"Sin," I repeated. "Baby? Can you come down from there?"

He hissed, and his eyes were all pupil, like he really was on drugs. He gnawed at the side of his can some more, worrying it with his teeth. Syrup dribbled out from the punctures, dripping sluggish trails down Sinclair's fingers. He licked the jagged metal, attempting to tear into the can and get at the fruit. He spat a piece of aluminum on the floor, and in doing so, he blinked. I watched in real-time as his eyes cleared, and he looked at the can in his hands, confused, as if he couldn't figure out how it had gotten there. "Royce?"

"Yeah, baby. I'm here. Why don't you come down?"

He jumped from the top of the fridge, landing gracefully on the floor. He still seemed reluctant to let go of his can. I wrapped an arm around his waist and tucked him against my side so I could steer him toward the bathroom. "Make yourself at home," I called over my shoulder at Priya. Good luck to her. It looked like Sin may have shredded one of my couch cushions.

I turned on the shower, testing the water temperature before guiding Sinclair to sit in the tub. "Can I borrow this?" I asked, gently prying the can of fruit cocktail from his twitchy fingers. I let the tub fill and went back to the kitchen, where I used my can opener to finish the job Sinclair's fangs had started, and poured the fruit into a little bowl, checking for fragments of can before returning to the bathroom. I handed Sinclair the bowl and he dug his fingers into the sticky, sweetened fruit and stuffed each piece into his mouth. Once he'd eaten and licked the bowl clean, he seemed to have calmed down a bit. However, he definitely was not in complete control of his faculties, so I sat on the edge of the tub and washed him gently, taking care to clear his mouth of pieces of label and syrup.

"I'm sorry," he said sullenly. "I'm so embarrassed."

"It's okay," I said, washing his scalp for no other reason than to soothe him.

"I'm not a child," he snapped, batting my hands away. "I just don't know what came over me. Of course, Detective Tanti is here, how humiliat—"

"Sin." I clasped his face between my hands, trying to get his attention. "Look at me."

"What?"

"You were eating," I said, my excitement barely controlled.

"I was—what?"

"You're in your human form," I said. "And you just ate that whole bowl of fruit."

Sinclair blinked, aghast. "I did, didn't I?"

I kissed him thoroughly, tasting the sticky sweet syrup on his tongue and reveling in it.

"Yes," I said, and my voice was thick. *This was going to be okay.* "It's working."

He smiled, so tremulous and sweet I couldn't resist kissing him again, pressing our foreheads together.

"I love you," I said. Then I jerked back, balking immediately. *Oops.* I stood, dropping my hands to my sides and backing away. "Um, I'm going to go to the store and get you some more fruit."

Sinclair looked at me, flabbergasted, but before he could form a reply, I bolted.

Priya sat on my sofa, giving the shredded cushion a fair berth. She yawned. "Everything okay?"

"Yeah," I said, though it wasn't. Why had I just said that? *Fucking idiot.* "Can you stay here with Sin? I have to run to the store."

She sat bolt upright, all trace of sleepiness gone. "What if he tries to eat me?"

"I won't," said a soft voice. Sinclair appeared in the hallway, wearing one of my old shirts and a pair of my boxers that had survived his purge.

Priya looked at me. "That's not super reassuring."

I sighed. "Sinclair? Promise you won't eat Priya."

He nodded solemnly. "I promise."

"Jesus Christ," she muttered under her breath. "Fine. Hurry back."

I fled the apartment as fast as I could.

————

SINCLAIR

I perched on the sofa beside Priya, who sat rigidly, her hands twisting in her lap. She let out a breath, puffing her cheeks up, and blowing nervously in an audible exhale.

"I'm sorry," I said quietly.

Priya's head jerked toward me so fast she cricked her neck. "For what?"

I gestured at the mess. "I didn't mean to frighten you."

A muscle went in her jaw, but she didn't answer. I got the distinct impression I was being tested in some fashion, but for the life of me I couldn't discern how to pass.

"Detective Tanti—" I began.

"Oh, come on, Sinclair," and here at least she shot me a smile, albeit a tight one. "I think we're a little past that, don't you?"

"Perhaps," I said carefully. "Priya—"

"You saved my life," she blurted.

"I did," I allowed, unsure where she was going with that.

"I am fucking *terrified* of you," she said. "Seriously. But I see how much you care for Royce. And I think there's a good man under all the blood and fangs."

"I like to think so," I said. Perhaps it was time to go for broke. "It's important that you trust me."

"Why?"

"Because, you mean so much to my Royce," I said. "He listens to you."

She laughed. "No, he doesn't. If he listened to me, he

would have run screaming in the opposite direction once we figured out who you are."

"Hmm," I said, unsure what to do with that information.

"Listen," she said. "I see what you're doing here. For him. That's enough to show me you're serious about this relationship. Just—don't snack on me on your cheat day, deal?"

I grinned. "Deal."

Priya was snoring by the time Royce returned from the all-night grocery. He entered the flat in time to find me tucking a blanket around her where she curled up on the sofa. I straightened and watched Royce set his bags on the counter. "Are you still hungry?" He asked.

I nodded. "Ravenous."

"Thanks for not eating my best friend," he said.

I rolled my eyes, crossing the room to stand in front of his offerings. He laid several things on the counter like he was waiting for me to choose. I selected a large item I knew to be called a pineapple, though I'd never had cause to sample one before, of course. I lifted it by its spiny leaves and braced the end against my other palm. Since I was, as I mentioned, ravenous, I went to take a massive bite out of the side.

Royce let out a strangled noise of surprise, and I sputtered, choking immediately on the rough, bark-like exterior of the fruit. I coughed through my mouthful directly back onto Royce's countertop. "What on earth?" I said. "Why would you buy me this?"

The skin was spiney and thick, and it felt like I'd eaten a mouthful of garden mulch. I stuck out my tongue, unable to get the wooden taste out of my mouth.

"You don't eat it like that," said Royce. "Have—have you never had a pineapple before?"

"Tropical fruit wasn't as readily available when I last had cause to consume produce," I said, embarrassed.

"No way," said Royce softly. He considered for a minute. "Okay, well, why don't you head to my room? I'll cut this up for you and bring it in. You'll like it. I promise."

I looked doubtfully at him, sticking my tongue out and brushing remnants of pineapple bark off it with my sleeve. The mirth in Royce's eyes made me scowl, but there was no real energy behind it. I turned and stomped off toward his bed chamber, and I heard his chuckles echoing through the air behind me.

I stripped down and sat in the center of Royce's bed, waiting. When he joined me, he carried a plate with yellow cubes on it, presumably the proper serving method for pineapple. The embarrassment of Priya seeing me in this state, plus making a dining etiquette blunder with the pineapple had me feeling out of sorts, pouty and mutinous.

With an indulgent smile and a sigh, Royce sat opposite me with the plate between us. He selected a morsel of pineapple, holding it between his fingers. I parted my lips obediently, letting him place it on my tongue. The fruit was bright, tart, and sweet at once, and as I sucked the juice from Royce's fingers I recalled my hunger, eager now to gobble the entire tray.

"It's better like that, isn't it?" said Royce.

I now lay with my head in his lap, and he stroked my hair. I huffed.

Royce's hand stilled, cupping the back of my skull. "Thank you," he said.

"For what?"

"Doing this." The muscle of his thigh tensed. "It's been

so hard for you, these past few weeks. But you're so strong, and you're doing this for me. So we can be together. It's..."

I recalled what Royce had blurted before he'd left me in his bathtub. He wasn't repeating those specific words, so I felt it best to allow him to pretend he had recalled them. I turned my head to kiss his thigh. "It's nothing."

"It's not nothing. You're amazing."

I was glad then that my kind did not blush; I merely smiled to myself and allowed Royce to continue petting my head.

"So, what was that, before?" Royce asked me after a while.

"Which?"

"You seemed..." he faltered. "Unwell. When I got home."

I laughed. "That's one way to describe it."

"Well?" Royce prompted.

I frowned, thinking. Recalling how I felt the moments before when I'd simply *ached* with desire to feed. I sat up suddenly, startling Royce. "I think—it felt almost like when I was first turned."

"What?"

"Yes," I said, mind whirring. "I was resting, and suddenly I felt *ravenous,* like I hadn't in decades. It was like my whole being whited out and all that was left of me was thirst."

Royce shuddered.

"Yes," I agreed. "It's fairly overwhelming. What's interesting is that I went for your strange fruit concoction."

"Yeah, and not my neighbors," said Royce drily.

I pinched his thigh, but in actuality, his joke hit a little too close to home. "I think this strategy of Mr. Ambrose's is truly rewiring my system," I said.

Royce hunched over me so he could kiss the top of my head.

The next morning, it felt like a fever had finally broken —the sun brought with it a clarity of mind, and a manageable hunger. I ate the remainder of the pineapple, *sans* tough exterior, and Royce grinned like a maniac as he offered me an orange.

"What?" I asked him, disconcerted.

"Do you know what that is?"

I hefted the citrus in my palm. "An orange?"

"Not just any orange—" Royce snatched it from me, and cut it in half. The interior was a deep crimson. "A *blood* orange."

I rolled my eyes. "Ha-ha."

Royce cut the orange into wedges for me and I had to admit, the deep red juice of the blood orange was truly delicious. I'd never had one of these before, either. Some of the juice ran down my chin, and I watched as Royce tracked its movement, his tongue poked out past his lip, the gesture appearing almost involuntary.

With a grin, I used my fingertip to brush the trail from my chin, and then I sucked the juice from it. Royce swallowed, his lips parting, eyes darkening.

Things had taken a *very* positive turn.

14

A HOMILY UPON FRUIT

ROYCE

After several nerve-wracking weeks, Sinclair seemed to have settled into his fruitarian diet. There were still things to which he needed to become accustomed. Sleeping at night really seemed to disorient him, though I had to admit I loved it because he looked pretty adorable with his face squished into my pillow, snoring and drooling. He'd also lost a significant amount of his strength and speed, now only able to move at an average human rate.

Aside from one dicey moment in bed, wherein Sinclair realized the handcuffs were actually physically restraining him and he panicked, things between us were better than ever. Once he became accustomed to his decreased physical strength, our kinky bedroom romps ramped up. Something about surrendering put Sin into a deep state of almost meditative relaxation. Sinclair loved submitting, and I loved his willing, needy obedience. I also really loved the after part; caring for him made me feel settled, deep down in my bones.

In the meantime, I was desperate to prove to him how much his sacrifice meant to me. I knew that, given his "druthers" he'd certainly have preferred his customary, natural diet and its accompanying powers. It also didn't escape me that he didn't bring up the fact that I'd dropped the L word the other day. It had just slipped out, and any time I tried to repeat it, I got all stupid and tongue-tied. So, I had to let it out in other ways.

"What is this?" Sinclair eyed the giant cellophane parcel doubtfully.

The thing I'd *thunked* down on the counter at Datura was indeed huge and garish, but I was far too excited to care. "Just open it."

Sinclair smiled at me, then set about plucking the shiny pink ribbon from the package, disentangling the cellophane and revealing—

"What is this?" He asked again.

"You tell me," I said.

"It appears to be some sort of...vertical cornucopia of cut fruit?"

"It's an Edible Arrangement!"

"A *what?*"

"It's like a flower arrangement, but it's fruit!"

Sin poked at a cut pineapple daisy. "Did you make this?"

"No," I said. "It's like a whole business."

His face clouded, and he bit his bottom lip. With fingers almost trembling, he reached for a skewer of a blueberries and grapes, removing it from the bouquet.

"What's wrong?"

Sinclair pointed at me with the skewer, drawing a shaky breath before answering. "Why did you get me this?"

My guts churned a bit at that. "I thought it was kind of funny," I said. "And I thought..."

"Thought what?"

"I don't know, Sinclair. I thought you'd like it!"

"I do like it." He nibbled daintily at a blueberry.

"Then what's wrong?"

"No one has ever gotten me something this thoughtful before," he whispered. Then he smiled crookedly. "Nor this odd."

I let out a breath, laughing. "Well, you know. I just thought. You like flowers..."

He next selected one of the daisy pineapples, twirling the skewer between his fingers before taking a large bite. "I do like flowers," he said, his cheek bulging as he selected several more pieces and ate them. "Thank you, Royce."

We spent the evening snacking on the arrangement, sitting cross-legged on the counter in Sinclair's shop, *Sixteen Candles* style.

With things between Sin and me settled at present, I could focus all my energy on this case. After hitting so many dead ends, I was trying to start at the beginning, to look at the fact pattern with fresh eyes and hope it would inspire something.

One afternoon, Priya had rolled her desk chair up to me, looking over my shoulder. She seemed to have unofficially attached herself to this case on the down-low, especially now that she and Sinclair had become friends. She also asked me a *lot* of questions about vampire stuff.

"Is it weird sleeping with him?"

"*Priya,*" I hissed.

"No, I mean literally. Like, snuggling up to a cold piece of marble."

I paused to think. "It's actually kind of nice," I said.

"Really?"

"Yeah, it's like..." I struggled to find the words. "It's like always having the cool side of the pillow to smush your face against."

"My god, that's beautiful," said Priya, giving me a sarcastic eyeroll. "Hey," she said suddenly. "Why don't you look at other jurisdictions?"

Switching between my love life and the case was giving me whiplash, but it was kind of how Priya's mind worked. "I'd have to go through Stark to request the files."

"Not if you went after the hard copies."

"The hard copies..." I frowned. What Priya said about other jurisdictions shook something loose in my brain. There was one thing all these weird threads had in common.

Stark had originally been a cop in Denver.

Sinclair had said Clay and his sadistic pals had moved here from another city—and I was willing to bet I could guess where. If I could get into the archive department at the Denver PD headquarters, I could maybe start tying some of these threads together.

"Royce?"

I looked up and resisted the urge to groan. For all of about five minutes, Sinclair had been cowed and embarrassed by the fact that I'd arrested him, considering I'd forced him—dickishly—to do a perp walk. However, he wasn't the kind to let something get him down for long, so once we'd made up, he marched right back in with his head held high, daring anyone to ask what had happened between us. It had been awkward at first because the story I'd told the other cops as to why I'd hauled my boyfriend in covered in blood was *wafer* thin, but for the most part, things had gone back to normal.

However, now that Sinclair had some limited tolerance for sunlight exposure, he showed up at any and all hours, with a few rather unorthodox accessories—namely, an enormous black, ruffled, lace-covered parasol. Coupled with his heroin-chic emo-rocker clothes, it was quite the look.

"Hey, Sin," said Priya.

"Detective Tanti," he said, offering her a slight bow.

"What're you doing here?" I asked.

"One of these days, I'm going to take offense to that question, my darling."

"Right—sorry. This just has me all—" I gave a noncommittal grunt and a frustrated wave of my hand.

"I understand," said Sinclair sympathetically. "That's why I thought I would drop by for lunch."

He set down a burger and fries for me, and pulled out a fruit cup for himself.

"Cheers," I said, grinning.

"Cheers."

"You two are disgusting," said Priya. She swung her leg over her chair and dragged it back over to her own desk.

"So, what is your current boggle?" Sinclair asked.

Despite the fact that it was daytime, and Stark wasn't here, I lowered my voice. "I'm having a hard time finding any pattern of evidence that will help us expose Stark and rescue Beckett."

While I pored over files, Sinclair stood behind me and rubbed the knots from my shoulders. Once, that might have embarrassed me, but honestly—right now, it just felt amazing to have someone in my corner who cared about me as much as Sinclair did. I reached up to cover his fingers where they rested on my shoulder, and turned to kiss his wrist. "Thanks," I mumbled.

He rested his chin on top of my head. "You're welcome."

I tilted my head to peer up at him. "Hey," I said. "What do you say to a romantic trip to Denver?"

———

SINCLAIR

"I will never understand humans."

"You were human," Royce pointed out.

We strolled arm in arm down furrowed rows of short, bushy foliage. I had my parasol and sunglasses to protect my face, which was still fairly sensitive to the sun. I did have to admit, it was lovely to walk outside in the sunshine, even if the direct rays were uncomfortable. "Still."

"I'll bite. Why don't you understand humans?"

"Well," I said. "We used to get all of our produce in this manner." I gestured at the land around us. Royce had arranged for us to spend the day picking our own fruit at an organic farm near our hostelry, just outside Denver.

"Okay, true."

"Then, street markets were replaced by supermarkets, and all fruit was shipped from across the globe to convenient, temperature-controlled buildings with a selection those from my time couldn't even fathom."

"Also true."

"And yet," I continued. "Here we are, out in the sun, paying for the privilege of foraging once more."

Royce stopped in his tracks, so sudden I almost fell over when he tugged on my arm. "So, you don't like the farm? I knew it was stupid."

"Hey," I said softly. I stepped close, cupping Royce's face to pull him into the shade of my parasol. "I love it. I would never have been able to do something like this without you. I'm only teasing."

"Yeah?"

"Yes," I said. I nudged his forehead with mine, looking into his eyes. "I love it. I am having a marvelous time."

To illustrate my point, I bit into a strawberry the size of a chipmunk. The juice in my mouth tasted of fresh earth and summertime.

"Just wait till we get back to the hotel," said Royce with a wicked grin. "I have something even more 'marvelous' planned."

I offered him a bite from my strawberry. "This will be hard to top."

He snapped his jaws, allowing the juice to run down his chin. "Just you wait."

Back in our room at the hostelry, a charming, cozy place called the Silverleaf Inn, I sat nervously on the edge of the bed. Royce had some big plans and was fussing around in the kitchenette of our little suite. "You better be naked by the time I get in there," he called from the other room.

A shocky thrill ran down my spine, and I peeled out of my clothes before moving to kneel in the center of the bed, knowing that was the position Royce liked me in whenever we played. Palms up, resting on my thighs. Knees spread. Vulnerable. Obedient.

I could already feel myself slipping into that strange, tranquil state of mind that I found so alluring. Royce emerged from the kitchen area, still fully dressed, bearing a heavily laden breakfast tray.

The tray was heaped with fruit, many I couldn't even name, and some I could name but could not begin to guess the flavor.

"I thought we could try something a little different,"

said Royce. His voice was husky, and the way his eyes raked over me with barely controlled desire had me simmering where I knelt. "If that's alright?"

"Of course."

Royce chewed his lip. He still experienced nerves in his role whenever we played this way, something I, of course, found endearing as all get-out. "Hands behind your back," he commanded. "Please."

With a small smile, I clasped my hands at the small of my back.

Royce withdrew a few things from his suitcase. "I'm going to restrain your hands," he explained. "And if it's okay, I'd really like to use a blindfold, too."

"A blindfold?"

He advanced on me with a few soft wrappings. Since the time I'd experienced real fear being restrained by hand-cuffs, Royce had pivoted to using delicate silk ties. I loved the way they felt against my skin, and Royce seemed to enjoy their aesthetic. He moved behind me on the bed, clasping my hands together and binding them securely. "Yes," he said. Once the knots were tied, he tested them ensuring they weren't too tight. Then he trailed his pinky down my spine. "You haven't tried a lot of these fruits before, right? I thought maybe we could do like, a taste test?"

I tugged on the restraints.

"I'll feed you," he clarified. "Sticky, sweet—I figured, there's something there, right?"

I laughed. "I think you're onto something."

"So, you'll try it?"

"Indeed."

Royce pulled another matching silk tie and wrapped it gently around my face, robbing me entirely of sight. The effect it had on me was a sudden one; I had never felt so vulnerable before. My other senses ratcheted to high alert. I could hear every one of Royce's breaths, the thudding of his heart. I *loved* it.

"You okay?"

"Yes," I said.

"And our safe word?"

"Begonia," I answered, with a small smile.

Royce pressed his lips to my forehead. I felt the air current moving a split second before the kiss landed. "You look so beautiful like this," he whispered, almost to himself. Had I been human, I might have missed it. Had I been human, I might have blushed.

I sensed rather than heard a rustling nearby, the weight shifting on the bed to indicate Royce was stripping down himself. My cock twitched, the charge in the air between us changing instantaneously, like my bare body could sense his, and called out to it. Royce steadied one hand on my knee and I jumped, startled. My other senses might be heightened, but I relied on sight as much as most predators did, and being suddenly in the dark entirely changed my perception of the room, of myself, of Royce—it was positively electric.

Royce carded a hand through my hair before dragging his knuckles down my cheek. His thumb came to rest on my bottom lip. "Open," he said.

I obeyed, and Royce dipped his thumb inside, just briefly. I was tempted, sorely, to close my lips around it and suck, but I knew better than to act without command. During our games, Royce could be so deliciously cruel in the way he wielded his power over me. Sometimes, it was worth enduring his ire, but we'd only just begun, so I resisted.

Something tart and chill landed on the tip of my tongue, and I gasped—nearly inhaling it. I had not expected it to be cold. Royce chuckled. "You okay, baby?"

"Yes," I said. "Just—it's cold."

It was like I could hear Royce's smile. "I thought that would add a little something. You like it?"

"It's tart," I said, chewing thoughtfully. "What is it?"

"It's called a golden berry," said Royce.

I swallowed and opened my mouth again.

"Good boy," Royce purred. The deeper into a scene we went, the easier Royce found confidence in his dominant role.

Another piece of fruit landed on my tongue, sweet this time. We moved through countless samples, and Royce was so clever, keeping me on my proverbial toes, alternating sour, sweet, different textures, so I never knew what to expect. Plum, peach. Lychee. Papaya. Grapes. Kiwi.

"Here," said Royce. "Bite."

The piece in question was larger, and when I sank my fangs in, the sweet juice seemed to explode out of it, running down my chin. Instinctively, I went to brush at the sticky trail with my finger, but was stopped by the restraints.

"Allow me," Royce rumbled.

I gasped as the tip of Royce's tongue pressed against the point of my chin, following the dribble of juice to my lips before he plunged it between them. Royce kissed me hungrily, sucking my tongue like he was trying to taste the fruit there. When he drew back, I said, "I liked that one."

"Oh yeah?" Royce kissed the corner of my mouth. "It was mango."

"Mango," I repeated thoughtfully. Never did I think I'd

ever get to taste a mango, or any of this really. There were a lot of things I never even dreamed of having, before Royce.

"More?"

"Yes, please."

Another slice of mango poked at my tongue, and as I nibbled it toward the center, I was met with Royce's lips. He stole another sweet, tropical, intoxicating kiss and my head swam. "*Hnnf,*" I said as he drew back, and I could feel the warmth of his breath ghosting over my lips, sticky with fruit juice and swollen with kisses. Royce fed me more mango as he kissed down my jaw, licking any juice that spilled from the corners of my mouth, then sucking on my earlobe just below the fabric of the blindfold. I hitched a little breath, and then Royce was feeding me his fingers, and I licked the juice from each and every one. When he held his palm to my lips, I cleaned it dutifully as well.

"*Fuck,*" Royce cursed under his breath, his nose buried in my hairline, and he dragged his teeth down the tendons of my neck, biting my collarbone. I could feel the heat of Royce's body moving closer, radiating the space between us and I squirmed, just trying my best to get nearer to him. I heard a clang, and Royce cursed again, and I knew the fruit tray had gone flying as Royce pushed me back against the pillows, invading my mouth with his tongue. The smell of fruit and sweat filled the air as Royce lavished kisses all over my body.

I had no idea what he planned and it was thrilling; I was utterly in his power with my hands pinned below me and Royce's weight pressing me into the mattress, and then all at once he was gone. I let out a startled noise, feeling exposed, alone—the sensation swooping through me like vertigo, but then Royce was there, his fingers below my chin, his lips on my ear. "Easy," he murmured. "I'm right here."

I twisted my head, searching for his lips and kissing only air, and the *snick* of a plastic cap caught my attention.

Royce kissed down my neck once more, dragged his tongue over collar bones, dipping into the hollow between them. When Royce nudged my thigh with the back of his hand, I spread my legs obediently to accommodate him, wanting him there, needing him there. Needing him close. His lips closed around one of my nipples, sucking hard while tracing the bud with his tongue, and I was so disoriented I had no time to react to the featherlight probing around my entrance before Royce pushed one of his thick fingers inside.

I melted into the mattress, surrendering entirely to Royce's wicked fingers—the way he crooked them just so, deep inside, sent pleasure flowing over my skin like static. He teased my other nipple before kissing down my chest, dipping into my navel, worshipping the vee of my hips until finally, blessedly, wrapping his lips around the head of my cock.

My shoulders twitched; all I wanted was to tangle my fingers in his hair and fuck his throat, but the silk ties held fast, chafing at my wrists as I tested their strength. Royce pulled off, teasing my slit with his tongue, knowing it drove me insane, all while his fingers twisted and stroked me from the inside out. He mouthed down my shaft, kissing as he went, before sucking my balls. Without stopping, Royce encouraged me to drape my legs over his shoulders, and then his tongue was *there*, too, like it was fighting with his fingers for access, and the differing sensations had me twisting and squirming. Eventually, Royce slowed his fingers, pulling back slightly to kiss inside my thigh, sucking the skin there as he pulled his fingers out, leaving me quite bereft until I felt the thick head of his cock take its place. I nearly wept with relief, but Royce made no move to breach my channel; he simply rested his hands on my waist, nudging my rim with his dick. "*Please,*" I whispered, trying to wriggle just right in order to capture his cock inside me. I hooked one of my legs around his waist, tugging him, trying to encourage him to get on with it.

Royce's thumbs made teasing, featherlight trails down the furrow where my thighs met my groin. "Christ, baby," said Royce. "Your body."

I may have made an impatient huff because Royce let out a low chuckle.

He leaned forward, and I felt him plunge his hands below me on the mattress. A few awkward tugs later and my hands were free, free to grab blindly for Royce and cling to him while he whispered absolute filth in my ear.

"Your body is the holiest fucking thing I've laid eyes on," said Royce, his voice thick with lust. "I can't believe you're mine."

"Yours," I agreed, digging my fingers into his ass.

"My greedy little monster," he said, sinking into me in one long, slow thrust. From the moment the head of his cock pushed past my rim I moaned, long and low until he was seated fully, right where he belonged, and I released a shaky sigh. "Not so patient, huh?"

I turned my head to the side, embarrassed. But I knew better than to assume the question was rhetorical. "No," I said. "I'm not."

Royce drew back and pushed in again. "Good," he said.

I clenched around him, like I could keep him there if I squeezed hard enough, and Royce choked off a little noise muffled into the meat of my shoulder. His hands roamed my sides, my belly, my chest, before he wrapped me in his arms and my world tilted on its axis, dizzying without my eyes to orient me, and I found myself vertical, impaled on Royce's lap. This time when I searched for his mouth I found it, our lips meeting in a messy tangle. "I love your lips," said Royce, biting one, tugging on it until I hissed. The muscles below my navel tightened in pleasure as the new angle allowed Royce to reach even deeper. I ground against his soft belly, my cock trapped between us and desperate for some friction.

Royce kissed my neck again, so fixated one might wonder which of us was truly the vampire after all, sucking and biting and moving toward my shoulders. "I love your freckles."

I braced my hands on Royce's shoulders, utterly lost to sense as I fucked myself on his thick shaft, so intent on chasing my pleasure I couldn't even answer Royce, despite the lovely things he was saying.

And he wasn't finished—it seemed he was very happy to let his cock-drunk mouth run. "Your eyes—I need to see your eyes..."

"What?" I gasped, distracted, trying to encourage Royce to adjust the angle of his thrusts just a bit so I could—

I blinked in surprise as light flooded my field of vision, assaulting me with the sudden influx of stimuli—adding to the already rich tapestry my body and mind were already experiencing. Royce slowed the movement of his hips, looking at me so intensely I was suddenly afraid I'd done something wrong. But then he cupped my face, brushing his thumb over my cheek. "I love your eyes," he said, softly.

"Oh," I said, ducking my head to escape the intensity of his gaze.

He picked up his pace once more, breathing heavily, but

kept his gaze locked on mine. "I love—*fuck*—I love this fucking fang," he grunted, using his thumb to push my lip back, exposing my canine.

Royce pushed forward, sending me back into the pillows, and was on me in an instant, his mouth and lips and hands everywhere at once as he let loose and fucked me, hard. For one of the first times in our relationship, I felt like I couldn't keep up. He drove into me with everything he had, like a man possessed. I felt my climax barreling toward me like an avalanche, and with each glancing blow to my prostate, I cried out, overwhelmed and feeling like all I could do was hold on to Royce for dear life and hope he didn't snap me in half. And he was still—

"I love that you get me flowers," he said. "I love that you followed me around. I love that you watch me sleep. I love that you—fuck, Sinclair, I just love you. I love you so—fucking—*much*—" And Royce unloaded with a hoarse shout, grinding his hips against my ass as he filled me up, showering my face and brow with kisses that still held a lingering taste of mango.

I was right there, and the tiny aborted movements of Royce inside me as he rode out his high, plus the shock at his confession sent me soaring, and I erupted between us, firing spurt after spurt of cum all over myself. Royce immediately dipped his head, licking every drop of seed from my chest before collapsing, half on top of me, breathing like a winded bull. He turned his head, his nose sliding over my cheek as he whispered, "And...I love the taste of your cum."

"Oh my *God*," I managed, finding my words at last. I covered my face with my hands.

Royce scooped me against him, rolling us once more so I lay draped over his chest, my head tucked up in the crook of his neck. When it seemed like he'd caught his breath, I trailed my fingertips up his ribcage. I hesitated, not sure my heart could take the truth, but I had to ask. "Did you mean it?"

"Yes," said Royce, without hesitation. "Of course, I did."

I turned my face to kiss his chest. "And you're not going to bolt out of here?"

"Not this time."

"Good," I said, feeling every muscle in my body sag with relief and contentment. "Because I don't think I can move."

Royce laughed, and the vibrations shook us both.

"And..." I paused. "I love you too, Royce Davis."

———

ROYCE

In a complete one-eighty from the previous evening, Sin and I found ourselves in possibly the least romantic setting on the planet: the archives room in the basement of the Denver Police department headquarters.

I glanced over at Sinclair, sitting cross-legged on the floor, and couldn't contain my stupid, dopey grin. He was, somewhat begrudgingly, wearing the t-shirt I'd bought him at the farmstand yesterday. It had a picture of a bee, a butterfly, and a bat on it, and it read "Love Your Local Pollinators." I'd laughed myself stupid when I saw it, and couldn't resist getting it for him. It might have been the only thing I'd ever seen him wear that had a color besides black.

"I think I have something," said Sinclair, pulling me from my sappy thoughts.

I set down the box of files I'd been holding and went to sit beside him on the ground. "Show me?"

He'd uncovered a series of folders for a big human trafficking bust that had been put to bed shortly before Stark had transferred to Douglas Crest. He was on record as the primary detective on the case and had even received commendations from the governor. The pictures in the files showed a setup much like the one Sinclair had described to me where he'd witnessed Beckett Taylor fighting to the death for, in Sin's words, table scraps.

"This says the man running the trafficking ring was someone called...Lance Fellows."

"I don't understand," Sinclair said. "Clay's name isn't anywhere on this file."

"Well," I said, "I imagine Clay either took control of the operation after this guy was arrested, or perhaps this guy was never guilty at all—and Clay had his good friend Stark pin the whole thing on a patsy so they could pack up and move to Douglas Crest."

"How long has he been doing this?" Sinclair wondered.

"What do you mean?"

"I think...I think Clay was turned a long time ago," he said, but I sensed there was something more he wasn't saying.

We looked at the pictures of the victims. In this instance, three young men and two young women, as well as several unnamed John and Jane Does, most likely reaped from the transient populations of the city. "We've got to get Beckett Taylor out of there," said Sinclair softly.

I shot him a look. "Based on what you've told me, Beckett Taylor has a pretty impressive body count racked up behind him."

"I don't believe he had a choice," said Sinclair. "You don't know what it's like—the hunger..." He gulped, and his hand went to the scar on the back of his neck, gripping tight.

"Be that as it may," I said, "What the hell are we supposed to do with him if we get him out? We can't send him home to his mother if he's as blood-crazed as you say. He'll tear her apart, won't he?"

"Well," Sin burst out angrily. "We have to do something! He deserves justice. Being turned...it shouldn't be like this."

"What do you mean?"

"It doesn't matter," said Sinclair, shuffling papers on the floor in front of him, refusing to meet my eye. "I'm just saying, we should try to help him. I could help him."

"Okay," I said, my voice calm and placating. "Okay, Sin. We'll try. I promise."

He nodded, but then he frowned as his eye caught on the photo of one of the victims. "Does she look familiar to you?"

I frowned down at the photo. "Marcy Kemper," he read. "I don't recognize the name from anywhere."

Sinclair's fingers swiped over the photograph, like he could divine something about Marcy Kemper by touching the image of her face, but if he had thoughts about it, he kept them to himself. "So. what now?"

"Now, we make copies of all of this and go home," I said. "And we figure out what the hell we're going to do about it."

We knew we had to act fast, but that was the extent of it. I couldn't imagine that Stark was going to let it go that Sinclair had made him, and working with at least three other vampires meant Sinclair and I were tragically outgunned. I explained my thinking to Sinclair on the drive back to Douglas Crest. We had to take Stark out of play. The sooner the better.

Maybe we could get some intel out of him before—I frowned, glancing at Sin where he reclined in the passenger seat, slouched down with the hood of his sweatshirt pulled up over his head, big sunglasses mostly covering his face. "Sin?"

"Yes?"

"How do we..." words failed me. I didn't want to ask something like this. But I needed to know. "How are we planning on taking Stark down?"

Sinclair didn't answer straight away. "In my travels, I've learned of a few ways of fully dispatching one of my kind," he said eventually.

I reached across the center console and let my hand come to rest on his knee. "Sorry," I said quietly.

Sinclair shrugged, but the air between us was tense as he continued. "Sunlight, eventually, will do it, but we heal quickly and Stark is unlikely to lay quietly under direct sun and allow himself to be cooked. Fire, I think, would do it as well—though on that I'm not certain. And..."

"And?"

"Beheading," he said, his hand clutching his own throat as if he could protect this vulnerable part of himself from our conversation.

"And that's it?"

He eyed me over the top of his aviators. "Royce, my information is woefully incomplete. This isn't the sort of topic one brings up at dinner parties."

"No, I guess not."

"There's also silver," he added, as an afterthought.

"I thought that was werewolves," I said.

He released a little scoff. "Bring that up to your little rodent friend," he said. "See where that gets you."

"Again, I don't think—"

"*In any case,*" said Sinclair loudly, "I don't know that we have time to craft some bespoke silver weapons."

"No, probably not. But we could bring some stuff with us to help." *Detective Davis, in the billiards room, with the candlestick.*

We drove some distance in quiet until Sinclair spoke up again. "Royce," he said.

"Yeah?"

"Are you alright with this?"

I gripped the steering wheel tight, and gritted out, "Which part, exactly?"

"All of it," said Sinclair. "We're...outside of the law."

"No, I'm not," I said. "I'm not okay with any of it. We're casually talking about killing my commanding officer. We're discussing the corruption, and the cases he's covered up. We're talking about risking our lives to save the life of a killer. We're talking about how to whack fucking *vampires,* Sinclair. No. I'm not okay at all."

I could feel Sinclair shrinking away from me, and I realized I'd been practically shouting at him in the tiny, confined space of the car. He didn't answer, just turned to stare out the window. Fuck.

The awkward silence gave me the rest of the ride to figure out our plan of attack. To be perfectly frank, it wasn't looking great. Stark was part of a coven of at least four vampires, and they had loyal human "familiars" working for them.

I had Sinclair.

Who wasn't even at his full, superhuman strength.

Yeah, this was going to go great. "I think I should hit Stark's place tonight," I found myself saying.

"Tonight?"

"Yeah," I said. "He should be working at the station, and I need to get some kind of edge here. Maybe he has something at his apartment I could use against him."

"Excuse me," said Sinclair. "I couldn't help but notice you saying '*I*' kind of a lot there."

"Sin—"

"Don't even try, Royce," he said flatly. "I can't let you go into a Vampire's nest without any backup."

"Well," I said, thinking. "Maybe you should consider..."

"Consider what?"

"Having a real feed. Before we head over there."

"*What?*"

"Sin, we are punching way above our weight, here. It would be great to have a full-strength vampire in our corner."

"No."

"But—"

"Royce, do you think this is something that I can just fall in and out of? It took me *years* to hone the control over my blood lust. I did it all alone because he..." Sinclair broke off, cleared his throat. "My sire had turned me and left me alone in the gutter. It wasn't pretty, believe me."

I kept my eyes on the road because I had a feeling he wasn't done. I also had a feeling Sin had a specific "he" in mind before he'd caught himself.

"I'm afraid if I went back to feeding from blood, it would be like starting over from scratch. I won't put you in danger like that, Royce. I refuse."

"Well," I said. "In that case, maybe you'd consider hanging back?"

The look he shot me had the power to melt steel and shrivel balls. "I'm with you. Always."

"Okay. But you have to be careful."

"Please," Sin scoffed. "I'll be fine."

"Yeah?"

"I'm crafty. I followed you for days and you had no idea."

Well, he had me there.

15

CARELESS AND
UNSUSPECTED POISONING

SINCLAIR

What I had told Royce was the truth. I had no idea how I'd react to returning to a diet of human blood, and to be frank, I wasn't even certain how my body would cope with the change. And then, assuming Royce wanted me to switch *back* to fruit again...there was only so much a gentleman's constitution could withstand.

But that was only part of it.

Royce's outburst reminded me that to him, my kind would always be monstrous. If I wanted to keep Royce, I had to do everything I could to separate myself from them. I didn't want to remind him I could be like that—feeding from human blood, hunting, killing. When the dust settled on this investigation, when we had unmasked Stark, stopped Clay, and with any luck at all, saved Beckett Taylor, I didn't want to be left alone, having driven away my beloved Royce.

It was vital Royce not leave me behind—I was determined that when we brought the fight to Clay, we took him alive. Initially, at least. I had to know. I had to know if he was the one who'd sired me and left me in the dirt like an earthworm, and had now come back to see how I'd evolved on my own. I wasn't certain which answer I wanted—but I wanted it.

I watched Royce drive, watched the little muscle going in his jaw, the white-knuckled way he gripped the steering wheel, and felt I'd made the right call. I could still help Royce plenty in my current state. As I'd said, I was still crafty. And I could still shift.

And I was still nimble as an acrobat, which was how I found myself crouched on the window sill outside of Lieutenant Stark's apartment. Royce and I decided to split up. I'd climb in through the window and unlock the door from within, allowing Royce to enter. We could search the place and relock his apartment without him being any the wiser.

Silent as the night itself, I pried open his window and slipped in, finding myself in the man's bedroom. When my feet hit the floor, I immediately knew something was wrong —but I couldn't place it as I crept across the carpet, through Stark's apartment. The man was aptly named; the place was very barren and sad. Utilitarian, but not well kept. The place was a mess, with dirty clothes, trash, and clutter littering almost every surface, giving the place a very strong scent.

A musty scent like an old forest, or a cave...

Something about that scent was off, but I couldn't quite put my finger on it. Moving into the kitchen, I saw that Stark had precisely one personal effect: a photograph on his refrigerator. It was a photograph of Marcy Kemper, the victim from the case file Royce and I had read in Denver. Her head rested on Stark's shoulder, and he had his arm around her. I realized where I had seen her face before—the two of them had near-identical smiles. I stopped in my tracks, realization slamming into me the same instant the sound of a gun cocking cut the silence. "Turn around."

I sighed, turning calmly to face Royce's boss, Lieutenant Stark. He had a gun trained on me, and if he pulled the trigger, it would definitely strike me center mass. I could hear the sound of Royce's footfalls on the carpeted hallway outside the apartment door. "You realize that won't kill me," I said.

"I imagine it would still hurt like a bitch, though," he said gruffly, his finger brushing the trigger.

Bang. I flinched, expecting to learn what it felt like to be shot in the chest, but the noise actually turned out to be Royce kicking down Stark's front door. Under other, less dire, circumstances, the action would have had me weak in the knees. As such, I just felt relieved.

Royce had his sidearm out, pointed at Stark.

"Royce," I said, but he ignored me.

"Detective Davis," said Stark, sounding frustrated. "You really are a pain in my ass."

"Yeah, well, unless you lower that gun, I'm going to be a pain in your gut," said Royce. "Like you said to Sin, it probably won't kill you, but it'll hurt like a bitch."

"Royce," I said again. "I think it might kill him."

"Sin shut—wait, it might—what?"

"You're not a vampire, are you, Lieutenant Stark?" I asked quietly.

Stark's hand shook, the one holding the gun, but he didn't lower it. He only set his jaw mutinously and didn't answer.

"Sin, what are you talking about?"

"Look at the photo," I said. "On the fridge."

"What the..." If anything, Royce looked even angrier. "Why do you have a picture of Marcy Kemper?"

"She's my daughter."

"Your..."

"Adopted, but yes. Marcy was my daughter." Finally, he lowered his gun, and Stark seemed to age a decade in the span of time it took him to scrub his empty hand over his tired face.

Royce still had his weapon up. "Why the fuck are you working for the guy who killed your daughter?"

Stark shot him a withering look. "I'm not working for him, you moron. I'm trying to take him down."

"You're a shifter," I said. It wasn't a question. It was the only explanation that made sense; the only way he could "pass" as a vampire. "A bat shifter."

He sighed. "Yes."

Royce cursed a blue streak, lowered his gun, and then said, "I am going to *kick* Thor's ass."

"Why?"

"Well, when you and I first met, I thought *you* were a shifter," Royce explained. "He put the fear of God in me about you, and said there *were* no bat shifters."

"There aren't many," said Stark. "I've never met another one."

"So...Marcy?"

Stark sat heavily on his sofa. "Yeah. My sister and her husband were killed years ago in a car accident, and I took Marcy in. She was the only family I had left, and that *bastard* killed her."

"Clay?"

"When I first took the case," he said, "I thought it was a matter of human trafficking. Which, it was, in a sense. But it was so much more than that, as you saw, Sinclair. When I tried to convince my commanding officer at the time that something paranormal was going on, he 'suggested' my ass right onto psychiatric leave. Marcy getting involved was just a cruel coincidence of fate."

"So what happened?" I asked.

"She died," he said bluntly. "By the time I was off leave and 'closed' the case, Clay had closed up shop and pinned the whole thing on a patsy."

"How did you know where they went?"

"The patsy," he said coldly. "A few well-placed knife cuts and he told me everything I needed to know. The guy was besotted with Clay. Thought he was going to become his vampire protégé."

"Jesus, Sir," said Royce.

"I think we're beyond 'sir' now, Davis."

"Still—"

"I am *this* close to gutting that fucking leech," said Stark, and I winced. "I don't really care about the state of my career after that. None of this is going to look too good for me, I don't think."

"We can help," I said. "We want to stop him, too."

Stark glared at me. "Sure," he said, gesturing between myself and Royce. "And then the two of you skip off into the sunset together? Human and vampire—can't imagine *that* not going great."

I didn't want to meet Royce's eye in case I saw there that he agreed with Stark. "You can't do this alone," I said, instead.

"I've done it alone so far," he said.

"You could have told me," said Royce. "You did to me exactly what your CO did to you—after the Ambrose family investigation, you buried it."

"I had to," said Stark.

My stomach turned as I recalled Stark drinking a toast of human blood to maintain his cover. This man had truly lost his grip.

"Why?" said Royce, firing up. "Thor and Cas deserved justice. All those shifters did—your people."

"My people," said Stark with a sneer. "You heard your little shifter friend say what he thought about someone with a pedigree like mine. My entire value to Clay and his cronies was my being a cop, and being 'in the know' about paranormal shit. And being able to bury it. He's planning on staying in Douglas Crest. He was born here, I guess."

It was on the tip of my tongue to press the issue, but Royce had other things on his mind.

"That's not possible, at the rate he's burning through victims."

"It is if he has a police lieutenant cleaning up his messes," said Stark. "I've been doing his dirty work for months."

"So, what was your plan?" Ironically, the more he learned of Stark's true motives, the angrier Royce was becoming.

"I was biding my time, getting closer to Clay. Waiting for my chance to take him down."

"And who cares who gets hurt in the meantime, right?"

The deadened, chilly look in Stark's eyes was answer enough.

"Well, that's fucking stupid," said Royce. "I have to imagine that's not why you became a cop. You were good, Lieutenant, I know you were."

"Please, Royce. You know as well as I do there aren't any good cops. And if there are, they sure as hell don't stay that way."

Royce opened his mouth, furious, but I cut him off.

"Regardless," I said loudly. "You don't *have* to do it alone anymore. We can help—we just need a plan."

———

ROYCE

I was so angry with Stark I could barely see straight, but at least we had the edge on Clay now. "Royce," Sinclair's quiet voice grounded me. He rested his hand on my knee.

"Sorry," I said. "I just—he doesn't give a shit who gets in his way. He just wants revenge, not justice."

"I think it's more complicated than that," said Sinclair. "You don't know what it's like for..."

"For?"

"For us," Sinclair said. "Vampires, shifters. Whoever else might be out there, doing their best to live in a world that has no room for them. We don't have laws, or systems in place to keep the peace. The only way we can get justice is...to take it ourselves."

I rolled that over in my head on the drive back to my apartment, but beyond that, we had to focus. Getting the drop on a vampire wouldn't be as easy as our half-cocked plan made it out to be, but the longer we waited, the more of a chance that Clay would decide having Sinclair in the know was a liability—or give Stark a chance to sell us down the river for a shot at his own personal vengeance. We had to act now.

I knew it was important to Sinclair to try to save Beckett Taylor. For my part, I wondered which would be harder for his mother to cope with—her son being dead, or her son being an undead killer. Part of me thought that regardless of the outcome, it might give her grief some closure if we told her a lie—that her son had been killed weeks ago. I didn't say as much because I didn't want to dash Sinclair's hope of reuniting the kid with his family.

We decided to go for Beckett first. If we could free him, there was a chance he could help us. It dismayed me that we'd found out Stark to be on our side in this conflict, but also that he did not have vampire strength. We could use a ringer in our corner.

Sinclair and I snuck over to Clay's hideout during the day, when the sun would be out and hopefully fewer vampires lurking near the bulkhead doors. Luckily for Sinclair, I could pry open the doors Clay had reinforced with silver, and we could get in and lock them behind us. The doors had been rigged to help soundproof the basement; after what Sinclair told me about what he'd witnessed here, it did not surprise me. Sinclair trembled beside me, and his tension set my teeth on edge. It was eerily quiet for a place that had witnessed such carnage. Even I could smell the remnants of blood. "Sin," I said, whispering even though we were alone, "Is it weird this place isn't guarded?"

Sinclair turned round, nervous eyes on me and said, "I think it's the kind of place that guards itself. Beckett was kept just past that door there," he pointed. "I imagine stumbling into that room has a fairly high looky-loo mortality rate."

I shuddered.

"Can he hear us?"

"You, probably," said Sin. "But he might be…dormant."

"Dormant?"

"If he's been starved enough, he might have gone into a sort of hibernation state. He won't rouse until he smells fresh blood."

"Jesus," I muttered under my breath.

The stench of the room was overwhelming, and every animal instinct in my body screamed at me to run, run from this place and never look back, but to pull off this ambush, Sinclair and I had to settle in and hide till sunset when Stark could get Clay down here. What would we do if they didn't show? Or if Clay refused to come down without his entourage?

The waiting was horrible, especially because Sinclair seemed to have entered some sort of zen vampire state wherein he wasn't moving at all. The guy was statue-still, and I was hyperaware of every single fidget I made.

Sin pulled on black leather gloves, and was armed with my grandmother's sterling silver carving knife and two-pronged meat fork, as well as a dodgy as fuck homemade flamethrower. He'd been thrilled to discover a video tutorial—"The youth of today are *so* industrious!"—on how to fashion one from a WD-40 can and a Bic lighter. I had my gun, and the best machete Home Depot could sell me. I also had one of Grandma Davis's cheese knives tucked into my belt, just in case. I really hoped they could withstand being used for combat, because she was going to have my hide if I damaged them.

Sin tensed further beside me, and several seconds later, I heard the creak of the bulkhead doors opening. I realized with a jolt that this was the first time I laid eyes on Clay. He was good-looking, in an *American Psycho* kind of way, and his eyes were cold enough to freeze blood.

We waited, watching as Stark led Clay across the basement floor and they discussed plans for the next fight. I started to sweat as they approached the door behind which Beckett was being held, tightening my grip on my gun. Like Stark had said—it might not kill a vampire, but it would hurt like hell, and at least buy me some time. I had to imagine it would take even a superhuman being a little while to heal from having his kneecap blown to shit.

"This is tiresome," said Clay suddenly. He brushed his hand over the handle of the door leading to the holding area. The door swung open with a soft click, and out stepped three armed men.

"What is this?" asked Stark, taking a wary step back. The alarm bells in my head blared.

Clay grinned as the three men flanked him protectively. "I thought it prudent to bring along my new familiars," he said in a bored voice.

Two of them walked around behind Stark, moving like hungry sharks circling prey. "Clay—"

"Having a lawman on the take was helpful," said Clay, and he snapped his fingers. The men grabbed Stark's upper arms. "But you've clearly outlived your usefulness. Why don't you come out, Sinclair?"

Sinclair looked at me, aghast, but didn't move.

"Come now, Lieutenant Stark," said Clay. "Did you really think you were fooling us?"

"What?" Stark struggled against the grip on his arms.

Clay stepped forward, dragging a finger down his cheek. "I'll admit, your ability to shift had me convinced... but the look on your face when we shared a toast the night we met, the revulsion. You couldn't hide it. The pleasure we feel—it can't be faked. Can it, Sinclair?"

Sinclair jerked his head toward me, his eyes darting to the basement stairs and back to me. I nodded in understanding. This plan was going to hell in a handbasket faster than even I could have anticipated. Sinclair stood up, crossing his arms over his chest. "How did you know I was here?"

I rocked onto the balls of my feet and shuffled past Sinclair's legs, waiting for my chance to slip out past the crate we had been using as cover and head for the stairs. Clay still sounded like these entire proceedings were little more than an annoyance. "Stark may be something a fool, but even he wouldn't be stupid enough to come here with *no* backup. At any rate—" And Clay fixed Sinclair with a penetrating stare. "I know your scent."

And before Sin or I could react, Clay had his fangs in Stark's throat, while the two men held his struggling body upright. Sinclair wasted no time, and dove forward, going for Clay while his back was turned, while he was distracted draining the life from Stark before my very eyes.

I drew my gun and pivoted on my heel, firing on the third familiar, who had his own gun trained on Sin. The guy ducked, and my shot lodged into the wall behind him. "Shit!" I dove back behind the crate as he fired back at me. His shot went way wide, pinging off the inside of the bulkhead doors with a deafening clang and a shower of sparks. I rolled out from behind the crate toward a support column, trying to get a better angle to cover Sin as he went for Clay.

Clay was still occupied with his teeth in Stark's throat, but when Sinclair approached, he shoved his meal away and whirled on Sin faster than I would have thought possible. He had his hand closed around Sinclair's throat, using his momentum to slam him back against the basement wall. My stomach churned as Clay nosed his way up Sinclair's neck, whispering something to him I couldn't hear. He got in Sinclair's face and hissed, which gave Sin a chance to pull his fun-size flamethrower from his jacket pocket and flick it to life.

The front of Clay's suit caught and he dropped Sinclair immediately, frantically attempting to put out the flames as they licked across the fabric of his vest. Meanwhile, I was nearly fucking scalped by a bullet winging close enough to ruffle my hair. I hit the deck just in time, and the shot clanged as it hit what I think was the water heater behind me. The plumbing hissed, spraying me with scalding steam. I cursed, shielding my face with my arm, temporarily blinded.

"*Royce!*" Sinclair was back, crouched at my side, pulling me out of the way of the leaking tank.

"I'm fine," I snapped. "Where's Clay?"

Sinclair poked his head out from where we hid, only to duck back down again as one of the guys took another shot our way. "He's heading for the stairs," said Sin. "We can't let him get—"

Boom. The sound of an explosion rattled my teeth. My ears rang, and an intense heat hit my face—sudden enough to make me flinch. Sinclair gripped my arm so tight I knew I'd have little bruises on my bicep. The leaking water heater had blown and hit the ancient fuse box, sending sparks flying into the dried-out old wood of the basement walls.

"I don't think Clay's getting out now," said Sinclair, and I was distracted by the pure terror in his eyes as he watched the flames. "The bad news is, I don't think I am—"

He ended his sentence on a soft cry, and it took a few seconds for me to figure out why. My brain caught up and my vision swam, and I looked down to see a huge red stain spreading slowly from my right side. "*Woah,*" I said, touching it. I hadn't felt the bullet hit, but when my fingers grazed the wound the pain hit me like a cannonball to the... well. To the ribs, I guess?

"Royce," said Sinclair. He peeled off his glove, cupping my face.

He was so pretty, I thought—but I couldn't focus enough to answer him.

"Royce! Can you hear me?"

"Yeah, Sin, I can hear you." I fought the urge to boop his nose. It was a cute little nose. *Shit.* I had to focus. Time seemed to slow, which was handy because my brain seemed to be slowing down too. I had to think of something. I couldn't leave Sin on his own and outnumbered four to one. Especially when one of them was a psychotic vampire. That actually gave me an idea—Sin was a few mouthfuls away from being a psychotic vampire too!

"Sin," I said.

"What are you doing—Royce, stop moving!"

I was attempting to roll onto my left side and expose the wound at my ribs. "Here," I said, wriggling my arm to pull up my shirt, exposing what must have been something really ghastly because Sin made a face and looked away with a shudder.

"Royce," he said, "You can't ask me to do this."

I looked around me, noting the spreading puddle on the floor beneath me. "Baby, I think at this point my blood's either going in your mouth or on the floor."

Sin's pupils were blown, and he clenched his jaw, shaking his head. The flames looked so pretty reflected in his dark eyes. My brain might be struggling, but I knew we didn't have time to dither. Bracing myself, I dug my fingers into the wound at my side, covering them with viscera, and before he could speak a word of protest, I shoved them into Sinclair's mouth.

16

POVERTY OF BLOOD

SINCLAIR

When Royce stuffed his bloody fingers into my mouth, my first thought was—*If we survive this, I'm going to kill him.*

Once the taste of his blood danced onto my tongue, my brain went entirely offline. I wrapped my fingers around his wrist, sucking each drop, each crimson morsel, nipping his thick fingers.

Royce slumped against the wall, ghost-pale, with his eyelids drooping closed. I turned away, pulling his fingers away from my face, even as I could feel his blood humming through my system. "Royce..." I said softly. I knew enough of blood loss to know Royce was running out of time. The fire had bought us a little breathing room while Clay and his cronies tried to gather themselves, and flush me and Royce out of our hiding place.

I knew he was right. If I didn't do this, there was a chance neither of us would make it out of here. Squeezing Royce's hand, I dipped my head and latched onto the gaping wound at his side. I drew pull after pull, every synapse in my nervous system feeling like it had been struck by lightning. I drank, and drank, my Royce nourishing me, his blood flowing over my lips, the taste so exquisite it brought a tear to my eye.

Dizzy, lost, it took Royce moaning in pain and pushing on my forehead to bring me back to my senses. I felt sick, aroused, and ravenous all at the same time. I had one, single rational thought left in me:

Get away from Royce.

Before I lost all my control, I pressed a kiss to his forehead, leaving behind a bloody imprint of my lips on his skin, which had gone an ashy grey.

My muscles twitched, cramping and convulsing—I imagined this might be like what one felt when they'd been recently jabbed with a syringe of adrenaline. I vaulted over the crate with ease, overshooting my jump a bit, forcing me to tuck and roll through the flames engulfing the basement. The smell of smoke, the taste of blood—I saw red. If I had a living heart, it would be pounding.

It was like time had skipped—and the next thing I was conscious of was a man's gurgling screams as I tore out his throat. My stomach was full—like a tick ready to burst, I felt fat and sated, my entire being engorged with blood.

Looking down at my hands, I realized I'd plunged my silver carving knife so deeply into the man beneath me on the floor that I'd snapped the handle. Empty-handed, I cast around for something—anything I could use on Clay, who was trying to use his jacket to suffocate the flames on the basement stairs. I recalled vaguely that Royce had a machete, but I was loath to approach him again in this state and I was afraid Clay would make his escape before I could retrieve it.

Advancing on him, my foot connected with something on the floor and I stumbled. Looking down, I saw one of the silver chains they'd used to restrain the fighting fledgling vampires. I wrapped it around my gloved fist, and the desire to wrap it around Clay's throat and squeeze until his eyeballs burst, filled my guts with a heat burning hotter than the fire in this basement.

Clay turned to face me as I swung the chain, and he lunged, taking me to the ground. He wrapped his fingers around my throat once more, squeezing tight. Clay was strong, but the fresh feed after so long without had my body tuning into its survival instincts, giving me the feral strength of a newborn vampire—so we were well matched.

Clay grunted with exertion, and after grappling furiously I wound up on my belly, Clay kneeling between my shoulder blades. "I can feel the fight leaving you, Sinclair," Clay hissed in my ear. He dragged his fangs over the scar on my neck. "I'd love to reopen this," he said. "But there really isn't time to indulge."

He shifted his weight, wrapping a forearm around my throat and using his strength to push me across the floor toward the fire. The heat on my cheek filled me with an animal fear, and I thrashed in his grip, trying to escape before he burned my face off.

I scrabbled on the earthen floor, my instincts sending my hands to brace myself against being shoved inexorably forward. Somewhere in my blood-addled brain, I recalled I had another weapon, the silver carving fork. I plunged my free hand into my belt where I had it sheathed, gripping it by the handle. I ignored the sting in my palm and stabbed back blindly, with all the unhinged strength I could muster.

Clay shrieked like a banshee, so I imagined I must have struck home. I still clutched the silver chain in my gloved fist. When he released me, I rolled onto my back and sprang to my feet, swinging the silver chain as hard as I could. It collided with the side of Clay's neck and he screamed again. When the free end of the chain whipped around, back toward me I caught it in my bare hand, the pain in my palm excruciating, but I did not drop it. I squeezed it tighter and yanked, pulling it back like a piano wire. Clay clawed at the metal burning the sensitive skin of his throat, his screams choked off as I pulled ever tighter. The smell of burning flesh—mine and his, mingling together—curdled in my stomach as I drew him closer, flexing every muscle in my body to hold Clay against me as he struggled. The sound of his flesh sizzling and the high, reedy wail he attempted to let out despite the chain cauterizing its way steadily through his vocal cords. Dimly, like it was someone talking to me from far away, something yelled for me to stop—to remind me I wanted Clay *alive*...but I couldn't stop. I wanted him dead.

Planting my feet, I clenched my biceps and with a rough jerk, Clay's head popped off his body and he crumpled in my arms like an abused Barbie doll. Shoving his limp corpse away, I dropped the chain as quickly as I could, and the burning metal peeled a good chunk of skin from my palm as it clattered to the ground.

I registered the sound of sirens approaching—thank goodness, because this building seemed seconds away from collapsing on top of us. *Us!*

I had to get Royce out of here—I had to. Fighting my way through the smoke, I was blind, traversing the basement only by the siren-call smell of Royce's blood, I found him slumped by the wall, deathly pale and eerily still. I gnashed my teeth, tossing my head in an attempt to ignore the tug in my gut that told me to feed again from the last few glugs of blood pulsating from Royce's wound. A trickle of it slid from the corner of his mouth, and I pressed a kiss to his lips, tasting it and feeling his weak breath rattling.

"*Sin...*"

I clutched at Royce's shirt, trying to keep him upright, convince him to stay awake. He was dying. I could smell it on him. How long did he have—minutes? Less. The urge to feed was driving me mad, my mind filled with a buzzing like a swarm of hornets. I nearly ripped myself in two as my instincts warred, burrow inside of Royce's skin and drink my fill, or run away to keep him safe, and then another voice in my head, searing across my brainpan, urging me to turn him. *Turn him, take him. Make him yours forever.*

"Sin!" Yet another voice, discordant, penetrated the fog. "Sinclair—what the—Jesus Christ."

Someone had arrived on the scene; someone had approached where I sat guarding my beloved Royce. I turned and snarled, throwing as much menace into the sound as I could, as a blinding light seared my eyes—a flashlight.

"Sinclair, you've got to go—" It was Priya, but what she was saying made no sense. How could I go? My place was here, dying in this fire with Royce, whom I had not been able to save.

Dying with the man I loved.

Was it not always fated to be so?

A stinging slap connected with my face, and I startled. My vision and mind cleared slightly as I looked into Priya's eyes. "Sinclair, you can't be here. I've got him. Run." She shouted the last word, and when I didn't move, she slapped my face again. "*Run!*"

I ran.

———

ROYCE

My head.

My ribs.

My...everything. I coughed, and the effort of doing so sent spasms of pain from my throat down to my toes. Maybe if I looked pathetic enough Sinclair would get me a mug of soup for my sore throat.

Sinclair! My eyes popped open and I sat bolt upright, calling out for him. Or at least, I thought I did. What really happened was that I gave a feeble lurch, and released a sad, wordless groan.

"Royce!" Priya appeared in my field of vision. "Holy shit, you're awake."

"*Nuhhh,*" I said. Had blinking always been so damn difficult? I was exhausted by the small act of opening my eyes. Before I could tell Priya to get Sinclair, I drifted back to sleep.

The next time I came to, blinking didn't seem as dire. I opened my eyes to see Priya passed out in a chair on the other side of the room. It took a good minute for my arm to get the message my brain was sending it—or at least that's what it felt like. With a grunt of effort, I picked up a magazine from my side table and threw it at Priya.

She startled awake and I grinned, though based on the look she gave me it looked more like a grimace. "We've got to stop meeting like this," I joked.

"Jesus, Royce. You scared the hell out of me." She came over and sat on the edge of my bed, the slight movement of the mattress to me felt like a ship churning on a stormy ocean.

I flinched, and she made to stand again, but I rested my hand on her leg. "Stay," I said. "I need a cuddle."

With a sigh, Priya gingerly leaned toward me, offering a hug like I was made of glass.

"Speaking of," I said, trying to sound nonchalant. "Where's Sinclair?"

Priya chewed her lip.

"Priya, what?"

"Maybe you should just rest before—"

"Priya."

"I haven't seen him," she said. "Since...you know."

I groaned again, shifting up against the pillows a bit. "I don't, actually. The last thing I remember is being slurped like a human smoothie while the basement was on fire. Everything is pretty hazy after that."

Priya hesitated, and I could tell she was planning her words carefully. "I only know what I saw when we got there," she said. "The place was burnt to a crisp, but it was pretty much out by the time we got there. Fire rescue went in to check for structural damage and I went down into the basement and..."

She trailed away, looking scared. It took a lot to shake her. "What?" I prompted.

"I've never seen anything like it," she said quietly. "It was horrible, Royce. I don't know exactly who did what down there but—the only ones alive were you and Sin."

I gulped nervously.

"He was messed up, Royce—covered in blood, snarling like a rabid animal. I didn't think he recognized me at first. I really thought he was going to kill us both. The look in his eyes... But I scared him off you and... I haven't seen him since."

My stomach fell. "Oh," I said absently.

"Royce," she said. "What the fuck happened down there?"

I screwed up my face, remembering everything that happened before I'd been shot and told Sinclair to feed on me to get his strength back. I gave her the gist—told her what we'd figured out about Stark, how he was playing Clay all along. Explained how my blood gave Sinclair the edge in the fight to keep us both alive. And if Sinclair hadn't been able to control his thirst—well, I'd been dying anyway.

When I finished my story, right up until the final, bloody kiss Sin and I had shared before I fully lost consciousness, Priya averted her eyes. I wondered what could be worse than Sinclair being AWOL and thirsting for blood. Whatever it was, she was reluctant to tell me about it.

"Priya," I said. "What's wrong?"

She chewed her lip nervously. "The good news is that you're getting all the credit for busting up Clay's 'human trafficking' ring."

"And the bad news?"

"They're pinning all of it on Stark."

"*What?*" I jerked in bed, trying to sit upright.

Priya placed her hands on my shoulders, pushing me back down. "Let it go, Royce. It's done."

"But—"

"I know it sucks, and it isn't fair, but he's dead—and the only thing you can do by telling the real story is send your own career up in flames."

I opened my mouth again and closed it.

"You know I'm right."

"This isn't fair," I said. "This isn't justice."

"I know."

Later, when Priya had gone home and I sat alone in my hospital room, watching HGTV reruns, I couldn't stop thinking about Lieutenant Stark. He'd done some bad things, and made some fucked up choices—but he'd been trying to dismantle this whole paranormal criminal element on his own, with no backup and no help. He'd made some hard calls trying to get it done—and he had been successful, in some ways. I thought of all the lives Sin and I had helped him save by taking out Clay. The fact that I was getting credit for all his legwork left a bad taste in my mouth. Stark didn't even have any family I could clear the air with—the only ones who'd know he wasn't just another corrupt cop were me, Priya, and Sinclair—wherever the hell he was.

By the time the last day of my stint in the hospital rolled around, I'd all but given up hope of Sinclair coming by. My heart seemed to have taken up residence somewhere in my kneecaps. With long hours to just sit in bed with my thoughts, I'd had plenty of time to dwell on a question that was slowly eating me alive.

Why hadn't Sinclair turned me?

The question was like a splinter in my foot, working its way into my bloodstream with a healthy side helping of infection.

Why hadn't he turned me? Based on what both Priya and the doctors had told me since I'd come to the hospital, a few more minutes would have put me beyond their ability to save. Between the smoke inhalation and the blood loss, things had been pretty dire. And still, Sinclair hadn't tried to save my life by turning me. No matter how many ways I turned the question over and over in my head, I kept coming back to the only possible answer. He hadn't wanted to commit to being stuck with me forever.

The more days that had passed since I first came to this conclusion, the more certain I was about it. Priya came to pick me up from the hospital when I was released, and she could immediately tell something was up.

"What's got you so mopey?"

I made a face but didn't answer.

"Sin still hasn't visited?"

"No," I said. "I think he's ghosting me."

"That doesn't make any sense," said Priya. "The guy is nuts about you. Anyone could see that."

"Yeah but..." I trailed off. Priya and I always played it a little coy when discussing Sinclair's otherness. "He could have saved me."

"He did, though—didn't he? He protected you. He fought off all those guys..."

"I'm probably just being stupid," I said, hoping it was true. "All these meds are making me loopy."

"I think you should give Sin the benefit of the doubt," said Priya. "After everything, I feel like he deserves that, don't you?"

"You're probably right," I said. But I didn't say what I was really thinking. *If that was true, why had he stayed away?*

———

SINCLAIR

"When can I see my mom?"

I passed Beckett a mug full of blood. His hand shook as he grabbed the handle, and gulped it thirstily. Those were the first words he had spoken to me since I'd smuggled him out of a silver cage in the basement of another abandoned building.

I took it as a good sign.

The blood I'd gotten from the apartment of the late Lieutenant Stark. He had saved the blood from the people he'd drained in the interest of maintaining his cover with Clay, packaged neatly in his freezer. God only knew why— perhaps if he had an unexpected visit from Clay. When I'd left the burning basement, I'd been mad with bloodlust, and it took all my self-control to make it to Stark's apart-ment. I'd seen the blood there when we'd searched his place, and since the poor man was deceased, I knew his abode to be empty. It let me gather my faculties, nurse a few pints of blood, and plan my next move.

Stark was dead. Royce was hospitalized. Things looked fairly bleak. However, at the very least, Clay was off the chessboard. I decided to start there and pay a visit to his cronies Randall and Louise. I tailed them for two days, observing every move they made. When at last they lead me to where Beckett was being kept, I took them out.

Swiftly.

Without remorse.

I now had Beckett stashed upstairs above Datura, and I was trying to get the poor lad ready to rejoin the world of the living.

"Soon," I said, hoping it was true. The kid had been turned a while ago, long enough that had he a responsible sire, he should be alright to walk among the living without massacring a crowd in the street. But Beckett had known nothing but starvation, darkness, captivity, and bloodlust for months.

I wasn't certain how soon he'd be ready to keep company with a human without posing a threat. And I was not about to test his restraint around his innocent mother.

He swirled his now empty mug, looking into its depths

like he wanted to read his future in the dregs. "I miss her," he said quietly. "She must be worried."

"She is," I said truthfully. "Worried sick. But this is very dangerous, Beckett. We have to get it right."

"I know," he said, but he looked miserable.

"We also have to figure out how much you want to tell her."

"What do you mean?"

"Well," I said carefully, "You're...different now."

"I'm a monster, you mean."

I crossed the room and grabbed his shoulder, gripping tight so I could stare him in the eye—a challenge, because Beckett Taylor was an absolute giant. "No," I said. "Just different. Trust me. I will help you through this."

Beckett's brown eyes were round, vulnerable. "I don't really have a choice, do I?"

"You do," I allowed. "But I can't imagine you'll like the outcome if you choose not to trust me."

He sighed and sat heavily on the chaise in the center of my living room. "You're the first person who's talked to me for months," he said quietly. "I barely even remember what it feels like to be human."

"I know," I said. "And after we reunite you with your mother, our next job will be to find you a good therapist with office hours after dark."

It had been about a week since I'd taken Beckett under my bat wing. Being someone's adopted sire required a lot of hands-on parenting, as it turned out, and I hadn't yet had the chance to get back to my beloved Royce.

Alright, perhaps I was avoiding him.

And besides, I still had questions that needed answering. I met with Priya after dark, in a parking garage like a classic spy film.

"Sinclair," said Priya, and she clutched some paperwork to her chest. She seemed reluctant to step closer to me, I realized with a pang. After what she'd seen of me, I shouldn't be surprised.

I held up my hands. "What did you find out?"

Her face twisted into a strange combination of fear, and sympathy. "They autopsied Clay," she said. "Even though his um, cause of death was pretty clear."

"And?"

She sighed. "He...he had a pacemaker. It didn't do anything anymore, obviously. But."

It washed over me like a wave. I wasn't one hundred percent certain when the pacemaker had been invented—but it certainly was well after I had become a vampire. Clay had not been my sire. I had been nothing to him, nothing more than an intriguing diversion.

It was almost funny. Clay had been so full of it. I almost laughed—but it would have come out like a sob.

"Sin...," said Priya. "Are you okay?"

And really, I was. So, Clay hadn't been my sire—just a pretentious madman. A monster through and through, no matter what era he'd been born in. I couldn't say I was sorry to learn the truth. In fact, I felt somewhat...numb.

Meanwhile, I knew I could no longer put off reuniting with Royce.

He had seen me at my absolute worst, and despite what I said to Beckett, my most monstrous. I hadn't been myself, but in some ways, I had been the most myself. I was afraid to learn what he felt about witnessing that side of me in terrifying technicolor. But now that my young ward was somewhat stable, I couldn't justify further delay.

While switching back to my natural diet was, by and large, a smoother transition than the reverse, there were some strange side effects. Peculiar lurches of hunger, regardless of when I'd last fed, kept me tense, always on edge. I also broke out in itching hives—that was a new one. I hadn't had a skin irritation in a century. As my body became once again accustomed to a nocturnal existence, even dusk and dawn had my skin breaking out red and patchy. Most distasteful.

On the whole though, by the time I felt comfortable that my internal restraint and discipline regarding human blood had returned, Royce had been in the hospital for several days.

This was inexcusable, but allowing myself into an entire building full of bleeding people would have been worse. Royce would understand that, once I made it up to him—if he could see past all the rest. One evening, after verifying his room number over the telephone, I climbed swiftly up the wall. Mercifully, Royce had a private hospital room. He was sleeping soundly, but my heart was in my throat when I saw that he was hooked up to all manner of infernal machines. The stubble upon his sweet face had grown in quite handsomely, and I longed to rub my cheek along his jaw like an affectionate cat. The windows only opened a bit, so I had to suck in my stomach to slip through. I landed on the floor in a crouch, listening for any sound of movement on the ward. When I confirmed the silence, I moved slowly and carefully up onto the mattress of Royce's bed. Without disturbing the mattress, or any of his various machines, I curled up on top of the scratchy blanket between his legs, resting my head upon his thigh to watch over him. I knew I could measure the beating of Royce's heart more faithfully than any machine.

Sometime in the night, his breathing changed seconds before he released a soft groan. I wondered silently if it was one of discomfort or satisfaction, until he wound his hand through my hair to cup the back of my head. His thumb moved in barely-there strokes across my scalp, and he gave a soft sigh before his breathing pattern told me he'd drifted off again.

Shortly before dawn, a tired-looking woman with kind eyes and bubble-gum pink scrubs entered Royce's room. It took her a moment to register my presence, exhausted as she was, but when she did, she startled. "Sir," she said, "how did you get in here?"

I faked a yawn and a stretch, sitting up so I could give her my most innocent of looks. "I'm sorry," I said. "I was visiting my boyfriend and I must have dozed off in the chair."

"But—"

"I woke up and it was so late, I didn't want to disturb anyone."

She frowned, grappling with my bull-shittery. Eventually she chose to accept it because the alternative was that I'd gotten past security in the dead of night.

"Well," she said. "I'm not going to send you out now. Our secret?"

I flashed her a winning smile. "I won't tell if you don't."

She proceeded to check Royce's vitals, and I resisted the urge to hover with immense difficulty. Royce came to as she took his temperature, making eye contact with me over the nurse's shoulder. He opened his mouth in surprise and the nurse clucked, reminding him to close his lips around the thermometer. I waited patiently—at least outwardly—for her to finish up and declare that Royce would most likely be going home today.

When we were alone again, I moved immediately to resume my place on Royce's mattress.

"Where have you been?" He asked at once.

I glanced at the door to ensure we weren't likely to be overheard. "Taking care of...the others."

Royce's eyebrows shot up. "By yourself? Sinclair, are you crazy?"

"I had to track them down and eliminate them before they left town."

"And how long, exactly, did that take?"

"Royce..." I started.

"I've been trying really hard to give you the benefit of the doubt here, Sin. Where the hell have you been? I—I almost died."

"I know," I whispered. "I'm so sorry I left you but I—I didn't know what I would do. I couldn't trust myself. And..."

"And what?"

"I had to find Beckett Taylor."

That startled Royce out of his anger, if only for a moment. "Well? Did you?"

"Yes," I said, with a small smile. I couldn't help but feel a surge of pride that I'd been able to begin helping Beckett. "I've sort of...adopted him."

"Hang on—you've, you've done what?"

"He never had a proper sire," I explained. *Like me.* "I'm helping him learn how to manage his hunger and thirst so he can have a real life again."

Royce glared at me, full-on scowled so hard I flinched away. "Well, of course, now I can't be mad at you, can I? You kicked evil vampire ass, saved the kid, and cleaned up the rest of the mess from this whole thing."

"You can still be upset with me," I said in a small voice. "I was somewhat afraid you'd never want to see me again after seeing me like—like that."

"Sin," he said. "You were amazing. We were totally pinned down—you saved my ass and kicked everyone else's."

I fiddled with the edge of Royce's blanket, not meeting his eye, but preening a bit at his praise.

"I'm still pissed you didn't come check on me."

"I know." I could sense there was something else on his mind. I cupped his cheek. "What's wrong, Royce? Talk to me."

His voice was tiny and vulnerable when he said, "Why didn't you turn me?"

Of all the things—this, I did not expect. "What?"

"I mean we hadn't talked about—but, I love you and—I figured," he stammered. I was shocked to see his eyes looking wet and glassy. "I could have died and you didn't..."

"Royce," I said carefully. "It wasn't the right time."

"Wasn't the right time? What if I'd died?"

I closed my eyes, unable to even imagine it. "Then I would have mourned, Royce. Fiercely, for the rest of my days. But I couldn't take your human life from you, without asking."

"My—what?"

"How could I take that choice from you?"

"Even when I was dying?"

"Especially then."

"I don't understand," said Royce. "Don't you...want me?"

"Of course," I said without hesitation. "But I want—need, rather—you to choose that life. It's not something I could have decided for you, Royce. My sort of life is not...it's not natural. It's not human. It's not life, even, not technically."

He frowned, thinking this over, but it seemed the hard look on his face had softened.

I leaned in, brushing a soft kiss to his lips. "I was turned, against my wishes. I didn't want this life. I'm grateful, now, to have met you—but I couldn't take away your chance at a truly human death. I hope you can understand that."

"Maybe," he said. "Kiss me again."

I smiled and obliged him.

"Alright," said Royce, settling back against his pillows. "If that's how it is, ask me."

"Pardon?"

"Ask me."

It clicked. "Royce," I said, a fluttering sensation behind my rib cage. "Will you...be mine, for always?"

"Yes," he said, eyes bright. "Of course, I will."

17
CURIOUS FACTS ABOUT RED

SINCLAIR

"You're certain you'll be alright?"

Beckett nodded. He'd settled in nicely to my flat above Datura, and didn't seem interested at all in pushing things or visiting the outside world. He had television, and books to keep himself occupied. The refrigerator was stocked with blood, should he hunger, but I was still anxious to leave him alone. "I'll be fine," he said.

"It could be a few days," I told him.

"I know." And here he smiled crookedly. "Go get some."

I felt like a nervous father, and I supposed in some ways, it was true. "You have my mobile telephone number," I said.

"Yes, Dad," he said, rolling his eyes.

Over the last week, his spirits had improved immeasurably, with the resilience and adaptability of youth. He'd spoken to his mother thrice on the phone, and I could tell he was dying to see her. I felt like it was almost time. He had enough self-control now to know when he *didn't* have control, and knew to extricate himself from a situation that seemed dangerous. I'd tested his boundaries with Royce, and Detective Tanti, both savvy enough that an escape would be possible if everything went to hell. I was strong enough to hold him back, as well. As soon as I'd brought Royce through his unholy transformation, I promised Beckett he could see his mother. And explain to her everything that had happened. It would not be an easy conversation, I knew. Their relationship would be changed forever, but they would *have* a relationship. It made me glad.

I arrived at Royce's flat just as the sun went down, jittery. He could still call this whole thing off. I flattened my hair nervously, adjusted the ribbon on the flowers I'd brought, and knocked.

Royce flung the door wide open before I'd managed to connect my knuckles with the door a second time. "Hi," he said, breathless.

"Hi."

We stood, staring at each other like newly matched chaps on our first courtship outing without a chaperone—that first date flutter, the fear, the stumble-tongued anticipation. I held up the flowers, and Royce accepted them with trembling hands. "You wanna come in?"

I burst out laughing.

Royce faltered, but he shot me a nervous sort of grin in response. "I don't know why this is so awkward. How many nights have we spent together, now?"

I stepped in close and cupped his cheek. "This is a bit different."

"No," said Royce softly. "No, it isn't."

He kissed me, hard and thorough. No hesitation. No fear. Royce kissed me like coming home. We shed our awkwardness at the door, and I had about a nanosecond to be insulted that my absolute masterpiece of a bouquet ended up on the carpet, but then Royce's arms encircled me; his tongue was in my mouth, and nothing else really seemed to matter anymore. In fact, when Royce spread his palm on the small of my back, pulling me hard against him, I stepped right onto the petals, crushing them beneath my feet without a single fuck to be given.

As always, Royce took the lead, pulling me with him as he walked backward toward his bed chamber. Our lips didn't part until Royce collided with the edge of his mattress, and he broke away to draw a shaky breath. I loved to see his eyes glassy and his lips plump and slick with spit. He panted, his gaze sweeping over me hungrily.

I placed a palm on his chest. "You're certain?"

Royce curled his fingers around mine where they rested over his heart. I felt a strange surge of grief that I would never feel it beat again, after tonight. I tried to keep that from my face, but Royce sensed something when he looked at me. "I am certain about you," he said. "I love you."

"I love you, too."

We kissed again, and my fingers found their way to the collar of Royce's shirt. To keep my hands steady, I worked slowly, undoing each button with reverence until I could peel the cloth from his shoulders. Stepping in, I kissed his chest, his shoulders.

Royce brushed my jaw with his fingertips, then used his knuckles to nudge my chin up. "Are you certain?"

I nodded.

"Then show me," he breathed, lowering his lips to mine.

I understood what he was really saying. Usually, Royce took the reins in bed. But now, here, tonight, he was placing himself wholly in my hands. His faith, his trust in me was intoxicating. I stilled, breathing him in, steadying myself. My hand still rested on Royce's heart, and I gave a slight push—a flex of my power, and sent him flying backward onto the mattress. He landed with a grin and a bounce, and I wasted no time stripping out of my clothes and climbing atop Royce's thighs. I hooked my fingers into the fly of his jeans and yanked, tearing the fabric and tossing it aside. When I had Royce naked, I blanketed him with my body, feeling the warmth of his skin, hearing the humming of his pulse beneath it. I kissed my way down his chest, nipping little marks into his skin, letting him feel my fangs. Every time, he gave a sharp gasp, and every time, I smiled against his flesh.

I veered away from his groin when I reached it—and smiled again at the sad huff he made. Taking my time to explore the vee of his hips, the dip of his navel, and the thick flesh of his thighs, I settled between his legs. I sucked my lower lip between my teeth, biting down, hard, as I remembered what I'd thought—what I'd *known*—the first night we met.

He was mine.

I trailed shaking fingertips over the scar I'd made when I first fed on him. It was soft and white, pale and delicate. Begging to be reopened. I met Royce's eyes, the fear and want in them igniting my prey drive, and I licked my lips. "Shall we begin?"

"*God,* yes."

To Royce's surprise, I swung around, straddling his hips to face his feet, and more importantly, his cock, which was delightfully hard and needy-looking. I twisted my neck, tossing a wicked smile over my shoulder at Royce. He let his head fall back with a groan, his large hands finding their way to my hips and squeezing. Bracing my hands on his shins, I leaned forward, nuzzling the base of his cock, breathing in the musky scent of him. I wondered how his scent would change, after. I was certain it would be just as delicious, but I wanted to make sure I absorbed every second of his human body, worshipping it for the last time.

Royce palmed my ass, squeezing and kneading my cheeks as I teased his shaft with sloppy, open-mouthed kisses. When I tongued the slit of his cock, he released a slow, shaky breath that ghosted over my hole. I shivered in delight and took Royce's dick deep into my mouth, slurping and sucking and tracing it with the tip of my tongue. Royce cursed softly before dragging his tongue over my hole, and I huffed and moaned around my mouthful. With my ass in Royce's face, the position was hardly dignified, but it did not matter, I was hard and aching when Royce drew my cock back between my legs, angling it into his mouth, allowing us both to suck in tandem—the push, the pull, the give and take, and then my eyes rolled when Royce did that thing with his tongue I adored.

I waited until he pulled off to catch his breath before I did the same, licking down his shaft and returning my attention to the pale, silvery scar on his thigh. I kissed the spot, hunger igniting me from the inside out while Royce dug his thick fingers into the meat of my ass. Before biting down, I laved the flat of my tongue over the scar, then sealed my lips over it, sucking hard on the skin there, leaving a fresh mark to serve as a target. Royce's fingers twitched, and his thighs tensed for a brief second before I pierced the skin of his thigh.

God, the taste of Royce. His blood gushed into my mouth from the punctures, and the pure, selfish, hedonistic joy of draining the sweet nectar that kept Royce alive had my entire body tingling. I released his thigh, lapping lazily at the beautiful crimson beads welling from the wounds I'd made. I rested my cheek on his thigh, watching, fascinated, as the blood rose, formed two perfect little ruby globes, before the surface tension broke and it ran down his thigh. I darted my tongue out, catching every precious drop before it fell.

The animal part of my brain woke, possessive and feral, and I dug into my meal once again, the warm gush of Royce's life flowing down my throat, smooth and sweet as honey. Royce hunkered down lower on the bed, sighing and moaning with pleasure as my venom flowed through his veins, and each weak, desperate sound spurred me on. I alternated between sucking his cock and sucking the blood from the wound on his thigh, and Royce just submitted so beautifully, allowing me to fuck his mouth. He sucked me with gusto, and I always knew there was a part of Royce that wanted to consume me, too—he would make the most gorgeous hunter, the most perfect mate.

When Royce finally spilled into my mouth, the taste of his seed and blood mingling sweetly on my tongue, I nursed his cock until it wilted between my lips. I straightened up, wiping my mouth on the back of my hand before turning to look at Royce, weak and pliant where he reclined against the pillows.

His skin was pale, ashen, and covered with sweat like morning dew. I'd been draining him for a while now, lost track of time as I disappeared into the pleasure of feeding, so I took a moment to take stock of the feverish way his eyelids fluttered, the frantic hum of his heart as it tried to make up for the loss of blood. The weak rise and fall of his chest.

"Is it time?" Royce slurred.

"Yes, beloved. It's time."

I spun to face him, and placed my knees on either side of Royce's head. With a flourish, I bared the interior of my wrist, bent my hand back, the tendons sharp, the skin paper thin. My fangs already distended from my feed, and I ran my tongue over one, staring into his eyes, searching for any trace of doubt. I saw none, so without breaking eye contact, I brought my wrist up toward my lips, and tore the flesh with my fangs. The taste of my own blood made me shiver. I brushed my finger through the wound, which bled sluggishly. Our blood was different than that of humans—thicker, aged, syrupy. With a smear collected on my fingertip, I moved to cradle Royce's head and offer him the first taste.

His tongue poked out, hesitant, and I leaned down to kiss the corner of his mouth. "The first taste will be...unusual." I pushed my finger between his lips, and he sucked lewdly until I pulled it free. "But the next..."

Still cradling his head, I brought the open wound on my wrist to his open, panting mouth and the droplets each fell upon his lips with a wet *splat*. Where Royce had been sliding under from the blood loss, the taste of me gave him a burst of energy, of want and desire—his first feed, I thought warmly, as he brought shaking hands up to grasp my forearm and draw me to his lips.

Royce latched onto the wound at my wrist, nursing the blood from my veins like it was the finest thing he'd ever tasted. Weak moans, helpless huffs and squeaks told me of his thirst as he drained me so hard and fast I grew dizzy.

"Oh, my," I said softly. With my other hand, I stroked his cheek, brushed the hair from his sweaty forehead. "Beloved, truly, you were made to be one of us."

When his hands went slack, I helped lower his head back to the pillow. His breath came slow and shallow, and the beat of his heart grew faint. I settled beside him on the mattress, resting my ear upon his chest to make sure I missed nothing.

Sure as sunrise, Royce's heart beat its last, and all I heard was silence.

————

ROYCE

My awareness began with the currents of air, and how they skittered across my skin, changing shape around me. I could hear them. How peculiar. Then, the feel of worn cotton below me, around me, and the press of something cool and soft against my side.

The smell of Sinclair came next, that smoke and winter scent but below that...the tang of copper. And with that, the hunger.

Thirst.

Need.

My mouth was full of sawdust and my throat burned, but both of those sensations paled in comparison to the ache in my gut, clawing, gnawing. I blinked and found Sinclair staring intently at me before a fond, warm smile broke over his face. I momentarily forgot my thirst as I stared at Sin's eyes. It was like I'd never seen them before; their grey-green color had transformed into a burnished, earthy silver that glowed and sparkled. His skin, the pale iridescence of it, somehow I'd never noticed before...

And of course, the pearly shimmer of the canine poking out over his lip. All brighter, crisper, sharper than I'd ever seen. It felt like waking up after years underground, and the first thing you see is the moon and the stars swirling through the sky.

Sinclair didn't speak; he simply continued brushing his fingertips over my face, touching my lips, my cheeks, tracing my jaw. I could feel the silken slide of his touch, but more than that I could hear his hand moving, smell the change in the path of the air around his arm.

I never wanted it to stop—until he shifted, reaching for something. When the object slid across the wooden surface of my bedside table I winced, releasing an involuntary hiss at the harshness of the sound that left my ears ringing in its wake.

"It's alright," Sinclair soothed. "You'll be surprised at how quick you get used to it."

And as he brought a wineglass into my field of vision, the only scent that could rival Sin's in terms of allure reminded me of my overpowering thirst.

"Sin..." I croaked, and I felt like my jaw had rusted like the Tin Man's. "Need..."

"I've got you, my darling," he said. Had his voice gotten more musical, somehow? I contemplated the possibility, until the clink of glass reverberated against my teeth, vibrating up into my skull. And then, at the first splash of warm blood on my tongue, I was gone. I sat up, fast enough to send Sinclair sprawling in surprise, and seized the glass. I chugged it like I was at a kegger, and it was gone far too soon.

"More?" I asked. The cup had barely taken the edge off my thirst.

"Not yet," said Sinclair, his voice tinged with sympathy. "It's a fearsome burn, but it will fade. You must pace yourself."

I opened my mouth again but all that came out was a

dry gasp. Shifting on the mattress, I made to set down the glass on the table but I misjudged the distance and slammed it into the surface, shattering the glass into a zillion crystal fragments.

I ignored it, though the sound of the glass set my teeth on edge. Sinclair left, presumably to get the dustpan, and his absence felt like a vacuum. I flung back the covers and followed him to the kitchen, and it seemed I'd only taken a step or two before I was colliding with his back.

"Oof," said Sinclair.

My momentum had squashed him against the edge of my kitchen island, and it was like I'd squeezed more of his smell into the air around him. I ran my nose up his neck, dragging my teeth along the side of his throat. He gasped in surprise, and I felt a burst of perfection on my tongue. Pulling back, I saw that I'd underestimated my new teeth— two shallow but bloody scrapes traversed the pale column of Sinclair's neck. My vision swam, and before I could stop myself, I'd plunged my teeth into the side of his throat, the flavor of his blood sticky-sweet and exquisite.

Sinclair moaned, letting his head fall back against my shoulder and exposing more of his skin for me to savor. A few more pulls and he squirmed in my arms, where I'd boxed him in against the tiled edge of the countertop. He turned, put a finger to my lips and whispered. "Slow down."

I nipped the pad of his finger in answer. "Can't."

"You must," he said, breathless. He covered the side of his neck with one palm. "Champagne and candy, remember? You'll make yourself ill."

I pried his fingers away, and I loved that I was as strong as him now. "I love champagne," I rumbled, before licking the blood from his fingers. "And candy."

When his palm was clean, I closed his fist and wrapped my hands around it so I could kiss his knuckles.

"How do you feel?" he asked softly.

"I'm not sure yet," I said honestly. "Thirsty. Hungry."

"That's to be expected, I think."

I flipped his hand exposing his wrist to the sky where he'd ripped it open to feed me, to turn me. It had already healed over, but it shone silvery to me in the dim light of my apartment. I kissed it. "...horny?"

Sinclair laughed. "Are you asking, or telling?"

"Both," I said. Suddenly, I noticed that Sinclair and I were both dressed. When had that

happened? "Did you dress me?"

Sinclair shifted awkwardly. "I wasn't certain of the protocol," he said. "Or how long you'd be...resting. I figured I'd lay you out with a little dignity, at least."

I kissed my way up past the scar on his wrist, to the crook of his elbow, his upper arm, his shoulder. "You are very sweet," I told him. "I love you."

"Still?"

"Always."

Sinclair clasped my cheeks in both hands and kissed me fiercely, and desire burned through my whole body, like a thing living beneath my skin. A hunger of a different kind.

I plundered Sinclair's mouth, and he offered the same, grazing my lips with his fangs. When I drew away, I realized something. In the first few moments of my new life, I'd already sampled the inhuman strength and speed Sin had been living with for a hundred years. Somehow, despite all we'd done together, Sinclair had managed not to snap my fragile human skeleton like a twig. "Sin," I said, mouthing along his jaw to whisper in his ear.

"Yes?"

"Can I ask you for something?"

"Anything."

"I want you," I said.

"You have me," said Sinclair, tipping his head back again so I could trace the tip of my tongue over the scrapes my new teeth had left up the side of his neck. "Though, not technically a question."

"No," I said. With a parting kiss to the spot below his ear, I stepped back. "I want you, and I want you not to hold back."

"What do you mean?"

I picked up a wooden spoon from the counter, and with the slightest pressure between my thumb and forefinger, it snapped. Sinclair flinched. "I know you are this powerful," I said. "I want you to give me...everything."

Sinclair blinked at me in surprise, but the next second my back slammed into the opposite wall so hard a picture fell off its hook and hit the carpet. I barely had time to grin before Sinclair was on me, fisting his hands into the front of my shirt and ripping it like crepe paper. He bit the skin of my shoulder, *hard*. I hissed in pleasure-pain, grappling with Sinclair's clothes. We stripped gracelessly, our clothing ruined by each other's grasping, frantic hands. Sinclair shoved me into the wall again, but I was ready this time, and I swapped our positions, pinning him against the plaster hard enough to crack it.

He hopped, wrapping his legs around my hips. His weight barely registered, and I licked and sucked the skin of his neck, biting hard and licking all the sensitive parts of him until we were both hard as hell. Sinclair had one hand tangled in my hair, and reached down between us with his other to stroke himself, but I seized his wrist. And his other wrist. He squirmed, but an electric thrill ran through me as

I realized I could truly hold him now. Sinclair seemed to come to the same realization; his eyes went wide, a startled, vulnerable expression crossing his beautiful face. The newborn predator in me combusted, and without breaking eye contact I moved his hands above his head one at a time. "You're mine," I whispered before attacking his mouth.

Our lips met, and to be honest, the kiss was mostly a tangle of fangs that tasted of blood.

If it hadn't already, that kiss would have stopped my heart. I moaned into Sinclair's mouth, and despite the fact that I had him trapped, he was eager and wiry and just as strong. He gave as good as he got, and my lips were swollen and kiss-bruised when I drew away. We ground against each other, my dick so hard it ached where I pushed it into the divot of Sinclair's hip. This position had its benefits, but I needed more hands.

I grabbed Sinclair by the waist, spun, and tossed him. I legitimately tossed him across the room. He landed on the couch with a bounce, and it slid the few inches to collide with the wall. I was on him before he could orient himself, flipping him to perch on his knees and his hands braced on the arm of the couch. I dragged my fingertips down his back, marveling at the pattern of freckles I'd examined so many times, that looked somehow so new, but beautifully familiar at the same time. It reminded me of the first time I'd seen him naked, and every time I'd seen him naked since that night. Just sheer amazement, dizzying disbelief that this perfect creature was here, shooting an impatient look over his shoulder like he didn't want to wait one more second, for *me*.

His perfect little ass looked good enough to eat, and before my brain could really catch up and process that thought, I sank my fangs deep into the flesh of one perfect cheek. Sin yelped, and I soothed the bite with my tongue, two tiny pricks of blood appearing amid the smattering of freckles. I paused, my forehead resting against Sinclair's tailbone, and I idly kneaded his ass, trying to collect my thoughts. It was like my brain was working on two levels, and my body only listened to one—the instinctual mind of a predator and all of its accompanying instincts.

I was still trying to gather myself when I realized with a jolt I'd already begun kissing my way down Sin's spine, moved my hands to spread him open. "Just trust yourself," Sinclair whispered. I glanced up to see him watching me over his shoulder again. "Let go, feel, and *do*."

So I did. I buried my face in Sinclair's ass, licking, sucking, even nipping the delicate skin around his rim. Sinclair remained poised and still, letting me have my fun and...*fuck*. If I'd thought I'd loved this before...

Every sound, every taste, every scent had the dial cranked to eleven. I could feel Sinclair's moans and gasps vibrating the air around me. I could hear his mouth fill with saliva, smell his precum. Holding him open with one hand, I reached around to jerk his cock where it hung heavy between his legs. He rocked back eagerly against my mouth. I could reliably take Sin apart with my tongue, but it seemed my new senses enabled me on a whole new level. The tensing of each muscle, each intake of breath—it was like my brain slowed down time and allowed me to react to every individual stimulus.

"*Royce,*" he breathed, and I wondered if my human ears could have heard such a soft, quiet sound. I released him, biting my own bottom lip when I took in the debauched picture he already made, and I barely had the chance to wish I'd grabbed lube ahead of time when I found myself in my bedroom, yanking open my bedside table hard enough to pull the drawer from its bearings. I tossed the drawer aside, annoyed, and returned to Sinclair, who hadn't moved from his position bent over the arm of the sofa.

When I resumed my post behind him, he craned his neck and I knew immediately what he wanted. We kissed again, softer this time, but longer. Sweeter. A kiss to get lost in. I realized that without either of us needing to breathe, that was an actual risk. So I nipped at his bottom lip, kissed his nose, and returned to the task at hand: preparing to pound his tight little ass into next Tuesday.

With my fingers slicked up, I breached Sinclair's rim. My fingertips came alive with sensation, and I watched fascinated, as they plunged in and out of Sinclair's hole. The way his skin yielded around my fingers, the way he was so warm inside, the furled skin of his rim squeezing tight around my knuckles—all of it felt new. If it felt like this on just my fingers...

It wasn't until I felt Sin baring down, fucking himself aggressively on my fingers that I realized I'd been at this for quite some time. Sin moaned and whined, but he did not ask or beg for me to move on. I got the distinct impression he wanted me to take my time, to explore, to relish this transformation and all that came with it. I loved him for that, and for so much else. But also, I wanted to bury myself inside him *now*.

And once again, my body moved obediently, eagerly, and my eyes watered with the pleasure of plunging my cock deep into Sinclair in one hard thrust. We moaned together, and the sound mingled in the air like music, and it was like I could feel his pleasure deep in my own chest. "Sin," I said, my voice a broken, wrung-out croak.

"I know," he answered, and he gripped the arm of the sofa with white-knuckled intensity. "*Hell.*"

I drew back, my eyes rolled, and I imagined I'd see actual sparks flying between us. The soft slick grip of Sinclair's channel was always divine, but this. *This.* As much as I wanted to savor this new, electric set of sensations, I couldn't help myself. I shoved forward, grinding my hips against him briefly before pulling out once more, watching the head of my cock slip out past Sinclair's rim. Then in again, harder. Deeper. Sin arched his back, pushing against me, and I moved my hands to cover his own, twining our fingers together and squeezing before I let loose and pistoned my hips hard and fast. The pace was brutal, and in my human form I never could have kept it up. So to speak.

But now, I felt like I could spend the rest of eternity driving into Sinclair and never, *ever,* ever tire.

"Yes," he said. "Please, do it."

I may have said that previous part out loud. The faster I moved, the hotter the flames licked up my spine, spurring me on. A shriek and a series of tears broke through my lust-filled haze, and for one horrifying moment I thought I'd broken Sinclair in half.

When I realized it was just the arm of the couch giving out, I wrapped an arm around Sin's middle, bracing my forearm beneath him to shield him from being squashed against the floor, and went right on fucking him. These new reflexes, I tell ya. Sin didn't even notice.

Braced on all fours he had some leverage and when he shoved back against my thrust, we bumped together awkwardly and he dislodged my rhythm. With a frustrated snarl, Sinclair shook me loose and I found myself on my back, Sinclair pushing my chest with one palm as he lowered himself down onto my dick. He squeezed me tight as he rode hard, posting up and down.

I used this vantage point to touch every inch of him I could reach. It was not enough. I slapped his hand out of the way and sat up, pulling him tight to my chest and plunging my tongue between his lips, tasting every moan, feeling every pleasured gasp as it poured from his mouth to mine. I filled my palms with Sinclair's ass, helping to hold him open so I could hit deep, deep, *deeper*.

My vision blurred, and when my lips found their way to Sinclair's neck once again, my entire world narrowed to two points, my cock in his ass and my fangs in his throat.

I lost track of the details after that, but awareness came back to me in a few unique pockets. Sin bent over my coffee table. Me on my knees choking on his dick. Us fucking on my kitchen island like it was a stage. Sinclair on his back on my table, stroking himself while I ate him out, his legs over my shoulders. His teeth in my thigh. His teeth in my bicep. His teeth scraping my nipple.

Teeth, blood, lips. Tongue. Fingers. Silver eyes and a dizzying array of freckles. Winter, copper, and smoke. Breaking glass, tearing fabric. Whispers of filthy love, and dark, beautiful confessions. The strain of springs and the sound of wood breaking.

When I finally came, it was with a shocking jolt of white-hot clarity, the entire picture screaming through my mind at once, like sucking Niagara Falls through a drinking straw. I was on my back, my hands clutching tight around Sinclair's narrow waist. His head fell back, one hand wrapped around his flushed cock as he came all over my chest. His lips parted to the sky like he was praying, and downy white feathers swirled all around him.

Maybe he was an angel, like I'd thought our first night together.

Wait, no. That was crazy.

When I came down from my dizzying high, softening and slipping from the clutch of Sinclair's body, I realized the feathers were from one or possibly more of my pillows.

Or should I say, former pillows.

And former comforter.

And...I looked around, and our union seem to have finally found its climax in the center of a crater. My bedframe had fully given up on life and lay in fragments all around us, littered with torn pillows and the shredded mattress debris. My arms went limp at my sides, and it seemed there might actually be a limit to vampire stamina after all. Static tingles of aftershocks skittered up my spine, and I shivered. Sinclair melted to the floor, sliding down until his head rested on my belly, and we both stared up at the ceiling.

We didn't speak for some time.

At last, I said, "That was..."

"Yes."

I tucked my chin to peer down at Sinclair, who looked at me with post-orgasm goony eyes and a sappy smile. "I love you."

"Yes."

I grinned and craned my neck to survey the damage around us. "I know we don't *need it,* really, but I think I want to replace my bed. So we have it. For purposes."

Sin stretched like cat in a patch of sunshine, and again, said, "Yes."

With a laugh, I propped myself up on my elbows so I could cup Sinclair's cheek and pull him in for a soft kiss. "Also, you should move in."

I had expected another thick, cum-drunk, *yes,* but Sinclair hesitated. His pause was like a bucket of cold water, ready to drown me in doubt, but then Sin cleared his throat and said, "Well, first, of course, you'll have to marry me."

That took a while to penetrate my brain. "You—I'll have to—did you just propose?"

Sinclair pulled me up so we sat staring eye to eye, smiling so big and so bright it *hurt* to look at. "Naturally, darling. I'm very old-fashioned."

EPILOGUE

ROYCE

"You don't think it's too much?"

I sighed. Sinclair had browbeaten me into this enormous marquee of a sign, and now he pretended like it had been my idea. "It's definitely too much," I said, but I smiled at it fondly. "That's why I like it."

He made a face. "I might change my mind later."

"As is your right."

The sign above the door of Sinclair's flower shop now read, "*Datura,* Private Investigations & Fine Florals," in a very impressive, and very ostentatious, script.

The new logo was creepy as hell, but Sinclair had loved it—a blooming flower with an eyeball in the center.

"Can we go inside now?" It was nighttime, of course, so for us to get a good look at the sign, we had Beckett standing beside us on the sidewalk holding a large flood-light to shine on it.

The idea had taken shape over the course of several weeks. I'd tried to go back to work once my "medical" leave of absence had ended, but I just couldn't stomach it. I'd gotten a medal of commendation from the mayor, and accepted it with as much grace I could muster—thinking of Stark and his mad quest for revenge. Thinking of Thor and Cas, who'd had no one to turn to and been through way too much. Thinking of Marcy Kemper and Beckett Taylor. Thinking of Sin, who'd been alone and hiding for so long.

So, I'd retired.

I couldn't *be* a cop anymore, not like this. The whole thing felt wrong, now. False. Like I had to bury this world that I was now *part* of.

Priya had been sad, but not surprised, and it had been her who'd actually put to words something I could do with this weird, awful *yearning* leaving the force had left behind.

"You should get your PI license."

It seemed so obvious, when she'd said it.

So here we were, Sinclair and I, partners in just about everything now. And we'd brought Beckett along for the ride because he'd needed a job and something to do with his time and his muscles and his desire to help. And he was kind of ours, now. Or at least, Sinclair's.

We didn't have any clients yet, but Sinclair didn't seem too worried about that.

There was a lot to work out—how could we feed, responsibly? How could we stay in Douglas Crest without drawing notice? But Sinclair didn't seem too worried about that, either.

"We've got nothing but time," he said, and it was true.

We had plenty of time to figure it out.

We had forever, after all.

THE END.

. . .

Thank you for reading *Dress the Neck Becomingly!* Want more of Royce and Sinclair? Join my newsletter to get a smokin' hot bonus scene! https://emmalinestrange.com/subscribe/

If you enjoyed this story, it would mean a lot if you could take a few moments to leave a rating or a review!

Curious about how Thor and Cassian met? Read on for a sneak peek of *Mighty Quill,* the first book in the *Saguis Et Fauna* Universe!

MIGHTY QUILL SNEAK PEEK!

CHAPTER ONE.

CAS

The posting was probably a prank.

It had to be a prank.

I flicked back to the pic I'd taken of the student center bulletin board.

"*Roommate wanted. Furnished room. Utilities included.*"

Below that, a price and a phone number.

And a name.

It *had* to be a prank.

"*Inquiring parties please text Thor Ambrose.*"

What the fuck kind of name was Thor? Were people actually named that? But the price was right and I was desperate enough to text the number and risk humiliation. Risk being butchered by some kind of Craigslist Killer wannabe.

I stood in front of the building, trying to convince

myself to go inside. The building seemed nice, more like a converted old multi-family house, far homier than a sterile high-rise. I double-checked the address, and when I couldn't stall any longer without being late, I buzzed the bell for number three, which did, at least, have a tiny name-plate beside it reading, "T. Ambrose."

I waited to be buzzed in and tried to conjure up the image of a person to accompany the name Thor. He was probably some big alpha male type, who'd turn everything into a damn pissing contest. His apartment was probably a disgusting bachelor man-boy hole with the aroma of sweaty socks clinging to every surface. He probably had the IQ of a potato, and hosted parties every weekend that would make sleep and studying impossible. I sighed.

The wooden stairs creaked as I ascended to the third floor.

I faced the door, still debating if I should even bother, but I didn't have much of a choice. Classes started in less than a week, and it was either this or live under a bridge, so I knocked.

The guy who answered the door stood a good head shorter than me, his frame was skinny, bordering on scrawny, and he drowned in an enormous green Grandpa sweater. He blinked up at me through shaggy dark bangs and thick, horn-rimmed glasses. I stared.

"Yes?"

"Uh—sorry. I'm Cassian. Rhodes. I'm looking for..." I choked on the name. It *had* to be a prank. "Thor?"

He slid his glasses up his nose, a small, tired sound escaping between his lips. "That's me."

"No shit?" I said, and immediately clapped a hand over my mouth.

He flushed and looked at his feet. "You'd like to see the

place, I assume?"

I nodded, feeling like the world's biggest asshole, and followed tiny Thor inside. The building was old, but the living room was huge and bright, with hardwood floors, lots of windows, and what looked like an actual fireplace.

"This is the living room," Thor told his shoes.

"It's nice."

Silence.

"Big."

He blinked up at me, the eyes behind his glasses big and brown, rimmed with long, thick lashes. The phrase "doe eyes" popped into my head, which, was weird. Thor turned and gestured vaguely behind him. "Kitchen," he said.

I almost drooled. The kitchen was small, but had a big, hooded Viking stove—a six top—and an island in the center to eat at. Everything shone sparkling clean and meticulously maintained, and I itched to get cooking straight away. After a year in dorm housing with nothing but a microwave, the little kitchen with the oversized range seemed like heaven.

Thor cleared his throat and took off down the hall, so I followed him. "My room," he said, pointing at a closed door down the very end of the hallway. "Bathroom. And your room."

I stuck my head into the bathroom, which, like the kitchen, appeared small but outfitted with beautiful new fixtures. The room Thor referred to as mine was spacious, had plenty of windows, and an inviting queen-sized bed.

"If you have furniture, we can put this in storage." He chewed the inside of his cheek. "Or bedding."

It was my turn to blush. I had budgeted for this school year down to the penny, which did not include new bedding. My stupid dorm sheets from last year would definitely not fit. Thor didn't seem to need an answer to that, however, as he turned on his heel and returned to the living room.

I followed, awkward silence thick on the ground.

"So," said Thor Ambrose, crossing his arms over his chest.

"So?"

He waved his hand toward the manilla envelope crushed between my bicep and rib cage. "Oh. Right. Here." He'd asked for a lot of materials: bank statement, personal reference, resume, and transcripts. Thank God he hadn't asked for records of my conduct at school.

I handed him the envelope, and he stuck out his other hand. "I'll be in touch?" It came out like a question.

"Sure, yeah. Thanks. It's great—I mean. The place." I had no idea why this guy made me feel so damn awkward. I shook his hand, and he gasped, a sharp intake of breath like I'd squeezed his delicate fingers too hard.

When I released his hand, Thor slid his glasses up his nose again. "Anyway." He clutched my paperwork and gestured at the door like he couldn't wait for me to leave. His big eyes darted away, then back to me, then to his shoes, so I took the hint. If I wanted to live here, I'd better not piss off my new roommate before moving in.

"Oh, well, uh. See you."

Back on the sidewalk, the knot of anxiety in my chest did not let up. I walked down the street, wrenched open the door of my ancient Impala, and drove back toward the shitty motel I'd been staying in while I looked for a place. I felt nauseated because my entire academic future now rested on the shoulders of a scrawny nerd in a cardigan.

———

THOR

It had started about two weeks ago, at lunch with my sister. Circe was my oldest sibling, and she'd gotten married last year to her mated partner from a totally respectable shifter family. Needless to say, as the oldest of the Ambrose brood, she was killing it.

"Dad's worried about you," she told me, sipping from her cappuccino.

"Yeah, right." I was the middle child, like Jan Brady. Most of the time, I did my best to escape the notice of my parents. Dad had no reason to be concerned.

"He is," she insisted. "I heard him talking to Mom about it."

"Oh?" Anything that stood out to my father was bad news. My entire goal in life was to fly under his radar. It was the least I could do as the resident family disappointment.

Circe eyed me over the top of her menu. "He thinks you're failing," she said bluntly.

My stomach tied itself in knots. "Failing?"

"Socially," she said. "For the most part. You live alone. You never go out. You haven't even tried to meet someone."

My parents had been trying to set me up for years, and I had yet to find anyone to whom I could form a mating bond. Being twenty and unmated put me well on my way to becoming an old maid, in their eyes. My siblings had both made great matches just out of high school, tying our lineage to other powerful shifter families, and our parents couldn't be prouder.

It was galling that they came down so hard on me, considering my parents hadn't begun their courtship until college. Perhaps my single life wouldn't be such a scratch on the family crest if it weren't for the other thing.

"I don't want to meet anyone," I said. "I love being alone."

"Do you really?" Circe scrutinized me as she spoke, like she could peer right past my eyes into my head. She had always been astute. I wouldn't go so far as to say we got along, but of everyone in my family, Circe had always been the only one who really saw me.

The truthful answer, of course, was no. I liked my space, but I didn't love being alone. I'd always hoped to find a mate, like just about everyone else in our world. But it hadn't happened, and I didn't mind my lonely life. It was quiet; it was tolerable. And it was infinitely better than whatever alternative I was certain my father was going to propose.

"Anyway," said Circe. "He thinks you're too immature— don't look at me like that, his words—to be on your own."

My mouth ran dry, the bite of crusty Italian bread in my mouth transforming to wet sawdust. *No, no, no.* The backs of my knees started to sweat.

"He's considering breaking your lease at the end of the year so you have to move back home. He thinks you need more social grooming."

And there it was. Gods help me. It took a moment of high, white panic before I could form my next words. "What do I do?"

"Well, you can start by calling Rafe Nardini."

I groaned. This fall, Rafe had enrolled in my school, Fremont University. He'd also just come out as gay, the only reason my parents had not fostered an introduction before this point. He was a year younger than myself, so my father had encouraged (nagged) me to "show him around campus," which was, of course, code for "lock him down and put a ring on it." Or rather, a mating bite. I hadn't called. In my defense, Rafe had not called me either. It was not hard to figure out why. I'd seen him around campus— tall, handsome, and popular. Running back on the football team. His *fauna* was an elegant Aesculapian snake, so he had that going for him too.

And me? I was nothing. Once I hit puberty, the time when our kind traditionally experienced their first shift into our animal forms, I had remained despairingly, resolutely, human. The emergence of one's *fauna* was a celebrated, sacred time for our kind—and, nothing about me was celebrated. Or sacred. When my sister had experienced her first shift into an elegant panther, a sleek and deadly predator, my father had gone misty-eyed and said she inherited his mother's speed and strength.

Then he'd look at me and say I inherited her near-sightedness.

My teen years were not happy ones. I'd learned since coming to college that the way shifters reared their young wasn't strictly...typical. Or ethical. But I shut that away in a teeny little box and moved on with my life. Because I was free. I had my own apartment, my own space. The thought of losing that and being brought back under my father's scrutiny was unacceptable.

When I hadn't undergone a shift, my father had tried all manner of things to "inspire" one, everything from spells to foul-tasting potions; anything he thought would unleash any latent animal instinct. Doctors in the know, holy folk of our order, and even witches were summoned and then dismissed as failures. As I grew older, my father's shame grew, and his methods grew more desperate.

He took any and all suggestions from the people we knew. For a while, he put me on a diet of raw meat. When I'd nearly died of a stomach parasite, he switched over to acorns and roots. He tried shoving me out the window, tossing me into the lake. Had my brother jump out at me in the form of his *fauna,* a massive grizzly. My father even stalked my footsteps himself as a wolf, trying to ignite the wild that might have merely been hiding inside me.

He'd even gone so far as to force me to camp naked in the woods behind our estate. That was the second time I'd almost died, of exposure in that case, and the last of his more drastic attempts. It had been obvious at the time he'd given up on me. I knew a year or two of relative peace, and when I was accepted to my parents' alma mater, where I'd have my own place, my own sanctuary, I had lit candles and incense and uttered tearful prayers of gratitude to our wild gods. I didn't consider myself religious, at least not compared to the rest of my family, but occasionally, when emotions ran high, I leaned on the crutch of our multi-theistic faith.

Now, my safe haven would be ripped away if I couldn't get my act together. The lunch with Circe had been a wake-up call. I needed a plan, and I needed my own money. If I could prove to my father I was not—to use his words—failing, all to the good. I'd call Rafe Nardini and I'd make an attempt to be more social. But I needed my own security net, as well. That way, if my father cut me off, I would be able to keep paying rent.

Or...perhaps I could move away from here. I could transfer schools and leave Douglas Crest behind. Be *normal.*

Be free. The thought terrified me almost as much as it thrilled me.

If I had a roommate, I could sock away their rent money, and if I could pass them off as a friend—even better. Cassian Rhodes was the fifth I'd interviewed. He seemed okay, all told, and really, *really* cute. My hand still tingled where he'd shaken it; his fingers were callused and warm, his hand dwarfing mine. The big hand suited his tall, broad frame. Between that and his thick, sandy hair, his dimpled smile, and freckles, I'd practically been swooning. And he smelled *incredible.*

My father had always said response to smell and touch were the most reliable indicators of mating compatibility. I tried to stuff that thought away. Cassian was looking for a roommate, not a suitor, and besides, I'd all but decided to leave this whole world behind me. I'd go through the motions and contact Rafe for a date, but after that, I hoped it would be a non-issue.

I shuffled through the paperwork Cassian Rhodes had brought with him. I saw he played for the hockey team, which made sense, given his body. He got surprisingly good grades. Based on his course load, he didn't seem the type to spend a lot of time partying, so perhaps he was the lesser of many possible evils. I typed a text telling him he could move in as soon as his deposit check cleared, but I hesitated with my thumb hovering over the send button. I didn't want to seem too eager; I'd already gone weak at the knees when he'd shaken my hand. I certainly didn't need to let him know I was thirsting over him, on top of everything else.

So, I decided to wait until tomorrow at least. I considered what my father would say about Cassian Rhodes.

Look at me now, Dad, I thought. *I made a new friend, and he's a popular jock. Isn't that something?*

***

Check out *Mighty Quill* to read the rest of the story!

ALSO BY EMMALINE STRANGE

High Fantasy Romance

Crown of Aster

Paranormal Romance

The *Et Fauna* Shifter Universe:

A Walrus & A Gentleman

Dress the Neck Becomingly

Short Reads

&Vixen

ABOUT THE AUTHOR

Emmaline Strange is the author of *Mighty Quill, Crown of Aster, A Walrus & A Gentleman,* and *Dress the Neck Becomingly*. She loves to write and read about smooching. She lives in Boston with her husband, dog, and cat, all of whom she loves to smooch. When not smooching, she can usually be found doting on her plants, baking, or watching far too much television. Ms. Strange is a lover of all things nerdy, from *Dungeons & Dragons*, to *Lord of the Rings*, to the MCU.

She enjoys iced coffee, long walks on the beach, complaining about her feet after long walks on the beach, and long sits on the couch to recover from long walks on the beach.

For updates on upcoming projects, come say hello on social media where she's always talking about writin', readin', and... well, not so much 'rithmetic.

facebook.com/EmmalineStrange

instagram.com/emmalinestrange

patreon.com/EmStrangeWrites